PR
for *The Swamp*

"This is fiction, but I wonder if some people in that most fiction-filled place, Washington, will feel that Jeff Grant is traveling a little too close to the truth. Anyway, you'll want to go with him. Jeff takes you on a journey into the heart and the guts and the cerebral cortex and the lizard brain of espionage."
—P. J. O'Rourke, author of *Holidays in Hell* and *Republican Party Reptile*

"A fast-paced, action-packed spy thriller filled with suspense and intrigue. The author, a CIA insider, weaves a tale that is compelling and authentic. There is espionage, politics, diplomacy, romance, technology, good vs. bad – all of it told through a series of twists and turns you would never expect. I can't wait for the sequel."
— Joanne Isham, former deputy director of the Central Intelligence Agency's Directorate of Science and Technology

"Only in Washington, D.C. can the laws of politics out-maneuver the laws of physics. CIA analysts are trained to understand both politics and technology so they can accurately infer intent. Discerning the difference between what might be possible and what is most probable requires well-honed tradecraft. This astute thriller weaves tradecraft, technology and human intrigue to bring to light the astounding lengths goverments will go to gain the upper hand. When it looks too simple . . . look again."
— The Honorable Jeffrey K. Harris, former assistant secretary of the Air Force and director of the National Reconnaissance Office

MORE
From The Sager Group

THE
SWAMP
Deceit and Corruption in the CIA

AN ELIZABETH PETROV THRILLER
JEFF GRANT

This is a work of fiction. Many of the details, places, characters, and events were inspired by real life. None of it really happened; none of the people really exist. Any resemblance to actual persons, events or classified information is entirely coincidental.

The Swamp: Deceit and Corruption in the CIA
An Elizabeth Petrov Thriller (Book 1)

Cover designed and illustrated by Siori Kitajima, SF AppWorks LLC

Cataloging-in-Publication data for this book is available from the Library of Congress
ISBN-13:
978-1-950154-24-1

Published by The Sager Group LLC
www.TheSagerGroup.net

THE
SWAMP
Deceit and Corruption in the CIA

AN ELIZABETH PETROV THRILLER

JEFF GRANT

THE SAGER GROUP

Artifex Te Adiuva

Contents

Author's Note

I retired from Northrop Grumman in July 2018, as the vice president and general manager of the Space Systems division in the Aerospace Systems sector, after being in that position for seven years. By that time, I had been working in private industry for over twenty years.

Prior to then, I spent twenty-two years at the Central Intelligence Agency, working in many different assignments in the Directorate of Intelligence, the Directorate of Science and Technology, and also as an office director in the Community Management Staff, working under then-director of Central Intelligence, Jim Woolsey. In these positions, I learned the extraordinary value of protecting *sources and methods*—and how hard it was to do so while making the data product of a valuable new collection capability available to the analytical community, while still managing to protect it from being revealed.

History is rife with examples of this conundrum, but the most famous is the successful breaking of the WWII German encryption system, Enigma, by Alan Turing's team at Bletchley Park. After breaking the German code, it was clear to the Allies that the fact the British had done so should not be risked by making this success widely available. The activity was known as the Ultra Program. To protect Ultra, the British intelligence service created a fictional MI6 master spy, Boniface, in order to ensure that the successful code-breaking did not become apparent to the Germans. Boniface, a fiction, was falsely credited with controlling a series of agents throughout Germany. Information obtained through the Ultra program was often attributed to human intelligence from the Boniface network in order to protect the new *source and method*. This idea of a misdirection forms the basis of my novel.

The current political circumstances we find ourselves in is the *rest of the story*—how can an individual who has repeatedly crossed legal and ethical boundaries survive when there is overwhelming evidence of his activities in the hands of the Intelligence Community? It can only be because the foreign intelligence collections that would prove his criminal behavior are protected, and the Intelligence Community are sitting silently on the sidelines, allowing his behavior to go unaddressed. The new sources and methods cannot be compromised, even to reveal the despicable and criminal behavior of a political leader.

After I retired, I had no firm plans, actually I had no plans at all. I was going to re-learn French, do some consulting, return to scuba diving throughout the world—and write a novel. I got a good start on the first three, but writing a book is not for the meek. I originally planned to write a book of nonfiction. I had been inspired by Dave Sharp, a friend and fellow sailboat racer on the Chesapeake Bay, who wrote of his experience at the CIA working on the Glomar Explorer activity, Project Azorian. His book *The CIA's Greatest Covert Operation: Inside the Daring Mission to Recover a Nuclear-Armed Soviet Sub* was a terrific read and told of the CIA's Directorate of Science and Technology's extraordinary accomplishments.

I originally thought I would write a book about my time at the National Reconnaissance Office. Not a book about the technologies and how they changed the Cold War... rather, about the people and how they made decisions to create the most amazing space systems that could be imagined. A book about teams of dedicated workers in the government and in an industry that made possible the impossible. But this was not to be, at least not yet. Instead, the unfolding political landscape and the urging of a former co-worker and friend,

Heather Laychak, challenged me to write this fictional story about what *could* be true.

When I told her I was kicking around the idea of writing a book, she sent me a link to a UCLA Extension writing class and told me to get off my retired rear-end and sign up for the class. I went online, looked at the syllabus, and asked myself, "What could go wrong?" I enrolled and found myself trying to write fiction—something I had really never done. But my UCLA teacher, Paul Witcover, and online classmates, were wonderful. My teacher was a very fair, but very tough grader—and my classmates were a terrific source of feedback and inspiration. One in particular, Adele Weinstock, who is very knowledgeable about US law enforcement and intelligence communities, provided keen insights and thoughtful inputs.

I have also been the beneficiary of other writers' support and feedback including: Jason Baum, Mike Sager, and P. J. O'Rourke. As the book matured, others brought their ideas and modifications to me, including Stephanie Schwartz, a professor at El Camino Community College, Jeff Harris, former director of the NRO, and Linda Zall, former senior official at the CIA. But I need to make a special call out for my uncle, Ronnie Kaintz, who spent his career as a boilermaker/welder in Pittsburgh, Pennsylvania—and who played minor league baseball, refereed high school basketball games, and wrote/published poetry. He read every word of my manuscript multiple times and methodically gave me his thoughts on the plot, characters, and everything else he could think to help with.

I cannot thank all of these dear friends and family enough.

I hope you enjoy reading the book at least half as much as I did writing it.

—Jeff Grant

PROLOGUE

Tuesday, August 8, 2017
Washington, DC

In August, Capitol Hill typically resembles a ghost town. The oppressive heat reminds residents and tourists alike of the metaphorical swamp that Washington is, having been constructed on top of an actual swamp. By August, the simplest of movements become onerous, weighed down by viscous humidity and morbidly still heat, so that any movement is akin to wading—wading through a swamp. In a city that moves slowly as a rule, the machinations of keeping the free world free grind to a virtual halt in August. Members of Congress escape the oven that is the District for their home states, glad-handing any constituents they can find along the way. Others jet off to exotic climes with aides and lobbyists in tow. Members of the Fourth Estate congregate on the nearby beaches in Delaware and Maryland, three hours from Capitol Hill, on a good day. Typically.

Tuesday, August 8, however, was not typical. Capitol Hill's pulse was elevated, a reflection of the raw emotions surging through that bastion of power, the heart of the federal government. On this day, most politicos had a palpable sense of dread, fear, and anticipation, but some were hopeful about the story Elizabeth would be telling. She and her Uber driver arrived in front the Russell Senate Office Building. The Russell is an icon of American democracy, named after the late Senator Richard Russel Jr., Georgian Democrat and noted segregationist in the 1960s. Inside the sedan, Elizabeth frowned for a heartbeat. She was sweating. It couldn't be the car; the driver had turned up the air conditioning the moment he picked her up outside her temporary residence at the Tabard Inn, the city's oldest continually run hotel. Only 7:50 a.m., and the day already seemed long. Had she remembered to use deodorant?

Elizabeth was wearing the first business suit she ever bought, worn to her interview for her dream job at the Jet Propulsion Laboratory three years earlier, immediately after she graduated from Cal Tech. She chose the conservative suit as a gift to herself when she was preparing to enter the workforce—lightweight dull navy, a long skirt, not too loose, not too tight. It still fit her athletic frame like it did the first time she wore it. At the JPL interview, Elizabeth had wanted the conversation focused on what she knew, not what she wore. Like today.

She ferreted through every pocket and cranny of her bag hoping to find a Kleenex. When she glanced down at her feet, she felt a wave of nausea for her faux pas worthy of an *Elle* column. "Oh, God. Unbelievable. One navy blue shoe, one black. Not today! Oh, not today!" Careers were at stake, including her own. Lives were at stake, including her own.

The sedan pulled away, leaving her alone to face a swarm of reporters. They surged. She thought they might knock her over. This was a far cry from her childhood fantasy of fame. Today, she was not on a stage in Stockholm. The King of Sweden was not presenting her with a medal. And, sadly, her grandfather was not by her side. She had anticipated the moment but not how large the buzzing cloud of journalists would be. Dozens of camera strobes, firing rapidly, momentarily distracted Elizabeth. She was taken aback by the cacophony of shutter sounds, cameras in continuous shooting mode. Video cameras silently captured her standing alone on the sidewalk as the media surrounded her.

The reporters blocked her path, indifferent to the fact they were causing a key witness in a congressional hearing to be late. Elizabeth spotted an opening and pushed toward the stairs in front of her, making eye contact with no one.

"Liz!" her former Agency boss, Frank, called out. He grabbed her hand, put his other arm around her, and guided her up the remaining marbled steps to the entrance. She felt relieved. For the moment.

Frank followed her through security, then put an arm around her again. "Thank you again for being here," she said.

More reporters and photographers were inside, jostling for position while thrusting boom microphones at her. It reminded her of her Cal Tech fencing tournaments. She wished she had her foil right now.

The reporters continued shouting questions.

"Elizabeth, what was your relationship with the former president-elect?"

"Ms. Petrov, were you a threat to CIA Director Plummer?"

"Liz... were you a part of a coup?"

"Will you be making a public statement after your testimony?"

"Elizabeth, did the CIA try to kill you?"

Don't answer, don't look at them, don't react. How could I forget deodorant? Did I comb my hair? I need to organize my shoes better, she thought.

Frank said, "Stay close and let me get you through." They made their way down the corridor more quickly as Frank strode purposefully through the throng, one arm around her, the other firmly outstretched, forcing the journalists to retreat. He looked like a Heisman-winning running back.

This chaos only foreshadowed the chaos to come, in a closed hearing before the Senate Select Committee on Intelligence that opened today with her personal testimony. Testimony that would detail why the president-elect had decided not to follow through with his inauguration and why people had died as a result of what she had discovered. And why the national security mechanisms and institutions of power in the United States of America would never be the same again. Never.

CHAPTER 1

Tuesday, June 14, 2016
Pasadena, California

In her office at JPL, Elizabeth reviewed test data from the most recent hypersonic lifting body test. The thirty-second test required weeks of preparation and was conducted in one of only two hypersonic air tunnels in the United States. The data was clear. Models were in error or the fluid flow rate and pressure sensors were mis-calibrated. Maybe both. Either way, they would need to run this test again. Another $520,000 spent with no progress. Testing hypersonic systems was not for the meek, or for those with cost and schedule constraints.

Carmen, the office administrative assistant called out. "Elizabeth, you've got visitors. Men in black suits. Have you done something wrong? Should I call a lawyer?" She laughed at her own joke.

Black suits on a hot day in Pasadena could only mean that they were not from Southern California nor clued into the JPL dress code of jeans, t-shirts, and flip flops. Elizabeth wore a t-shirt from the JPL gift shop that read "MARS 2020" and a pair of faded 504 Original Levi jeans from a consignment shop. Most women her age wore jeans with pre-made holes. She couldn't bring herself to conform to a fashion fad that made no sense to her.

"*Otpravit' ikh obratno*," Elizabeth replied. Speaking Russian annoyed Carmen, but it was a game the two of them had played for years.

Carmen called back. "You know I don't understand Russian, and I am not going to learn to. Did you just order a vodka tonic?"

"*Nyet*. Send them back. But warn them—I am knee-deep in real work here." Elizabeth answered.

Two men in matching suits appeared at the door of her small office. The tall one spoke. "Hello Ms. Petrov. I'm Ralph Fallows, and this is Chuck Lansing."

Ralph must have a dog; his black suit had light-colored hair all over it. Golden retriever or yellow lab. *Looks like my Tova's hair*, she thought, as she looked down and brushed a short blonde hair off of her jeans.

"Nice to meet you, and please—call me Elizabeth."

"Thank you, Elizabeth. It's good to finally meet you," Ralph said. *Finally?* Elizabeth thought.

"Thanks for seeing us without an appointment. We work for the Central Intelligence Agency. Can we talk?"

"Sure..." Elizabeth replied cautiously.

"Do you mind if we shut your door so we can talk privately?"

"No, not at all," she said. But she wasn't sure she meant it.

They gave their credentials to her—apparently CIA identification cards. She had never seen CIA identification cards, so she had to just trust that they were legit. She held the ID cards and realized, these two could be from anywhere.

"Please, have a seat," she said.

They both sat in chairs by her desk.

"Liz, let me get right to the point," said Ralph.

"It's Elizabeth."

"I'm sorry. Of course. Elizabeth, we're here to discuss an opportunity for you to join the CIA. Your expertise is needed at the Agency."

"I'm a physicist. There are plenty of us out there. Are you sure I am the person you're looking for?" she asked.

Chuck spoke for the first time. Elizabeth noticed the long scar above his right eye extending back towards his ear. He had been in the military, she guessed. Probably Iraq or Afghanistan.

"Oh, yes, Elizabeth. Without a doubt, you're the person we want to talk to. Your educational background and experience are impressive, and your fluency in Russian makes you unique. And we need you. The nation needs you."

"Me? The nation? Chuck, why does the CIA need *me*?"

Chuck leaned back as Ralph smiled and responded. "I'm sure you are aware of the progress of the hypersonic research and testing in both China and Russia. They're both close to fielding operational systems and are bragging about it."

Chuck nodded. "Putin actually had a press conference last year claiming the Russians are close to fielding new long range conventional and nuclear weapons systems that can't be stopped by the US anti-missile systems."

Elizabeth was aware of some of the progress in Russia. She had read many Russian academic papers on the subject, and it was clear that hypersonic research was a focus of the Russian R&D community. Being fluent in Russian was a great advantage—she could read recent Russian publications online without waiting for translations. However backward Russia was in many other areas, it had great physicists, aerodynamics programs, and focused research efforts. She was not, however, aware of how Russia had weaponized the ability to maneuver hypersonic vehicles to deliver warheads, both conventional and nuclear, at extremely long ranges.

"Yes, I am aware of some of their research into the area. But what does this have to do with *me*?" Elizabeth asked.

Ralph leaned across the desk and, in a hushed voice, said, "We really don't have the analytical tools and skills to fully understand these new systems. Our experience is founded in understanding and countering ballistic weapons. The last sixty years of our focus has been on monitoring the development and deployment of their ballistic systems, both land and submarine-based. We don't currently have the capabilities to confidently understand and counter the threats posed by these new hypersonic delivery systems."

Chuck added, "We're here to ask for your help to address these critical intelligence questions—"

Ralph interrupted. "We're putting a new team together to join WINPAC, the Weapons Intelligence Non-Proliferation Arms Control Center, at the CIA. You were recommended to us because of your extraordinary analytical skills, knowledge of hypersonic flight, and Russian language fluency. The Agency is pulling together a team to produce a National Intelligence Estimate, an NIE, by the end of this year on the emerging class of new weapons system, and we want you to be part of this team."

"Who exactly recommended me?"

The suits ignored her question, and Chuck continued the sales pitch. "We've waived our normal recruiting process for this special assignment. That doesn't happen very often, but because of the urgency of the NIE and the fact that we are behind—"

"This is straight from the top," Ralph interrupted again.

Chuck nodded. "Normally, you would apply, we would spend a year or two thinking about it, then another year conducting a background investigation, and you would have a job offer six months later. But for you and others we're recruiting for this team, we've already conducted an Extended Background Investigation and are prepared to make a firm offer once you successfully pass a counterintelligence and lifestyle polygraph exam. We've got a polygraph office near LAX and have an appointment set up for you for tomorrow."

Elizabeth had spent nine stressful years getting her B.S., Masters, and Ph.D., all at Cal Tech. The speed with which she completed her degrees impressed both her professors and fellow classmates and was indicative of not only her academic skills but her focus and commitment to completing projects ahead of schedule. She came straight to JPL out of Cal Tech and planned a career working on advanced fluid dynamics, publishing her research and teaching part-time. Going to work for the CIA was not in her career plan. She had pushed through undergrad and graduate degrees in record time because she didn't allow herself to be distracted from her goals. This sounded like a major distraction.

"Can I stay in Southern California?"

Ralph shook his head. "No, I am afraid not. You'll have to leave and join us back at CIA headquarters in Northern Virginia. The team is already partially assembled and setting up shop in the OHB, the Old Headquarters Building."

Chuck said, "The parking sucks, the offices are cramped, the hours are long, but the people you will work with are top notch—just like you. You'll be in a position to make a difference, Elizabeth, a big difference for our nation and our allies."

The very concept of being recruited by the CIA to work on a project in her academic field intrigued Elizabeth, but she had always been deliberative before making significant decisions. "I need to think about this. Can you leave me a business card or...?"

Chuck looked amused and said, "No business cards, but here's a number. This conversation needs to be confidential, please. Don't tell anyone about our discussion. If you choose to come to the Agency, you will probably be brought in undercover. You know, you won't be able to tell friends, neighbors, and family you've joined. We try to obfuscate the type of talent we are hiring, so we'll provide you with the details of story you'll tell then."

Ralph said, "Or you might be an open employee—"

"Open employee? Undercover?" she asked.

"Also, there may be other assignments requiring you to be undercover, not an openly identified employee of the CIA. Then you would have a cover story to tell your friends, co-workers, and neighbors. You know—a deception."

She could not recall a time when she couldn't be honest with her grandfather, her *dedushka*. The one person in her life whom she trusted and confided in. Could she do something, know something, that she would be forbidden to share with him?

"I have to talk about this with my grandfather. And maybe my dissertation advisor."

Chuck said, "Of course, talk to your grandfather and Professor Anderson. He recommended you to us. We're very close to Cal Tech and JPL."

"I had no idea," she said.

Chuck raised an eyebrow. "For decades. For decades."

"And, after I talk to my grandfather and consider moving forward," Elizabeth said, "I will have a lot of questions about exactly what the job would entail, the current status of the project, where I would fit in the organization, who I would be working with... also, I would need to arrange a sabbatical from here."

Chuck smiled. "Professor Anderson said you were a very pragmatic person, but some of the details you'd be seeking are highly classified. We'll answer the ones we can, but you will have to trust us."

She would remember those words in the coming months clearly. "Trust us."

CHAPTER 2

1989-2014

Brighton Beach, New York and Pasadena, California

Elizabeth arrived into and grew up in a close Russian emigrant community in Brighton Beach, New York. She initially had many close playmates and friends but matured faster than most and grew bored of children's distractions easily.

While her eight-year-old playmates were asking for American Girl dolls for Christmas, Elizabeth wrote "Estes rockets" on her wish list. Her favorite kit was the SA-2061, the Sasha, a multi-staged rocket which, when launched with two E-series rocket engines, could reach more than 2,000 feet in altitude.

When she and her grandfather launched the rockets along the shoreline near Brighton Beach, they were very careful to avoid the air traffic into and out of JFK International Airport. They launched between arriving and departing aircraft and loved seeing their rocket's contrails reaching up into the sky.

Through binoculars, they watched the stages separate and the parachutes deploy. They regularly lost nose cones, sections, or entire rockets. Every time they lost one, Elizabeth looked forward to figuring out what went wrong before building and launching the next one. And building them was as much fun as launching them.

She called him *dedushka* and he called her Yelizaveta. *Dedushka* was a term of love and affection that small children in Russia used when addressing their grandfather or any elderly person held in high regard. He had been in her life for as long as she could remember. He referred to her in the elegant Russian version of Elizabeth.

She knew little about her parents. When she raised questions about them to her grandfather, he was artful in his confusing responses.

"Oh, Yelizaveta, they loved you very much, and I am sure they still do, but they weren't able to come to the US with us. I wish we could talk to them, but it isn't possible now. Maybe in the future," he said. "You look just like your mother, but I don't have any pictures of them to show you."

He was much better at answering questions about math or science. Her grandfather was the only parent she had ever known, and he had taken an active role in every part of her life. She wondered about her parents, but she did not feel a loss. She hoped someday to know more.

In 1989, when she was three, she and her grandfather had fled the USSR as Jewish refugees for the United States. Part of yet another Jewish diaspora, abandoning their home and their roots for a safe but disrupted life. He considered moving with Elizabeth to Israel, but when his visa was approved to the United States, he jumped on the opportunity, and they moved to New York's Brighton Beach. His work there, exporting US electronic devices, was very successful, enabling Elizabeth and him to enjoy a comfortable lifestyle. He had a gifted sense of technology differentiators and knew when a product made in the US would be successful in the international markets. He served as a broker to US manufacturers and grew the business until he sold it when they moved to California.

Recognizing that young Elizabeth had a borderline obsession with science and could solve complex mathematical equations well above her grade level, her grandfather gave her a series of books by Richard Feynman, a renowned physics professor at Cal Tech. While she didn't understand all of the concepts, she was able to grasp much of the math. Reading the books instilled a love for physics and determination to one day attend Cal Tech. Her grandfather tutored many of her high school friends. Unlike the way any classroom teacher could, he helped all of his tutees appreciate math and science by transforming concepts into relatable real-world examples.

"Приходите сразу со своей книгой по физике и бумагой!" he called out. She grabbed her physics book and paper.

"Yelizaveta, today we practice partial differential equations. You'll need these someday."

"Oh *dedushka*, I do these just for fun and to spend time with you," Elizabeth said.

Elementary school, junior high school, and high school math and science were all simple to her. As a sophomore in high school, she augmented her studies with classes at the local community college. She applied to one university only, and when she was accepted into Cal Tech, they moved to Pasadena together. Her grandfather's business success allowed him to focus on his garden and cooking, but a car accident in California six years before had left him with a broken femur that healed successfully but slowed him down.

After graduation, she bought the somber business suit and scored the JPL interview. Within days, she was working at the Jet Propulsion Laboratory as an engineer specializing in maneuvering hypersonic vehicles in the exo-atmosphere. Her fascination with hypersonic flight had started with her interest in rocketry but blossomed when she came to understand how little was known about it. The history of manned flight was dominated by aircraft flying at altitudes up to 12 miles high, and manned space flight primarily dominated by spacecraft operating between 150 and 400 miles above the earth. There was very little knowledge about and flight experience operating in altitudes between 12 and 150 miles. Hypersonic flight, over five times the speed of sound at altitudes usually between fifty and eighty miles, allowed glide vehicles to operate at extremely long ranges and with stunning maneuverability by skipping off of the atmosphere much like a stone can skip across a pond. The challenges were, of course, much more difficult than skipping a stone. The extreme temperatures and airflow dynamics made controlling these glide vehicles a scientific and engineering challenge. Elizabeth had been drawn to a field where she could blaze a trail and influence the fundamental knowledge of hypersonics.

In addition to nurturing her math and science skills, her grandfather was her confidant, her mentor, her guiding star, and her moral compass.

CHAPTER 3

Tuesday, June 14, 2016
Pasadena, California

Elizabeth phoned her grandfather, Alexi Petrov, from her office, and he answered after a few rings.

"*Dedushka*, are you going to be at home this afternoon? Or will you be off tutoring?"

He had continued his tutoring activities after they moved to California, hoping to help every child he could come to see the beauty and mystery of understanding the universe through a fundamental knowledge of how things worked. He passionately believed that a solid background in math and physics were essential to any career. He reveled in telling anyone who would listen that the highest scoring Medical College Admissions Tests were from college graduates with undergraduate degrees in biomedical engineering or physics and the highest scoring Law School Admissions Tests were from college graduates with degrees in mathematics. He was zealous in his cause, encouraging all high schoolers to establish strong math and science backgrounds, especially if they wanted to pursue a career in law or medicine. His tutoring services were always in high demand from parents who wanted their children to do well on standardized tests, and he enjoyed focusing on children who could develop a love of math and physics.

"*Da*, Yelizaveta, I will be home this afternoon. But why can't it wait until you get home this evening?"

"I really can't say over the phone. I'd rather talk to you in person."

"This old man would love nothing more than to see you this afternoon," he said. "I will be here, are you coming soon?"

"*Dedushka*, I'll leave as soon as I can," Elizabeth said.

She checked her calendar and saw no meetings of importance. The day was going to be filled with data analysis that she could do from home, if needed. She called out to Carmen that she would be gone for the rest of the day, walked to her car, and drove to the home she shared with her grandfather. The drive was not long enough—a rare event in the Los Angeles area— to allow her to collect her thoughts and think through what advice she was really seeking.

She arrived at the house and went straight to her grandfather's study. He was not there, but her yellow lab, Tova, rushed out of Elizabeth's room and greeted her like she had been gone a month. "*Dedushka!*"

"I'm here, in the backyard." Alexi was sitting in his favorite chair looking out over the flower and vegetable garden. "Так приятно видеть вас сегодня днем, какой приятный сюрприз." (It is so nice to see you this afternoon.)

She gave him a big hug. "The roses are beautiful."

"The flowers love this time of year," he said. "Not too hot, not too cold, but no rain at all. They need our care."

Elizabeth dragged a patio chair over next to him.

They sat silently for a few minutes. While silence made most people uncomfortable, Elizabeth and Alexi had, over the years, spent quiet time together without feeling any need to speak aloud. Elizabeth had learned this was a gift in most settings.

Finally, she spoke. "I need your advice."

"Need my advice, you say? I remember giving you a lot of advice over the years, but I never remember you saying that you needed it."

"I was visited at the office today by two men from the CIA, and—"

Alexi sat straighter in the chair. His face tightened. Her grandfather interrupted, "What did they want?"

"It was an unusual meeting. They showed up unannounced and said that the CIA wants me to go to work for them," she answered.

"To work for them?" he asked. "Why would they want you to work for them?"

"Yes, they said they want me to join a team working to assess new Russian hypersonic weapon systems. I would have to leave JPL and move to the East Coast.

"Move?" he asked.

"Yes, to Virginia. The project is supposed to be finished this year. I haven't asked yet, but I think I could arrange for a sabbatical from JPL, then leave the CIA and return to Pasadena when the project is finished," she explained.

"I am not so sure you can ever leave the CIA," he said. "Are you telling me of your decision or are you asking me for my advice?"

"I would never make such a decision without getting your advice, *dedushka*. What do you think? Should I leave, should I join the CIA?"

He leaned forward in his chair and took her hand. "This is now *our* country and when *our* country calls, heed the call and serve. Serve our adopted country proudly and do everything you can to help. You and I thrive in this country because others before us have heard the call and served."

She reached into her pocket and felt the piece of paper with the phone number on it.

"Thank you, *dedushka*. This is probably going to move very quickly. They seemed eager and asked me to call and let them know."

"I understand," he spoke slowly. "How did they come to find you?"

"They said there had been a long relationship between JPL and the CIA, and Professor Anderson had recommended them to me."

"I wonder why he'd do that?" Alexi asked.

"They said it was because of my academic background and fluency in Russian," she replied.

"Ahhhh... I am not surprised," he said. "I'll miss you dearly, but I knew this day would come when you would go into the world on your own and serve a higher calling. I know you will make a difference in the world."

Elizabeth fought back tears. "I won't be gone long, and I'll call you often. And maybe visit, too!"

He sighed as she bent over and wrapped her arms around his neck.

"This opens a new chapter in your life... in our life," he said. His expression was unchanged. She expected a tear from him, but there was none.

"I need to get back to the office. I'll be home by six tonight," she said, knowing she needed some time on her own.

"Perfect. I'll prepare a special dinner to celebrate. Sausage in cabbage leaves and boiled potatoes!"

***

On her way back to her office, she called Professor Anderson.

"Elizabeth! How are you doing? How is your project going?" he asked.

"Honestly, behind schedule and not making the progress I expected," she replied.

"Ah, the turbulent world of dealing with science, budgets, and customers," he laughed. "I am sure you'll get back on track. What's up?"

"I was visited by two men from the CIA today. They said you had recommended me to the Agency?"

"I did. They moved quickly. I have quietly done work for them over the years, both research and providing feedback on attendees at international conferences," he explained.

"But why me? Why would you recommend me?" she asked.

"As I came to understand the problem they were dealing with, I easily concluded you would be an essential addition to their team."

"Professor Anderson are you sure?" she asked.

"Well, very few people know this, but when I was about your age, I spent the better part of a year working on a very controversial project for the CIA trying to fully understand the capabilities of a new Russian aircraft, the Blackjack bomber."

"What was the controversy, and why you?"

"Seems everyone in Washington had an opinion about whether it had the range and payload to be a credible strategic bomber, a threat to the continental US," he replied. "And all of the opinions were driven by politics and the policies that would be put in place, including negotiations with the Russians."

"I had no idea."

"Yes, so they formed a team of independent, objective scientists and engineers to provide an assessment to, well, inform the defense and policy-making community."

"And, how did it work out?" she asked.

"Very successfully! We pissed everyone off, I think. The Department of Defense, the CIA, State, and all of the defense contractors chomping at the bit to build a new class of weapons to protect against it," he answered. "The bomber is still in service, and over the decades, we have seen our assessment proven out."

"Amazing, Professor Anderson, really amazing," she said.

"You should take this opportunity. I think they need you."

"I will," she said. "I have spoken to my grandfather, and he thinks the same."

***

She returned to JPL, walked down the hall to her boss's office, and asked, "Busy?"

"No, come in," he said.

Elizabeth told him what had transpired earlier that day and got the response she had been expecting: finish up her analysis of the most recent test, figure how to make the next test successful, serve the nation, and then come back to JPL as soon as she could. Her job would be waiting.

She returned to her office and sat at her desk, rolling the piece of paper from Chuck nervously in her hands for a few minutes. Then she picked her phone and dialed the number.

"I talked to my grandfather, Dr. Anderson, and my boss, and I've decided to accept your offer," she said.

Chuck could hardly contain himself. "Terrific news, Elizabeth! They'll be excited to have you join the team."

"So, what's next?"

"Your polygraph. Be at 14771 Howard Hughes Parkway at ten o'clock tomorrow, Suite 340. Near LAX. No phone, tablet, or laptop."

"What should I bring, what should I do to prepare?" she asked.

"Prepare? Just be honest with them and prepare to be challenged," he said. "Your polygrapher will want to know a lot about you. Expect him to drag you through some dirt, but I have been through eight of these and, while painful, they are survivable."

"Whom should I ask for when I arrive?" she asked.

"They will be expecting you. Just arrive on schedule, and you should be through a few hours later. Give me a call when you are done."

"Thanks, will do," she said.

CHAPTER 4

Wednesday, June 15, 2016
Culver City, California

She found the building and Suite 340 and arrived twenty minutes before her appointment. There were no signs indicating this was a CIA facility or a polygraph center. She signed in with a receptionist and then took a seat on an uncomfortable, flimsy plastic chair. A muted FOX channel played on a television that no one appeared to be watching. She had expected a more professional environment. There were others in the room: two men in business suits, a ponytailed guy in khakis and a polo shirt, a young woman wearing way too much make-up with a tattoo on her right arm and a stripe of green in her hair. *Right out of the bar scene in Stars Wars*, thought Elizabeth. Like in a doctor's office, an inner door opened into the waiting room. Now and then, a somber looking person—a polygrapher,

Elizabeth assumed— stuck his or her head out into the room and called out a name. The person to be polygraphed would slowly make their way to the open door and walk through it to be tested. She never saw anyone leave.

"Ms. Petrov?" a young man called out. She rose, walked his way, and introduced herself. "I am Elizabeth Petrov," she said, extending her hand to shake his. His hands were warm. *A nice start*, she thought.

"It's a pleasure to meet you," he said. "My name is Andy. Follow me, please."

He led her down the hallway to an office with a desk and two chairs. Her chair was overstuffed with wires hanging over the back, connected to the laptop on the desk. A large mirror hung on the wall. *Probably where others watch the session or where video equipment is located*, she speculated.

"Is this your first time being polygraphed?" he asked.

"Yes, I am afraid it is," she replied.

"Oh, don't be afraid, I don't bite," he said. "This won't take more than a couple of hours. We'll be dividing the test into two sessions. The first will be about you and about the lifestyle you have led. We'll take a break after this first session and then move into the counterintelligence part of the polygraph. That part will focus on foreign travel, contacts with foreigners, and whether or not you have been cooperating—or plan to cooperate—with anyone to the detriment of the United States. After the first session or at any time you need, we can take a break so you can use the bathroom or have some water. Please sit. I'll be attaching some monitoring devices to you. Are you comfortable?"

"Not really. But do what you have to do."

He attached the electrodes to her fingers. "These are to measure conductivity," he said. Then he attached an expandable band around her chest, "This is to measure respiration." He applied a blood pressure cuff to her left arm. "This will measure heart rate and blood pressure. Any questions?"

"No."

"After I inflate the blood pressure cuff, I will ask a series of questions, and you need answer only 'yes' or 'no.' The only response I want from you is 'yes' or 'no.' Understand?"

"Sure," she responded.

"Please, answer either 'yes' or 'no,'" he said.

"Yes," she replied.

"I will keep the cuff inflated for only two to three minutes at a time, so we'll try to use this time efficiently with you answering as many questions as you can, truthfully, during this part of the test."

She had never seen anything so crazy in her life. This thing couldn't detect lies. It could measure blood pressure, heart rate, respiration rate, and sweating, but not lies!

She understood telemetry, test data from complex systems that helped engineers and scientists monitor the performance of equipment. She could not imagine how the limited data from the three simple devices connected to her body could indicate whether or not she was lying. Instead, the devices merely measured her biometric responses to the question asked.

Andy was preoccupied with making adjustments on his laptop and reviewing papers in a thick file with her name on it: Petrov, Elizabeth M.

She had led a boring life to this point. No illegal drugs. Well, almost no illegal drugs. There was that one party after the homecoming football game when she was curious about what it felt like to be "high," so she had joined classmates in an evening of cannabis-induced stupor. Fun, but not fun enough to repeat. *She would not admit to this caper*, she thought. She also had engaged in no criminal activity and mostly only traveled abroad to scuba dive locations.

The polygrapher noted her skeptical look. "You don't think this works, do you?"

"I am sure it does whatever you say it does."

He began inflating the pressure cuff. "Are you ready?"

"As ready as I will ever be."

"Please, just answer 'yes' or 'no.' Are you ready?" he asked.

"Yes," Elizabeth answered.

He asked if Elizabeth Petrov was her name. Was she a graduate of Cal Tech? Did she work at JPL? Was her birthday November 15, 1989? Simple questions with easy answers. But then the polygrapher began branching out into lifestyle questions. Drug use, criminal activity, lying, and whether she abused anyone's trust. She answered all of them with simple yes-no responses, and he seemed satisfied.

Andy released the blood pressure for the seventeenth time and said, "Great job, Ms. Petrov. We are making great progress. Let's take a fifteen-minute break before we begin the counterintelligence part of the test. Would you like some water, or do you need to use the bathroom?"

"Some water would be great," she said.

Andy handed her a bottle and said, "I am going to take a break and will be back in fifteen minutes. I will be reviewing your results with a supervisor to ensure quality control and consistency."

Andy left the office, leaving Elizabeth to sit in the chair with no distractions. She was actually starting to nod off when Andy reappeared, "Okay, I was right, we are through with the first part of the test, and we'll now move into the counterintelligence session. Ready?"

"Yes," she replied.

He asked about her travel. France, Mexico, Belize, Statia, Grenada, and Roatan. She was an avid scuba diver and, whenever she could, went to warm, clear waters for her diving adventures. Andy quickly got bored with her diving trips and moved to a new area. Her foreign classmates at Cal Tech. He questioned her over and over again about her Chinese national classmates and her professors with foreign backgrounds. Their names, their affiliations in China, their travel habits, and her continued contacts with them. Often, she answered a question only to hear him repeat it again a minute or two later.

"Ms. Petrov," Andy said. "Your responses to these questions are showing inconsistency and deception." He continued probing her about the Chinese citizens at Cal Tech for another hour before saying, "Ms. Petrov, let's take another break and then go into the final series of questions."

"Sounds good," she responded. "But this time, I will take advantage of the ladies' room."

"Okay, follow me to the receptionist. She'll escort you to the bathroom and bring you back here. I'll take a few minutes to review your results. Be back in fifteen minutes."

Elizabeth thought, *Escorted to the bathroom? Really?*

She was back in the office by the time Andy returned, reporting that the last session had been successful and they only had one other area to discuss. He reattached all of the sensors and began a surprising line of questioning.

"Is your grandfather's full name Alexi Vicktor Petrov?"

Elizabeth was startled. "Yes," she answered uncertainly.

"Did your grandfather work for the Soviet Union government?"

Where is he going with this? "I don't know," she replied.

"Please, just answer 'yes' or 'no.'"

Elizabeth said, "I can't answer 'yes' or 'no,' I don't know!"

"Was your grandfather in the KGB?"

"Are you kidding me? The KGB?"

"Please, just 'yes' or 'no'! Does he stay in contact with anyone in Russia?"

"I don't know!"

"Has he maintained contact with friends or co-workers from Russia?"

"Yes."

Andy relieved the blood pressure cuff. "Good. Let's talk about who he stays in contact with." She spent the next thirty minutes detailing their friends from her childhood in Brighton Beach. Although Andy took notes, Elizabeth was confident she was being recorded by a microphone somewhere.

He asked, "Are you ready to start again?"

"Yes. And, how much longer are we going to be here?" she asked.

"We could be here a long time," the polygrapher said. "A long time."

"I think I'll be here a short time. I am getting tired of this," Elizabeth said. "A very short time."

Andy replied, "I will reframe my questions to start with the phrase, 'Are you aware...' That will make it quicker, I think."

"Okay."

"Are you aware of your grandfather staying in contact with anyone in Russia?"

"No."

"Are you aware if your grandfather has a presence on Facebook or any other social media site?"

"No."

"Does your grandfather use a social media presence to maintain contacts with former co-workers in Russia?" he asked.

"If I don't know if he has contacts in Russia, and if I don't know if he is on social media sites, then how in the hell would I know if he uses Facebook to maintain contacts in Russia? I am tired of this bullshit."

"Well, if you're tired, we'll have to reschedule for when you're feeling better."

"I didn't say I was tired, I said I was tired of this bullshit."

"Then we'll plan another session," he said calmly.

Elizabeth unbuckled the chest strap, unpeeled the blood pressure cuff, and pulled off the finger sensors. "You won't need to. I am out of here."

"You are making a big mistake!"

She stood up wordlessly and walked out of the interview room. The door out of the waiting room had a cypher lock, and she could not leave that way without the combination.

They locked me in, she thought. She turned around and saw the polygrapher behind her.

"The exit is two doors to your left," he said.

***

She found it unlocked and that it opened directly into the parking garage.

She exited the office and walked purposefully to her car.

"Fuck them all," she said aloud, "All of them!" Her phone rang before she started the engine. It was Chuck.

"Well, now, Elizabeth, you certainly made an impression," Chuck said. "The polygrapher and the Office of Security are not happy with you."

"I don't care whether they are happy with me or not," she said. "Dragging my classmates, my professors, and for God's sake, my grandfather into this is beyond despicable. I don't want anything to do with an organization that operates this way!"

"Elizabeth, I apologize. The security folks are a unique bunch and can be challenging, but you passed the poly," Jim replied. "You passed just fine."

"Well, I don't know if you guys passed my test," she said.

"Hey, this is the strange part of our rite of passage. You won't have to deal with this again for at least five years, probably longer. I took the liberty of dropping off a new employee package at your house this morning and met your grandfather. He is very proud of all of your accomplishments and excited about your future."

"Okay..." she said.

"The paperwork will explain moving details and when and where to show up for employee orientation. We have you scheduled to begin in Langley a few Mondays from now, say July 11. Can you make that work?"

She thought about packing and driving across country with Tova. "I can make that work."

"Excellent. And please call me if you have any questions."

"Will do," she replied. *What could go wrong?* she thought.

CHAPTER 5

Saturday, July 2, 2016 to
Saturday, July 9, 2016

Pasadena, California to McLean, Virginia

Her move to DC was uneventful, mostly because she owned so little, and her car did not break down on the cross-country drive. She piled all of her belongings into her aging Toyota, put Tova in the front passenger seat next to her, and headed out of Los Angeles to connect to I-40 East in Barstow. The highway was over 2,500 miles long and terminated in North Carolina. Much of the interstate in the West paralleled the famed Route 66. Unfortunately, she would not "be getting her kicks on Route Sixty-Six" this trip. She wanted to get across the country in six or seven days of driving. Elizabeth wished she had more time to explore the old highway, but she needed to get to Virginia and didn't want to spend too many days with Tova in the car.

As she entered the open spaces of the West, she wondered why, with all of the unoccupied land available, all the housing was packed so tightly into Southern California's coastal areas. After only an hour of driving, she was driving eighty miles per hour alongside few cars but lots of trucks heading east.

On their first day of travel, they made good time and stopped at a nondescript motel near the Meteor Crater. The motel clerk took an interest in her travels and asked, "So, young lady, where are you and your dog heading?"

"To Washington, DC," she said.

"Whoa! You have a long way to go," he said. "Spending any time here in Arizona?"

"'Afraid not. Need to get there to start a new job. We'll be leaving here early tomorrow morning."

"Really too bad. The Meteor Crater is only five miles from here and is a once in a lifetime sight to see. You could drive right up to it and walk the rim, won't take you more than thirty minutes."

Elizabeth thought about the opportunity to see the results of a hypersonic impact, thought of the irony of driving right past it to develop an assessment of the impacts of hypersonic weapons and the impacts caused by them.

"Thank you," she said. "Sounds like a great idea. I'll check it out before we get back on the highway."

She ate a blue plate special—meatloaf, mashed potatoes, and green beans at a local diner and took the leftovers back to the hotel to supplement Tova's dinner. He was happy for the treats. They slept well, later than she intended. After getting coffee from the motel lobby, she and Tova drove to the Meteor Crater. It opened at 7 a.m., and she was one of the first visitors of the day.

Elizabeth was amazed by the size of the crater: over a mile wide and more than 500 feet deep. The evidence of the tremendous impact—created not by a nuclear explosion but by the kinetic energy of a large object at hypersonic speeds striking the earth—was massive. Although the earth's atmosphere protected the planet from small incoming objects, large asteroids, like the one that hit here and caused this crater 50,000 years ago, created an effect of over ten megatons of explosives. The Meteor Crater was a big dent in the earth. The Chicxulub crater that impacted the Yucatan Peninsula over sixty million years ago created a crater more than ninety miles wide in a catastrophe of many species' extinctions, including the dinosaurs.

After admiring the view and taking some selfies, they climbed back into her trusty Toyota, drove back out to the highway, and headed east.

***

Elizabeth was somewhere near Little Rock, Arkansas, a couple of uneventful days later, when she picked up an archived satellite radio show. Howard Stern was interviewing a flamboyant, egotistical businessman running for president who was bragging about the Miss Universe contest that he sponsored and controlled.

"You won't find rocket scientists; you won't find brain surgeons. What you'll find are the most beautiful women in the world," he said.

"And they do wear bikinis and thongs, right?" Stern asked.

"They wear thongs, they wear bikinis, they wear high heels," he replied. "They wear just about everything that you're not supposed to wear because that's not politically correct."

"Right, the show is totally politically incorrect," Stern said.

"Totally politically incorrect. You know Miss America went to politically correct and their ratings have been nosediving. They're not allowed to wear heels. They're not allowed to wear shoes. They have to wear these very large bathing suits in one piece. We don't do that. The problem with Miss America, you know the girls are talented, they do *have talent, but it's very tough to find great beauty with great talent, and they do,"* he added.

Elizabeth chuckled at the thought of entering the Miss Universe contest as a rocket scientist who rarely wore heels, and then only modest ones. But she did think women in heels were very sexy.

The interview moved on to the businessman's sexual prowess.

"They say that more people were killed by women in this act than killed in Vietnam," he said.

"Yes, that is true," Stern replied.

"You know, you get criticized for that statement, but that statement is very easily true," the businessman added.

Stern responded, *"I even went as far to say that you're braver than any Vietnam vet because you're out there screwing a lot of women."*

"Getting the Congressional Medal of Honor, in actuality," said the presidential candidate. *"I'm having a good time, but Howard, you know the one negative: It's very, very dangerous out there."*

"Yes, it is." Stern agreed. *"It's your Vietnam."*

Elizabeth couldn't believe it. A candidate for the US presidency and presumptive Republican nominee, who had avoided serving in the military and going to Vietnam, saying he considered himself worthy of receiving the Congressional Medal of Honor for having avoided contracting sexually transmitted diseases. He was unelectable, she concluded.

***

She arrived into McLean, Virginia after seven days of driving. Flyover country was beautiful. She wished she had been able to spend more time exploring.

She planned to live in a hotel for a few weeks and then find an apartment near CIA headquarters in Langley. She found a Residence Inn that welcomed pets and negotiated a weekly rate. It had a small kitchen and a dining area, so she could make dinners and enjoy them with Tova in her room. She arranged a side deal with the hotel housekeepers to take Tova out a twice a day for bathroom breaks and to stretch his legs.

She missed her grandfather. She called him every night, but she missed him already.

Tomorrow, she'd start her new job.

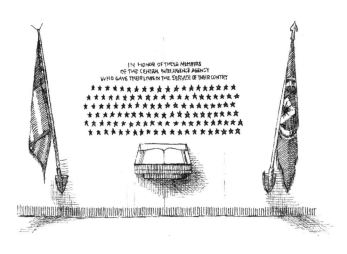

IN HONOR OF THOSE MEMBERS
OF THE CENTRAL INTELLIGENCE AGENCY
WHO GAVE THEIR LIVES IN THE SERVICE OF THEIR COUNTRY

CHAPTER 6

Monday, July 11, 2016 to October 2016

McLean, Virginia

Elizabeth's first day at the CIA started at eight o'clock in the morning. She joined a group of fellow new employees in what they called the "bubble" for an orientation/indoctrination session that lasted until mid-afternoon. The "bubble" was a free-standing structure outside of the OHB that looked more like an igloo than an auditorium. There, she was photographed and received her CIA badge. She filled out life insurance forms, tax forms, emergency contact forms, and health insurance forms. She received perfunctory briefings on CIA history, security, sexual harassment, and workplace rules. After all of the new employee activities were completed, she met her new boss, Frank Quintero, and was escorted into the OHB. Frank was average build and wearing a collared short-sleeved shirt and khaki pants. He had reading glasses on his forehead and a tie on that ended too far above his belt. His broad, welcoming smile and firm handshake made him instantly likeable.

"Elizabeth, it is great to have you on the team," Frank said. "I'm glad you're here. We really want to crack this problem. Walk with me. I'll show you around the building and then our offices and your workplace."

Immediately to the right, they passed a statue of Revolutionary War hero Nathan Hale, the nation's first spy who had regretted he had only one life to give for his country.

"Hung by the British in 1776 at twenty-one," Frank said. "We honor those who worked in the business before us. It's important to not get caught when spying."

Inside the headquarters building, Frank pointed out the CIA Memorial Wall just in front of the armed guards and the badge reading machines. The marbled wall was easily thirty feet high and a hundred feet long. In the center was a pedestal with a book of names, and there were stars carved into the wall between an American flag and a CIA flag.

"One hundred twenty-six stars," he said. "This wall is a tribute to our heroes, the men and women in the CIA who gave their lives for the mission and their country."

What had she gotten herself into?

***

Frank led her to an elevator past an employee gift shop, credit union, and Security Operations Center. As they entered the elevator, Frank pointed to the left and said, "The library is there. They are good and can get anything you need or want." They exited the elevator on the fourth floor and went to a room protected by a push button cypher lock. Frank showed her the combination to get into her work area: 1-2-3. She entered a large room with few windows and very few offices. Small work cubicles took up most of the space in the room. Then she noticed the paper. Mountains of paper! As she was led into her work area, she could not believe the towering piles of paper on the desks throughout the bullpen. Stacks of multi-colored paper piled so high they reached over the tops of cubicle half-walls. An inadvertent bump might set off a weighty, cascading five-foot-high row of dominos. *Why so much paper? Don't these people have computers and digital storage? Don't they have filing cabinets?* she wondered. As she turned into the row that contained her cubicle, she noticed some of the piles started on the floor! Was she working with a group of hoarders? She left behind a modern, paperless setting at JPL and now seemed to have entered a time machine that took her back decades. At her cubicle, she was relieved to see a computer and multiple phones of various colors on her desk.

"Your new home. And look, Liz, we have your name on your cubicle."

"Thank you, Frank," she said. Then she read the plaque on the cubicle wall. "I am eager to meet the team and get started, but—it's Elizabeth, not Liz."

"Oh, sure." Frank smiled. "I'll get it changed."

***

Elizabeth's second day began with meeting Frank's team, working under the internal, unclassified name of Cloud Spinner. The project brought together many elements of the Intelligence Community—NSA, CIA, NRO, DIA, DNI, NASIC—into a task force to understand the Russian hypersonic glide vehicle weapons program. Vladimir Putin had just announced the new system he called Avangard during his annual presentation to the Duma in March 2016.

She was one of about thirty people on the Cloud Spinner team. The project would produce a National Intelligence Estimate, referred to as an NIE by Agency veterans. The NIE was to be completed by the end of the year and would shape policy decisions, investment priorities, and negotiating strategies in the US. The estimate would be delivered to the National Security Council and Congress and would represent the consensus view from all elements of the Intelligence Community regarding this new class of weapon system, its effectiveness, and its vulnerabilities. Frank went around the room and introduced everyone to Elizabeth, encouraging them to say a few words about themselves and their responsibilities on the team. She recognized some of the names from research they had published and was truly impressed with the team she was joining.

After the meeting, Frank suggested Elizabeth take time in her cubicle to read the detailed reports and preliminary findings the team had developed so far. The office IT guy, Ray, was at her desk and showed her the tedious process of logging on to the secure network.

"Here, this is the reading library site where most of the files you would want to start on are found. For more help navigating through the documents, I suggest you ask any one of your stablemates," Ray said.

"Thank you," she replied. "The file structure looks straightforward."

She began the process of drinking from a proverbial firehose, consuming enormous quantities of data on a broad and deep spectrum of the subject. She was deep into a report on the most recent Avangard test when she heard a voice to her right.

"Hey Liz. I'm Tom Jenkins, a fellow traveler in this strange land." A young, muscular guy in jeans and a pink button-down Brooks Brothers shirt with "TMJ" monogrammed on the cuff peered over the cubicle wall. "Welcome to paradise. Sorry I missed meeting you a few minutes ago. Had a car issue to deal with. Let me know if you need any help sorting through our files or have any questions."

He rolled his chair to her cubicle opening. "I've been here for seven months. Joined the Agency from Draper Labs and MIT. You know, that *other* tech school!" he chuckled. "Navigation is my specialty. We are a tough bunch here in Cloud Spinner but only to keep each other on our toes. Your reputation precedes you. Wicked smart and obsessive about details. We're happy to have you here!"

"Thank you!" she said, deciding not to tell him today that her name was Elizabeth. "I recognize your name. I'm familiar with some of your research and publications. I really thought the work you did on star sensing and stellar navigation through ion charged plasma was really insightful."

"Any questions so far? I know you've only started, but first reactions can be very helpful."

"Yeah, I do have a question, as a matter of fact. I'm troubled by our lack of confidence in many of the key metrics: overall range, cross-range maneuverability, terminal guidance, and payload mass estimates. How can they have developed such a complex program and be so close to fielding a system like this, and yet, we still know so little about it?"

Tom nodded. "Three reasons. First, after 9/11, we stopped watching the Russians so closely and focused on the Middle East and counter-terrorist activities. Second, we've been focused on ballistic delivery systems, the types the Russians started building in the 1950s and that form the backbone of their nuclear deterrent."

"Seems we have a long history of being behind our adversaries until a crisis motivates us," she said.

"Third reason. We've been far more interested in watching North Korea and Iran build the systems of yesterday than investigating the Russians building the weapon systems of tomorrow. The Russians can now deliver both conventional and nuclear weapons against fixed and moving targets, and our systems cannot detect them, predict where they are going, or counter them. In short, we screwed up. Now it's catch-up time."

"From my perch at JPL, I'd never have imagined that'd be the case," she sighed. "Thanks for the cheery news. I'm going to get back to my reading." She returned to reading reports on the Avangard system produced by the many agencies working to support the estimate.

Elizabeth found the myriad of classification systems controlling the information they needed for their models and weapons system assessment daunting. The National Reconnaissance Office, Defense Intelligence Agency, National Security Agency, State Department, and all the military services had elements of control over who saw the data they collected from both spies and technical collection systems. For the most part, no raw data was available to the Cloud Spinner team. They had access to intelligence reports that had been created by the agencies who collected the data, not the raw intelligence. Data that was filtered by a process no one could understand—by someone who decided what the *all-source analysts* needed. Since their computers were not allowed to contain information from multiple agencies and sources, the information was disseminated on paper with each system having its own uniquely colored cover sheet and rules for protecting its content.

"This is insane!" she observed to no one in particular. "How can we generate a confident assessment of Avangard without an unfiltered view of the raw data? Is there no peer review of our product?" she called to Tom over the cubicle wall.

"None at all, other than by idiots who know half as much as we do about the system. Anyone who knows enough to review our work is on the Cloud Spinner team."

What could go wrong? she thought—again.

***

Elizabeth made friends quickly, and her work ethic and intellectual capacity put her in high demand. She became a go-to person for the team. Even though her specialty was aerodynamics, her other gifts in math, computer programming, and clear, analytical thinking made her a useful contributor to many of the sub-teams—propulsion, navigation, thermal control, aerodynamics, and payload working on the assessment. The sub-teams developed assessments of parts of the Avangard system so that a complete view could be produced for the NIE. The days turned to weeks and then months.

Ballistic weapon systems had, for decades, been designed to attack fixed targets such as dams, power plants, hardened military facilities, and cities. But Russia's new generation of hypersonic system, with its extraordinary maneuverability, now added the ability to evade current missile defense systems and the opportunity to strike moving targets. Formidable. Elizabeth's main responsibility was to develop a model of how the Russian weapon might work, grounded in the laws of physics and considering many variables: the booster size, the hypersonic glider construction, and the atmosphere in which it likely flew. She struggled over working with intercepted data that had been interpreted by some other agency and trying to converge what she could discern from it with the known limits of material science, flight controls, and the thermal effects of traveling at the incredibly high speeds.

As Elizabeth came to understand the full range of the Avangard system capabilities and flexibility, her level of concern grew. At an afternoon meeting with the team, Frank asked her to share her most recent modeling results.

"I think our uncertainty in some of the key performance metrics we are calculating is still too wide to be certain, but even at the mid-range of what we predict is possible, this system easily evades the US Navy's ship-based SM-3 and the Missile Defense Agency's anti-missile systems deployed in Alaska. I don't think we have anything deployed or in development to counter the Avangard."

While the team focused on assessing the capabilities of the Avangard system, Elizabeth had, in her spare time, modeled its effectiveness against deployed U.S. missile defense systems with sobering results.

Elizabeth told Frank and anyone on the team who would listen that many of the intelligence reports contained incomplete or incorrect data. The telemetry collects helped but were still missing large segments of test data from the flights. Some intelligence reports contradicted each other. Which should she believe? Others just made no sense. If the Agency was spending money for this garbage data, then they were getting cheated.

CHAPTER 7

Friday, October 21, 2016
CIA Headquarters

Frank called her into his office.

"Liz—" He was smiling.

"Elizabeth."

"Elizabeth, your work here these last months has been nothing less than spectacular. We'd never have developed such an accurate understanding of their test program limitations, challenges, and successes without your dogged persistence."

Elizabeth smiled back, but cautiously. "I don't think we can claim any kind of success yet, Frank. There are still strange disconnects and ambiguities in our analytical results as well as contradictions and major holes in the source reporting. It really causes our confidence in key performance parameters to be much lower than it should be at this phase. You know, in academia, we'd never publish a final report with such low confidence."

Frank shrugged. "Such is life in our business. We sometimes produce assessments that are less accurate and more incomplete than we'd like, and we keep moving. That's why we use words like may, probably, could, and possible. You get my drift?"

"Yes, but it's troubling to the novice."

"Then you will like my news. There's a new opportunity for you to access data—from an unusual source."

"Really? More data?"

"What I tell you next is unique. In fact, it's the first time in my career I've done this," Frank said. "I've been bringing your concerns about some of the reports we've been using to my boss and to the head of WINPAC. Your keen insights onto the nuances and inconsistencies of the reporting have caused some of our folks to try to reconcile the questions you have raised. I think our translators and the first phase assessment team of some of the intelligence reports we get are struggling with some of the technical nuances of the Avangard system."

"I think so, too. Any one report might look okay on its own, but it is hard to weave together a coherent story without knowing about the credibility of the IR. We need to be able to weight them when we see disconnects."

"We know. And as a result of your insights and your Russian language skills, you've been approved for unfettered access to a unique raw intelligence source we've been using to develop many of the Cloud Spinner intelligence assessments," Frank said.

"That sounded promising. I appreciate your trust."

"You know how sensitive new collection sources are. Giving you, an all-source analyst newbie from WINPAC, this kind of access is really unprecedented," he added.

Elizabeth sat upright in the chair, her back not touching the frayed faux leather back. "I'm flattered."

"I can't tell you more, I'm not read in," Frank said. "You'll be on your own."

Elizabeth could hear hesitancy in his voice.

Frank took his glasses off and added, "I've been told you have an appointment this afternoon at 1 p.m. in 5F43. When you come back, tell me what you can."

***

She skipped lunch and arrived at the door to 5F43 five minutes early.

Her stomach growled, and she immediately regretted the decision of only drinking coffee and not eating lunch. One of the pleasant surprises of the headquarters compound were meal options. The large dining facility was outfitted like a food court in a shopping mall, with a large variety, high quality, and low prices. She was told this had not always been the case, but when the Agency recruited millennials who refused to eat cafeteria food that was worse than they had suffered through in college, many new employees left the compound for lunch at local eateries scattered throughout McLean. Once Agency management recognized the potential security issues of employees talking shop while eating at a favorite restaurant and the inefficiency of a large chunk of the workforce leaving campus halfway through the day, they made a major investment in the food court.

The doors along the hallway had no identifying labels so she was uncertain which Agency Directorate she was meant to enter. The door marked 5F43 was closed and secured with a spun-off safe lock. She noted the opening/closing log, a paper record of when the door had been opened and closed, accompanied by the initials of who had done so. The log showed the room had been opened infrequently by the same person, initials "SF."

Elizabeth heard footsteps coming down the hallway towards her and turned. She saw a very attractive woman, maybe five years older than herself, who looked like a swimmer or maybe a volleyball player, with broad shoulders and a muscular physique. Four-inch heels, skirt a little short for the office, manicured nails, perfect eyeliner. *Nice,* Elizabeth thought. The heels brought her to Elizabeth's height. The woman extended her hand and looked directly at Elizabeth with intense green eyes. *This woman spent some time at the salon.*

"Sandra Friedman."

"I'm Elizabeth Petrov. Nice to meet you."

***

Elizabeth looked at Sandra's badge. Her number was NK 345. Elizabeth's was PS 258, so she estimated that Sandra had joined the Agency a while earlier. Frank's badge was GL 218. He had been at the Agency for decades.

Sandra opened the vault door, turned off the alarm system, and motioned to Elizabeth to follow. The vault door was armored, and the room inside contained a glass house. Elizabeth had heard about this type of security measure in US embassies in some countries but never imagined it existed inside the Agency compound.

Carrying a large manila envelope, Sandra led Elizabeth into the room within the room. The glass house held a conference table with six chairs. They sat down opposite each other. It was acoustically isolated and had no copper connections. Any attempt to monitor the room or its occupants would be easily detected. This conversation was going to be private.

Sandra opened the envelope and pulled out forms printed with Elizabeth's name.

"You have been approved to be accessed into a new security compartment. The process is similar to others in which you have already been working, but this new compartment is unique because of the collection techniques and how we get the data back to the Agency. I'll tell you more after you sign here and initial in these four locations." Sandra pushed three separate, color-coded forms with different cover sheets across the table.

"The new compartment you are being read into is called Klondike. And don't give me any shit about the ice cream bar, either. The Klondike Control System has a trigraph—KLO. You'll see this trigraph on every document or computer display containing information protected by the Klondike Control System. The control system's very existence is not acknowledged outside of the control system. So, you cannot tell anyone who has not been briefed that this system exists, what its name is, or what its trigraph looks like," Sandra said.

This feels a little like double secret probation in Animal House, Elizabeth thought.

"The KLO Control System protects exquisite capabilities that the Agency developed to monitor and exfiltrate voice conversations of key individuals by using specially modified electronic devices. These devices are not obvious recording devices, so they are often kept in close physical proximity to our targets. The other briefing statements you signed are for two specific programs controlled within the KLO system. "Any questions so far?" Sandra asked.

"Tell me about the new capabilities first," Elizabeth said.

"The first: the Whitehorse program, bi-graph, WH. We developed a way to modify automobile key fobs to record and transmit voice data—in addition to their real job of unlocking doors and starting cars. You'll see the headers and footers of documents from Whitehorse are striped purple. It is critical that these documents never be reproduced without these markings," Sandra said.

"I am beginning to understand the piles of different colors and cover sheets now," Elizabeth said.

"After Snowden's revelations, our targets became keenly aware of the many vulnerabilities of cell phones and our ability to exploit them. So, while our adversaries keep their cell phones away from sensitive discussions or remove the batteries, key fobs stay in their pockets and purses," Sandra said.

"Key fobs? Amazing that we can add that kind of functionality into such a small package," Elizabeth observed.

"Yep! We're able to collect and record hours of conversation and then use Bluetooth connections with unwitting cellphones to exfiltrate the encoded audio files. Those are then sent covertly to our server, right here in this vault, where we use auto-translation algorithms and keyword search algorithms to filter the collections. As you can imagine, the volume of information can be daunting. We take extreme measures to protect this unique, new source and method of collection," Sandra explained.

"How can you know whose key fob to modify? When do you do it? Isn't the battery life decreased noticeably?"

"Slow down!" Sandra smiled. "I am just a case officer—a spy—who targets high value assets in Russia and elsewhere. My daytime job is developing targets for the Klondike System to be used against. We're pretty rigorous about how we decide who to go after—the constraints on our system are the backend translation and sorting out what people actually mean."

"Makes sense," Elizabeth said.

"I don't know the details of the technology, but I can tell you this material is pure gold! We have modified almost *all* key fobs on cars going into targeted countries—in fact, into most countries! But we only activate a small number of them."

"How can that be?" Elizabeth asked. "How have you modified almost all key fobs?"

"We created a front, a company that operates as a real commercial company but is controlled and funded by the Intelligence Community. We call them *proprietaries*," Sandra said.

"So, the CIA creates a company that appears to be a legitimate company," Elizabeth said.

"Almost. It *is* a legitimate company," Sandra said. "In this case, a rare, successful joint operation between the CIA and the NSA. The company operates a foundry here in the US that manufactures gallium nitride electronics and sells them worldwide for many different customers and uses. So, we're able to avoid attention by already being a leading chip provider in the relatively esoteric world of gallium nitride and indium phosphide devices. Gallium nitride on silicon chip is all the rage now. High efficiency, low power, and high reliability chips. Great for many uses, including the key fob market, which we have focused on and now own. We hide in plain sight!"

"I know the technology well," Elizabeth said. "Those semiconductors are referred to as 3-5 devices because of where they are on the periodic table. They have electronic features that were initially in high demand for many defense programs and now exist in consumer electronics."

"One of the biggest problems we've had to deal with was getting the State Department and Commerce Department to allow us to export the microelectronics without too much oversight."

"I can understand," Elizabeth said. "They were probably worried about the chips ending up in other countries' defense industries."

"Yep, and we sure as shit weren't going to brief those Commerce and State idiots into Klondike. We have been at this for a few years and now offer our chips at prices that our competitors can't touch."

"I had no idea we could do something this bold and get away with it," Elizabeth said admiringly. "How can the foundry employees not know?"

"The employees there have no idea they are producing chips designed by a team at the National Security Agency and subsidized by US taxpayers. They sell our key fob microelectronics to the suppliers that car makers use for their key fobs. Our microelectronics are buried in the car makers' supply chains. As long as we meet our contract commitments for production rate and quality, we'll remain the world's premier supplier of personal monitoring gear. Ford, GM, Mercedes, BMW, Audi, Toyota—almost all cars come with a special CIA key fob. Badda bing, badda boom! And just like a pager—remember those?—we can enable or disable the voice monitoring function of our key fobs anywhere on the planet by sending an encrypted broadcast signal hidden in the GPS waveform that only assigned key fobs respond to."

"And no one knows?" Elizabeth asked.

"Anyone physically examining the device would never see or detect the additional functionality. Now that you are being briefed into the program, that makes 317 people who know of its existence. Only a few dozen have access to the raw collects."

"Un-fucking-believable!" Elizabeth said. "You have hijacked the world's automobiles' key fobs?"

"Yep, we have." Sandra smiled. "And that's just the beginning. The key fobs have GPS tracking functions that we can enable, also."

"Amazing!" Elizabeth said. "Really amazing!"

"We can activate key fobs when they get within geofences we establish."

Sandra stood. "So, Elizabeth, the transcripts of some of the discussions we have accessed come from raw voice captures via key fobs. Many of our targets have cars with dedicated drivers, so too often, their driver's key fobs are not in the room during a sensitive conversation, and sometimes our targets are guarded in their discussions while traveling in the cars."

"Then how do you get the key fobs into areas where the sensitive discussions are happening?" Elizabeth asked.

"These dicks all love their muscle cars, their show cars— Ferraris, Lamborghinis, Porches, Maseratis—and they would never let their driver behind the wheel of their macho machines. These guys love to drive fast and show the world how important they are with cars like this. They carry those status key fobs wherever they go."

"Makes sense," Elizabeth said.

"So, we collect conversations and locations of many principals and the people who are nearby," Sandra said.

"Both men and women?" Elizabeth interrupted. "I thought Russian women didn't drive as much as Russian men do."

"You're right," Sandra said. "Russian women don't drive much, so it's mostly men we collect from in Russia. If you spoke Arabic, you'd hear every Middle Eastern prick bragging about his money, his cars, and his women. They keep their key fobs with them at all times!"

"So, what will I have access to?" Elizabeth asked.

"Many audio recordings from key Russian leadership. These are very evil people. You'll hear them discussing many criminal activities in addition to their hypersonic program you are working on. And, perhaps more importantly, you can help us target others for monitoring. I speak Russian but am not that fluent."

"How can I do that?" Elizabeth asked.

"Easy. If you hear them talking about someone you think we should target, send me the name," Sandra answered. "We have hacked the Russian vehicle registration database and can move to activate his key fob."

"And then?"

"We can literally enter a vehicle VIN number and send a wireless signal to the key fob for activation. And just like that, it starts recording conversations. We experiment with our targeting, but after we find a keeper, you know, someone we mine gold from, we target them for sustained collection," Sandra added.

"Sounds like thousands of hours of voice files to sort through," Elizabeth said. "How do you know when to listen to a target?"

"After we identify a target, we use specially designed filters to eliminate background chatter, like televisions and radios, and specialized algorithms to narrow our searches—you know, who they are talking to, keywords, times, et cetera. Far from perfect, but it works and is getting better," Sandra said.

"It's like the CIA has their own Siri or Alexa."

"That's exactly right. We actually have both and more," Sandra said. "The voice recognition algorithms create text files that you will be able to search and read. You wouldn't be surprised at which companies have developed this for us, but that's in a separate compartment within the Klondike Control System, and you are not cleared for those accesses."

"I understand," Elizabeth said.

"You'll be able to search for voice collection databases by time of collection, location, keyword search, or speaker."

"This really is remarkable," Elizabeth said admiringly.

"When you read an intelligence report based on Klondike collections, it will falsely cite a source for the information—"

"Give me an example," Elizabeth interrupted.

"Like, it may cite a Russian diplomat at an embassy cocktail party, or a US scientist returning from an international conference, or some other technical collection system," Sandra replied. "It's essential the information gets into the hands of analysts like you, but we also need to continue to keep Klondike under wraps."

"I see. This helps explain the disconnects in so many of the IRs," Elizabeth said.

"Yes. When it became clear we were providing conflicting data to your team, it was decided to brief one analyst from the team into the raw data," Sandra said.

"And that's where I came in?" Elizabeth asked.

"Your combination of technical skills and Russian language skills made you the obvious choice," Sandra said. "You're now the bridge between the Klondike program and the Cloud Spinner team. You'll be working with me to make sure all of the relevant data gets out of the Klondike program and into the Cloud Spinner assessment, all while protecting the Klondike collection methods."

"This is just amazing," Elizabeth said.

"Yes, it is amazing—but it's more important to protect Klondike than it is to allow our broader analytical community to get access to the program data. You'll have access to the information that you need, but sometimes we won't be able to further investigate and validate the information that you get. And you have to live with that. Klondike must be protected at all costs."

"And the other Klondike program?" Elizabeth asked.

"It's called Dawson City, bi-graph DC, same classification rules as WH. By the way, both programs are NOFORN and ORCON, meaning no one who is not a US citizen can know of this, under any circumstances, and the CIA controls all data dissemination from this source."

"Understood," Elizabeth said.

"We are using similar technology, but the Dawson City program modifies Fitbit activity trackers to enable them to monitor voice conversation."

"Fitbits can be bugging devices?"

"Our engineers determined that the sensors in Fitbits and the acoustic transmissibility of the cover glass work not only for monitoring arm movement, counting steps, measuring heart rate, and oxygen levels. By changing the filter characteristics in the software, we can get reasonably good voice monitoring from these sensors. The device works out to only about 250 Hz, so voices sound indistinct, but the intelligence value of the data has been extraordinary!"

"Now I know why the CIA doesn't allow Fitbits and heart rate monitoring devices in the building," Elizabeth said.

"Exactly," Sandra said.

"And everyone carrying a car key fob or wearing a Fitbit is wearing a wire."

"More or less."

"My Fitbit is in my car," Elizabeth said.

"Where it should be," smiled Sandra. "The system is a bit more complicated than Whitehorse. It requires getting the location of the phone that works with the Fitbit. First, we geo-sort the phones focusing on locations where we think targets will be, like key government facilities in Moscow, for example. We then use a hacked Fitbit app."

"You hacked Fitbit?" Elizabeth was incredulous.

"We have an arrangement with the company. They are very patriotic."

"Also, there's another Klondike program that's been developed and is having some success. You haven't been approved to be briefed into that one because we don't have any Cloud Spinner data from it yet. At least we don't think we do. I will check and see if maybe we can get you read into the program," Sandra said.

"Thanks—I think," Elizabeth said.

"Now, you'll be able to directly access and task recordings and transcripts of key targets and the people they associate with—business colleagues, family, neighbors, and people they are fucking. We just need one person in a target's circle to have a key fob on them or be a Fitbit loyalist."

"I am really proud we can do this," Elizabeth said.

"You cannot use this raw data in any finished intelligence report or cite where it came from. Your boss knows you have been accessed to something special. You'll have to be circumspect with him about this."

"Understood, "Elizabeth said. "But he's a good guy."

"Of course, he is, but you cannot reveal anything about Klondike to him."

Sandra went on. "In order to access the raw data, you'll need to come to this room and use this audio equipment. This is the only place you'll be able to hear the actual voices and read the transcripts. You'll have a unique login password and are already set up with access to the vault security systems and the computer system in this room. Access is 24/7. The conversations are all in Russian. Translations can be difficult. Any other questions?"

"Can I start tonight?"

***

Elizabeth returned to her office and sat at her cubicle, mulling over her meeting in the vault and what to tell Frank about her new program clearances.

He appeared at her desk a few minutes later. "So, what can you tell me?" he asked.

"Actually, very little. I've been given access to a program I can't say anything about that may allow a clearer view of some of the Cloud Spinner issues we grapple with. I'll be spending some time in another part of the building, I think mostly in the evening, but still working on Cloud Spinner."

"Really, you can't say anything?" Frank asked.

"I have been told not to say anything about the additional accesses I've been given. I can tell you the name of the employee who briefed me, if you want to discuss this with her," Elizabeth offered.

"No need." Frank raised his hands. "I understand." But he clearly didn't approve._

She finished her day in the office in a brainstorming session with her co-workers trying to better understand the mass fractions of the fuel quantity, the propulsion system, the glide vehicle, and the warhead. In earlier days, understanding these factors on the many generations of Soviet ballistic missiles the CIA had been assessing had been a straightforward process, but the new maneuverability of the hypersonic systems made it almost impossible to deterministically calculate these factors. While the warhead size was key, the maneuverability of the system at various stages of flight was also essential for assessing whether or not the hundreds of billions of dollars that had been spent on missile defense since Ronald Reagan began the "Star Wars" program had been wasted. As the Cloud Spinner team left for the day, Elizabeth made plans to continue hers.

***

Even though it had been a long Friday in the office, Elizabeth returned to the vault after ending her day in the isolated cubicles of WINPAC. She added her initials to the door log, disarmed the security system after only two attempts, logged on to the computer system in the glass room, and plugged in her headphones. She found a detailed document with a chronological list of conversations intercepted over the last two years that highlighted the principals, dates, and locations of the discussions. She started with audio files from July of 2016 in the Kremlin.

Muffled Russian, missing words, and voices that lacked easily identifiable characteristics. The recording was not very good. This was hard. The transcripts in the file folder were clearly machine translations, rife with misspellings and misinterpretations. Included in the file was the IR that had been released, citing a Russian military attaché in Switzerland as the source of the information in the conversation. As she had heard endlessly from her team, the government spent billions of dollars for collection and pennies for processing and analysis._

Sitting at the computer, she saw that the true origin of the report was Whitehorse. Sifting through the voice intercepts was extremely tedious, and she wasted a great deal of time listening to complaints about traffic in Moscow and birthday party plans. Finally, at the beginning of her third hour, she heard an argument from July 23, 2016 between two men, identified by the auto-translation function as the Russian

Minister of Finance Boris Davidov and the Minister of Defense Sergei Polichuk.

"Go fuck yourself if you think we'll spend another ruble for your fantasy! You promised to finish testing this past spring. I'm done with you and your bullshit. I will not authorize any more money for your engineers to polish this turd!" Davidov said.

"We've been successful in three of the last seven tests. Putin has committed publicly to this system being deployed," Polichuk said.

"Three of seven! Again, go fuck yourself! Your program is a failure! And I don't give a shit about Vlad's commitments," the finance minister argued.

"The program is not a failure. We have already succeeded in the hardest tests. With only two more tests, we can have full confidence in the system. In these last tests, we can combine three key performance objectives together to have necessary confidence in the system: a real warhead with fusing, maximum range, and extreme maneuverability. The program will be a success," the defense minister responded.

"Surely, you can't claim the program will be a success after the costs have tripled and results are more than five years late," Davidov said.

"Without these tests, we may have to limit our initial operational deployments. In order to be a credible deterrent, the fucking Americans must understand what it can do almost as well as we do. We need to fund the team for four more months and 170 million rubles," Polichuk said.

A sound that might have been a fist pounding something that sounded wooden and heavy—a table? "I'll give you ten weeks and 30 million rubles. We go to production in three months, or I kill the program. And then I come after you for being a corrupt leader of the aerospace industry in Russia, and you'll be spending the rest of your miserable existence on the planet in a Siberian gulag."

The friction between the minister of defense was unmentioned in the filtered reports. Elizabeth already had found useful information that would help interpret reports and a possible reason for some report contradictions and discrepancies.

"Then we have an agreement? Ten weeks and 30 million rubles?" Polichuk confirmed.

"Yes, that's what I said, and you better get out of my sight before I change my mind," Davidov said.

"I brought a bottle of vodka to toast our success. Just in case we found a way forward," Polichuk said.

She heard the sound of liquid pouring and the clink of glasses and then, "Nastrovya!" said in unison.

"So..." Polichuk began. "What else has been keeping you busy here in the Kremlin?"

"Oh, the same bullshit. Lies, liars, and charlatans all find their way to my office. There has been a strange one though. A US businessman, a special US businessman. He has promised to make us all rich if we allow him to build a hotel complex on Red Square," Davidov answered.

Elizabeth sat upright. This was not in the transcript.

"You say special? Why special?" Polichuk asked.

"Because he is the Republican nominee for the US presidency!" Davidov exclaimed.

"Really? We'd let an arrogant US businessman develop a project in Moscow? I can't imagine the boss would agree," the defense minister said.

"In addition to making the required deposits into our Swiss bank accounts, he promised each of us an apartment in the development. He was working this deal before his nomination. I don't think this project will go far, but if he wins the presidency, we'll have him by the balls and who knows what we'll get from him! Maybe sanctions lifted and recognition of our little adventure in the Crimea," Davidov chuckled.

Polichuk sounded baffled. "Can you believe that Americans would actually elect such a person as their president? A corrupt womanizer who covets money?"

"I can't think of a president they've elected that this doesn't describe," Davidov said.

They laughed. A clink of glassware.

"It is a crazy world when in one meeting, we plan the funding and development of weapons to destroy the US, and in the next meeting, we

plan how to benefit from their capitalism and blackmail a US president,"
Polichuk observed.

"He doesn't realize we have recorded every conversation he has had
with us and videotaped his dalliances with his prostitutes. When the
project is completed, we will take ownership of his development as our
own," the finance minister said. "He is a child, he doesn't realize who
he is fucking with. While he may aspire to spend time here in Moscow,
it will be in Lubyanka, as a guest of the FSB, not in his fancy hotel.
We don't think he'll win against her, but if he does, he will be easily
manipulated. We know she is totally corrupt, she sold access to cronies
who contributed to her charitable foundation—"

Polichuk interrupted, "And used a private email server to keep her
communications hidden—but not from us! What an idiot!"

"Yes, we hacked her server, and she knows we'll be torturing her
with slow, embarrassing leaks of her emails," the finance minister said.
"Perhaps we should see if we can help him win? You know, put our
intelligence services to work to help his team."

"Great idea. I'll give Demetri a call and see if he can help. I'll need to
check with the boss though and make sure he's okay with this."

Elizabeth sat in stunned silence. She had just heard a new,
crucial fact about the Cloud Spinner program—and, more
disturbingly, heard two Russian leaders planning to influence
the upcoming US election and blackmail the corrupt candidate,
should he win.

It was late and she was hungry. She went back to her hotel
to try to figure out what to do.

CHAPTER 8

Monday, October 24, 2016 to
Tuesday, October 25, 2016

Old Headquarters Building

Monday morning came too soon after a quiet weekend exploring the area. Elizabeth and Tova spent Saturday hiking through Great Falls and Sunday taking a day trip, a two-hour drive from McLean to Old Rag, a granite outcropping, where they made the climb to the peak and enjoyed the leaves starting to turn in the Shenandoah Valley. The isolation and time away from her desk gave her the chance to plan her next moves at the Agency. She did not sleep well that weekend.

***

The Cloud Spinner team started early at an 0700 stand-up meeting for those who could make it. A tactical review of the last workday, a look forward to progress made in producing the NIE, and an opportunity to pass on any thoughts and questions to the team both as a whole and individually. Elizabeth liked the process. Not the hour.

"I still don't really understand the last test results," observed John, one of the older analysts on the team. "On one hand, we think we saw really extraordinary cross-range maneuverability in the HGV, but when we model the mass of the vehicle, it seemed far heavier than we would have expected for this test. Like they had a full payload onboard. Why would they conduct a maneuverability test this early in the test program with a heavy payload in the airframe? In the last thirty years, we've seen them be very incremental in their test approaches. Hopefully, our collection in the coming year will be much better so we can improve our estimates."

"Perhaps they're accelerating their test program, reducing the number of tests before going into production?" Elizabeth asked.

He considered her idea and shook his head. "I really can't see them going into production and fielding these weapons without more confidence."

"Maybe they've got serious schedule and budget pressures and are planning on software updates to the system to improve performance and reliability—you know, like iPhones and Teslas," Elizabeth responded.

John dismissed her. "No, I think we can count on another year or two of testing and at least eight more flights before they commit to production."

Elizabeth bit her tongue. "Perhaps, but what if they were to be less incremental—you know, incorporate more than just one key performance parameter into the same test? Then they could be only one test, two at the most, away from deploying operationally. They may be relying on advanced computer modeling to generate the necessary confidence and not need as many physical tests. This is the approach we are taking this year at JPL."

The team looked at her silently. John looked away. *No need to argue*, thought Elizabeth. The coming months would allow the team to better assess the Avangard capabilities and vulnerabilities. And, they needed more data to produce the high confidence NIE the director of national intelligence was counting on.

Back at her cubicle, Elizabeth called Sandra and asked to meet in the vault.

***

"What's up?" Sandra asked.

"I spent Friday evening here listening to an audio file from July. A discussion between Davidov and Polichuk about the Avangard program. Davidov was pissed about the program overrun and schedule slips."

Sandra laughed. "Just like every friggin' program our aerospace industry touches. Another way of life that we and the Russians share. Program overruns and schedule slips by the defense industry bloodsuckers."

"Davidov threatened to cancel the program, but they ended up coming to an agreement to spend 30 million rubles to complete testing in ten weeks. I think they will fly, at most, two more tests and then go to production. I told the Cloud Spinner team that I didn't think we have another year to collect flight test data and that production will start much sooner than they currently are forecasting." Elizabeth sighed. "The team ignored me and thinks the test program will be like the ones we have seen over the decades. Many, many tests before operational deployment. But if we don't place the highest collection priority on the next test or two they conduct because we think we'll have many more chances to collect results of many more tests, we may miss collecting essential performance data.

"So, what do you want to do?" Sandra asked.

"Help the team understand that we have limited time and limited data collect opportunities, so it can focus."

Sandra nodded. "No problem. We'll get a sanitized report out today crediting a HUMINT source. You know, a spy? So the team will know quickly."

"Great! This will allow Cloud Spinner to get the highest priority collection from other systems," Elizabeth said.

Elizabeth liked Sandra. No BS. Issue raised, action taken, problem solved. And she really liked those heels. Elizabeth was more of a cross-training shoe kind of woman, but Sandra looked great. Elizabeth would have to get to a nice shoe store and pick up a pair of pumps. And then figure out how to walk in those things.

"Yes. One other thing. After Davidov and Polichuk made a deal on a new budget and schedule, they drank a lot of vodka to toast their agreement and talked about another deal the Kremlin was working on. A US businessman is trying to build a hotel development on Red Square and has promised money and condos to Putin and his team as part of accelerating the approval process. Should this go to the FBI?"

"No," Sandra shook her head. "We don't involve ourselves in petty behavior like this, and we would never jeopardize Klondike material just for a graft and corruption investigation. Not in our job jar. We need to focus on these new weapons systems. Everything else is just noise."

Elizabeth countered. "This isn't just noise, though. This is criminal behavior. This is international and domestic criminal activity that I've uncovered."

"Hey, this isn't what you're looking for, and you have to let it go. If he is corrupt, he will eventually be caught by the FBI when he screws up in the US," Sandra said.

"But this guy is running for president. He is the Republican nominee. He might win."

Sandra sighed. "I'll get that report out for your team this afternoon. Really? That idiot is bribing Russians government officials. That is really stupid—and criminal. But she is a shoo-in. She can't lose."

"I am not sure," Elizabeth said, "She has a lot of baggage herself and is hated by many."

Sandra repeated herself. "He can't win."

Elizabeth rolled her eyes to the sky in a look of frustration.

"Thanks, Sandra, I look forward to seeing the sanitized report."

***

Elizabeth returned to her cubicle and immersed herself in historical data collects and the physics-based model ambiguities. It was obvious that the Russians had developed and tested a system, knowing the limits of US technical collection systems, and were intentionally feeding information in palatable chunks to US intelligence sources. The Russians revealed some of the key performance details of their system but kept other critical features of the Avangard unknown. They encrypted some telemetry, but not all. They seemed to want the US to understand some aspects of Avangard's performance capabilities but were being selective about what they revealed.

Elizabeth called out across the cubicle for Tom. "Do you think the cross-range distance is limited by thermal maximums or by aerodynamic stresses?"

His voice floated back. "Both. But the warhead mass uncertainties make it impossible to understand which one it is."

Elizabeth updated her software modeling tools to incorporate a complex Monte Carlo simulation with payload mass as the dependent variable. She would program and run millions of simulations comparing the actual tests results already collected with a payload mass varying from zero to the known mass of Russian nuclear warheads. She suspected the results would be controversial with the team, but if the technique worked for casinos in Las Vegas, it should be good enough for the Cloud Spinner team. The runtimes for the calculations would be hours, and she hoped she would see results by morning.

***

She left the Cloud Spinner teamwork area early with the Monte Carlo runs underway and returned to 5F43 to listen to more Klondike audio.

She screened the summaries of recent collections and saw one between Polichuk, the minister of defense, and an unknown woman. She opened the file and saw the collect was from October 2, 2016. She put her feet up on the desk and opened the file.

She heard groaning and the sounds of love making. Audio porn. *What a crummy way to make a living,* she thought. The sounds died down quickly. Polichuk sounded like he had an orgasm. The woman? Elizabeth was unsure. She heard footsteps.

"*I have to go home now, and I have to be gone next week,*" *Polichuk said.*

"*Why do you have to leave next week? You promised me you'd take me to London,*" *the woman complained.* "*I've rearranged my schedule, and now you say you can't go, and I'm stuck here in Moscow.*"

Polichuk said, "*I have to be in Tyuratam for a very important missile test. This is the last test of a very important system, and I must be there to witness the results. My balls are on the line.*"

"*Your balls are on the line with me too, you asshole,*" *she said.* "*I know you are a bigwig in Moscow, but to me you are just a piece of meat.*"

"*The test cannot be rescheduled for your London shopping trip. And I'm coming into a great deal of money, US dollars. Putin is sharing the spoils of a deal he made with a US businessman for a big development in Moscow, just next to Red Square. My share is in a Swiss account. We'll enjoy London later!*"

Elizabeth struggled to hear the conversation. The collection was weaker, so probably from a Fitbit rather than a key fob.

A key fob would be in a pants pocket, strewn on the floor far from the pillow talk. A Fitbit would be on the woman's arm, next to their heads, near their bodies, and capturing most of their conversations. She obviously wanted to get credit for her physical activity against her daily goal. Thank goodness for fitness nuts.

Elizabeth was pleased to learn of the upcoming HGV test. It was probably the last before production and might provide important answers. Some in the Intelligence Community would take the uncertainties and conclude the system's performance to be at the high end of the range; others would presume it at the low range. Everyone in Washington had an angle to play that revolved around each agency's priorities and program funding. The Missile Defense Agency would want billions more to counter the system, the US Navy would be in a perpetual state of denial now that their carrier battle groups were at risk and could not be defended, the USAF would want to replicate the new capability, and industry would smell blood in the water and clamor for new program starts.

She was troubled about Sandra's indifference to the corrupt US businessman. The guy was bad news. How could someone who was bribing Russian officials and subject to being blackmailed possibly be a serious candidate for the US presidency?

She pulled the headset back on and spent the rest of the evening listening to Russian leaders planning to nuke the US. She wondered again about this being a strange way to make a living.

**

The next morning, Elizabeth asked for time on Frank's calendar.

"So, what's going on?" he asked. "You look tired."

"I need some advice," she said. "The new program I've been read into has some extraordinary information on Cloud Spinner that I'm able to bring to bear in our analysis, but I've also become aware of illegal activity by a US citizen that could be of grave consequences to the country. I don't think anyone at the Agency could care less."

"Tell me exactly what information you've become aware of and how reliable it is," Frank asked.

"I can't tell you anything," Elizabeth said. "I've agreed to protect all of the information and the control system that protects it."

"Then you're wasting my time," he said, twirling his glasses. "I'm really not interested in solving hypothetical problems for you. Go to the people who read you into the program and tell them your concerns but leave me out of it."

"I have," Elizabeth replied. "But I was told it wasn't the Agency's problem and to focus on the Cloud Spinner project."

"My advice is to take their advice."

"But the consequences are, well, insane!" Elizabeth frowned. "To ignore this could really hurt the country."

"Liz, we can't solve all the problems we find." Frank put his half rims back up on his nose. "Let's focus on Cloud Spinner."

***

She left the Cloud Spinner team area early to return to the glass house. She searched the data base for all conversations with Davidov. There were hundreds. She suspected that the minister of finance was the best source for information about bribes from the US businessman.

She opened an audio file of a conversation between Davidov and Putin from August of this year.

"What it is that he wants?" Putin asked. She was surprised at how tired he sounded in these private conversations.

Davidov spoke. "He is seeking the rights to develop the Old Mint into a hotel with restaurants and apartments. He wants it to bear his name, of course. He claims he will do the same thing for the Red Square area as he did when he developed the Old Post Office building near the White House in Washington. That property is opening later this year and by most accounts will be successful."

Putin asked, "What's in it for us? Can he be trusted?"

"Of course, he cannot be trusted." Davidov said. "He has many bankruptcies and spent a fortune on lawyers litigating with everyone—his investors, his contractors, and his employees. That is why he will borrow all of the money necessary. Deutsche Bank is fully supporting this project."

Putin laughed. "The Germans will finally enter Red Square. They couldn't get here with their Panzers but will arrive with their Euros."

"Since he can't be trusted, we've been very diligent at building an extensive Kompromat file. We have all of his bribery conversations on audio and all of his nights with his whores on video. Each night he's been in Moscow, he's sent his security guy to the Night Flight Club to select one or two women. He has no idea that we've controlled all of his and his team's engagement with us."

A Kompromat file was a detailed package of dirt the Russian intelligence services developed on everyone they could to influence their behavior—much like the infamous Hoover files. The Russians were diligent in collecting material to gain influence. Years before, the Russians tried to blackmail Indonesian President Sukarno with videos of him engaged in sex with a group of Aeroflot flight attendants. When the KGB showed him the video and made their demands, he laughed and asked for copies of the tape. He was proud of his stamina and, as a professed polygamist, thought publicizing his performance would enhance his reputation in Indonesia. Elizabeth wondered if such a file would be met with the same reaction by this guy.

"Why would such a person run for the US presidency?" Putin asked. "And could he win?"

Davidov answered. "Ego, combined with money and power. He cares only about his personal and family's interest. And although he has won the Republican primary, no one thinks he'll prevail over the Democrat."

"I agree," Putin said. "I detest her. She is corrupt and a worthless piece of shit. But perhaps we could help him win?"

"We've actually thought about it. Recall that we have been funding a Ministry of Defense team, a very sophisticated computer network attack team, here in Moscow to better prepare for cyberwarfare. Our cyber efforts during the 2014 invasion of the Crimea had some success, but we have gotten far better since then. We could divert the team to the US election and see if we can help him get elected. If we were to succeed, we have a US president as your lapdog," Davidov said. "Your башка!"

"Do it!" Putin said. "And get me a copy of those video tapes."

Elizabeth had not heard the term башка for many years. башка, *bashka*. In English, chump. The chump. A chump. Putin's chump.

Putin was hoping to influence the election and have his chump in the US White House.

She had to act.

***

She returned to her cubicle to use her red phone, the one used for classified calls, and left Sandra a voice mail asking to meet in the vault that evening.

Then she returned to the vault to listen to more conversations. These Russians leaders were scum. Lying, cheating, backstabbing scum. They were the swamp of Moscow. Their focus on money, power, women, and total disregard for the Russian people sickened her.

She looked up at the clock and saw it was after 9 p.m. Although she had not found more revealing audios, she was learning about the characters of these soulless Russians leaders. Money and power, power and money. That is what drove them. She was tired and sore from sitting in a crummy chair when she sensed someone entering the outer room. Shadows changed shape, and then Sandra appeared at the door to the glass house with a pizza box in one hand and a bottle of red in the other.

Elizabeth hadn't realized she was hungry until this moment. Almost on cue, her stomach rumbled.

"Impressive that you can carry a pizza in those heels." Elizabeth smiled.

"I hope you like pepperoni and a cabernet? If not, more for me!"

"I could eat the box, and I love a good red," Elizabeth replied.

They ate the pizza and sipped the wine slowly.

Sandra asked, "So, you called earlier today and said you wanted to meet. I am glad you did. What's going on?"

"It's been a long day. I've learned things I shouldn't know, and I'm tired." Elizabeth rubbed her eyes. "I need to tell you about the intercepts I listened to last night."

"Later, later," Sandra said.

She stood, walked behind Elizabeth's chair, and began massaging her neck and back.

"Oh my God, that feels good," Elizabeth said. This encouraged Sandra to work on Elizabeth's aching neck and back muscles more aggressively. She continued down her arms, her lower back, and close to her breasts. Elizabeth sighed and relaxed as Sandra began a more sensual massage. Elizabeth had never been with a woman before but was curious about an encounter like this. She actually had not been with many men before and those she had been with were mostly boring. Sandra could be an experiment. Perhaps a dalliance. Elizabeth had never had this kind of opportunity. Sandra's hands slipped lower. Elizabeth sighed and leaned back in the chair, inviting Sandra to continue.

Sandra continued applying her strong hands, kneading and caressing Elizabeth's neck, shoulders, and back. She reached around and began stroking Elizabeth's breasts and kissing her neck. Elizabeth responded by pulling Sandra's head closer to her neck and turned to kiss her.

"We can't do this—can we?" Elizabeth moaned. "Can we...?"

Sandra cupped Elizabeth's breasts as Elizabeth reached out to Sandra's thighs. They kissed passionately. "... get away with this? I am not your boss! Of course, we can."

"But what if someone comes in?"

"Here? We won't be interrupted," Sandra whispered.

***

The rest of the evening in the vault was both a blur and memorable for Elizabeth. The time passed way too quickly.

"I have never had an experience like this, that was at least five firsts," Elizabeth said quietly. "I really didn't expect this to happen. I didn't even imagine this."

"I think we might be good for each other. I was thrilled to be with you tonight," Sandra replied.

"Me, too. You are so beautiful, and your body—and heels, make me crazy," Elizabeth answered.

"Let's call it an evening," Sandra said.

"Let's call it a fantastic evening," Elizabeth smiled.

Before they left the vault, Sandra gave her a lingering goodnight kiss. They rode the elevator to the first floor in silence and gave each other a knowing smile as they separated and left the building through different entrances to get to their distant cars.

So, this was what it was like to work at the CIA. Analyze Russian weapons designed to kill Americans, uncover a corrupt politician, and be seduced by a sexy co-worker and amazing lover. If only she knew this before. She would never have settled into JPL with all of the nerds and geeks. She would have stayed back East and enjoyed the seasons.

CHAPTER 9

Wednesday, October 26, 2016
CIA Headquarters, Corcoran Street

Last night with Sandra was confusing for many reasons. Having a one-night fling or perhaps even beginning a relationship with a co-worker. Being with a woman for the first time, something Elizabeth realized felt right, natural, and much more satisfying than her few dates with men had been. And then there was Sandra's dismissal of an issue that seemed paramount to Elizabeth: the corrupt businessman running for president. All that confusion swirling in a pleasant fog of desire took her mind off of Cloud Spinner and the *bashka* problem.

Ironically, that morning she was required to attend a workplace sexual harassment training meeting in the conference room after completing the Agency's mandatory online training. She quickly learned how to game the system and complete her mandated one-and-a-half-hour minimum training time in less than thirty minutes.

After, she stopped at Frank's office.

"Got a moment?"

"Sure, come on in," he replied. "What's up?"

"I need to spend more time working on the compartmented project I got briefed into. There are critical areas related to Cloud Spinner that need to be further evaluated," she lied.

Frank looked unhappy.

"I understand," he said. "Take whatever time you need, but—I'd appreciate you trying to attend the 0700 stand-up every morning, especially if you're out of the loop for a few days."

Elizabeth nodded. "Done. This morning was a bit of a struggle."

Elizabeth returned to her cubicle and called Sandra but got her voice mail.

"Good morning," Elizabeth said, trying her best to sound professional. "I am going to be in 5F43 for most of the day and would appreciate it if you have a few minutes to stop by. I have some additional thoughts I'd like to cover with you."

***

She returned to the 5F43 and noticed she had not signed the security log last night when she closed the vault. A security check at 3:45 a.m. flagged the fact that the vault alarm had been secured and the door cypher lock engaged, but the open/closing log had not been initialed. "Shit," she muttered. Her first security violation. A note on the door instructed her to call an internal number to clear up the issue. She opened the vault door, disabled the alarm system, and called the security office.

"Good morning. Elizabeth Petrov calling from 5F43. I just entered the room and disabled the alarm, but there was a note on the vault door asking me to call and speak to Gordon."

"Yes, ma'am!" said a cheerful male voice with a slight Southern drawl. "Gordon Haver here—thanks for calling. Let me look at the security log and see what was going on there last night." Elizabeth heard the clicking of a noisy keyboard. "It looks like one of our roving officers noted the door log open at an unusual time, confirmed the alarm was set and the lock secured, so she knew the office was empty, but she saw that the door security log was incomplete."

Elizabeth said, "Gordon, this was my mistake. I left very late last night and secured the vault but neglected to complete the log."

Gordon did not sound particularly upset. "Thank you for clearing this up. We aren't allowed to access the room unless there's an immediate emergency. The Office of Security has a master key to ensure we can gain access, but we'd never abuse such a privilege. We just noted the discrepancy and wanted to let you know."

"Thank you very much for doing so. It won't happen again," she said. "I hope I won't be issued a security violation for this."

During her new employee orientation briefings, she learned that security violations like this would be treated harshly and could result in permanent notes in personnel files, time off without pay, and even termination.

"Not a problem, Ms. Petrov," Gordon said. "Knowing you were here working so late is enough for me to just let this go with a verbal warning. If there is ever anything I can do to help you, please reach out and let me know."

She had dodged a bullet. Maybe.

Elizabeth entered the glass room and started reviewing transcripts and listening to audio files. She was able to find significant discussions about the *bashka*, including a phone call from Davidov to his banker with account numbers and funds transfers. She kept notes on a paper pad, highlighting the names, dates, amounts, and transferred amounts.

Sandra came by the room in the late afternoon.

"Hi, I just got your voice mail. What's going on?" Sandra asked. Then she gave Elizabeth a long look. "I really enjoyed our evening last night."

Elizabeth was unsure where to start. The *bashka*, Cloud Spinner, or what she was really thinking about: last night.

She stood crossed the room and gave Sandra a long kiss. Sandra responded passionately.

Elizabeth motioned to Sandra to sit in her chair and pulled another over for herself.

"When I talked to you about my concerns about the corrupt US businessman, you said not to worry about it. You said that our focus was protecting Klondike and understanding Cloud Spinner."

"I did."

"Well, I disagree."

Sandra frowned.

"I gave Frank a watered-down version of what I was worried about. He was dismissive of my concerns and said I should listen to you."

"But you didn't, did you?" Sandra asked.

"No. I spent the day reviewing audio files and found something big. I was going to talk to you last night about it, but we... got... well, distracted."

Sandra looked perplexed.

"I need your thoughts, maybe your help," Elizabeth said. "Davidov and Putin are assembling a team in Russia to help the *bashka* get elected president."

"The what?" Sandra asked. "The *bashka*? What is a *bashka*?"

Sandra's Russian did not include nuanced terms like this.

"*Bashka*. Russian vernacular for chump. Putin's nickname for him. I found a detailed conversation between Davidov and Putin discussing the compromising material they have on the *bashka*, how he can be blackmailed with it, and how they're going to use the Russian military's cyber warfare teams to aid in his election."

"I need to hear this," Sandra said.

Elizabeth found the audio file, and they both put headphones ones while she played it for Sandra.

"Holy shit," Sandra said.

Their eyes met as they both realized the importance of the file.

"Before we talk about what to do about this, I need to understand where you and I are," Elizabeth said. "Last night was good. I am attracted to you. Was that just a...?"

Sandra put her hand on Elizabeth's leg, "I am very attracted to you and hope to see you again. Is that your question? One and done, or should we see each other?"

"I guess it is," Elizabeth replied. "I would really like to see you again."

"Dinner tonight? My place? I live near Logan Circle, in the city."

"I'd like that. And we need to talk about what to do about this *bashka* issue," Elizabeth said. "Can we do that at your house?"

"Absolutely, let's figure it out together," Sandra said. "Parking in my neighborhood sucks, so how about I pick you up here when you're done, and we go together?"

"I need to go home and take care of my dog. Pick me up there?"

"Sure, what is your address?" Sandra asked.

"The Residence Inn off of Old Dominion in downtown McLean," Elizabeth answered.

"You're living in a hotel?"

"Me and my yellow lab. I just haven't felt the need to find a permanent place to live yet."

"You don't feel committed to the Agency yet, hm?" Sandra asked.

"Not really," Elizabeth admitted. "I was really only asked to come to work on Cloud Spinner."

"We should talk about your career tonight, then, too," Sandra said. "I'll be there at 1830."

"*Tovarisch*, too?" Elizabeth asked. "I hate to leave him alone for so long."

Sandra shrugged and said, "Of course. *Tovarisch?* You named your lab Tovarisch?"

"Yes, Tova for short, my *comrade*," Elizabeth replied. "I can't imagine living without a dog, a big dog! Big in size, big in ego, and big in protection."

***

Sandra arrived a few minutes early. Elizabeth and Tova were waiting in the hotel lobby. Elizabeth held a leash in one hand and a bottle of red in the other. Sandra drove a Tesla Model 3, an all-electric sedan with little room for a shedding yellow lab. Sandra looked at her all-black interior and Tova's long, yellow hair.

Elizabeth saw Sandra's displeasure and said, "I'll get a portable vacuum for you, or loan you mine. He does shed a bit."

Sandra's eyes lingered on Elizabeth's trim figure in jeans and a tight, white t-shirt.

"Don't worry," she smiled. "You're worth a little dog hair."

Rush hour traffic down the GW Parkway into DC was snarled, which gave them time to talk.

"Where did you grow up?" Sandra asked.

"Brighton Beach. Only child. Raised by my grandfather who emigrated with me from the Soviet Union in 1989. Born in Moscow and now a US citizen."

"Where are your parents?"

"Still in Russia, as far as I know. I've not seen or spoken to them in over twenty-five years. My grandfather says they viewed me as an accident and a burden in their lives. He was at the front of the Fourth Wave of Jews that fled Russia. My grandfather felt strongly that if he didn't leave then, he would never be able to. He knew I would have greater opportunities in the States. Told me he rescued me from going to a Russian orphanage."

"Shit, I'm so sorry to hear," Sandra said. "What a difficult time."

"I was very young when we left, so I really only know the US. The love and caring my grandfather provided me was enough. Of course, I do wonder if I have siblings and how my parents are," Elizabeth said while she struggled with Tova in the back seat. He wanted the window down.

"That explains why you understand Russian so well."

"I grew up thinking it was normal to speak two languages. My grandfather only ever spoke to me in Russian. My schools in New York were all in English."

"How did he make a living in the US? How did he support the two of you?" Sandra asked.

"He was in international trade; you know, an importer and exporter, but has been retired for many years," Elizabeth said. "Your turn."

Sandra laughed. "I'm so boring compared to you! I grew up in a close Jewish family in the suburbs of Pittsburgh. My father was an executive at US Steel, and then our world collapsed when the mills shut down. But at least after that, we could then breathe the air and go boating on the Ohio and Monongahela Rivers."

"I have never been to Pittsburgh, but I love the Penguins," Elizabeth said.

"Me, too! I love to watch a good hockey game. The Caps are a great team, too. Let's plan on going to a game!" Sandra interjected.

"Yes! I'd love that. But more about you now," Elizabeth said.

"Well, I had a completely traditional family life in every sense. Then I told them I was bisexual. Rattled their world but they have come to be accepting and supportive. The suburbs suffocated me, and I knew I needed to live in a city—you know, like, diverse, vibrant, limitless opportunities.

"Understand, for sure." Elizabeth agreed.

"Then, I got accepted to Georgetown and studied international affairs and business. Minored in Russian. It killed them I didn't go to Carnegie Mellon or Pitt—but sometimes the bird has got to leave the nest."

"Yeah, I got thrown out of the nest at an early age."

Sandra winced. "I'm sorry, honey. That really shouldn't happen to anyone. Maybe I can help figure out what happened in Moscow that would have brought you here under such circumstances."

"Hah, here we are, two single Jewish girls ready to change the world. Go figure!" Elizabeth said.

"My roots are in Poland," Sandra said while maneuvering through an accident site. "My grandparents survived the Holocaust and got to the US—you and your grandfather were just a couple of decades behind us.

"Perhaps we should just speak Russian to each other from now on?"

"*Nyet*. I could never keep up with you," Sandra laughed.

"But that's how you'll get better," Elizabeth countered.

"I thought the mix of Russian and business at Georgetown would be a good combination toward a decent career. Senior year, one of my professors suggested I apply to the Agency and, well, the rest is history."

Tova stretched his torso between the two front seats demanding some attention.

"He's used to riding up front. We made it across the country with him as my co-pilot," Elizabeth laughed. "What kind of assignments have you had?"

"You really can't talk about this with anyone, but I'm a case officer, a spy."

Elizabeth laughed. "Isn't everyone?"

"Not really. Most Agency employees are open employees or have light diplomatic cover. I'm under deep cover, a special category called Non-Official Cover. A NOC."

"Knock?"

"N-O-C. A NOC. Most Agency employees stationed overseas get official cover and diplomatic passports. NOCs are usually just businessmen and women with regular US tourist passports, so if we get caught, we see the inside of a prison. Or worse."

"Can you tell me where you've served, what kind of assignments?"

"Sarajevo, Morocco, Kabul. Most recently, Kiev. I'm sorta cooling my heels for a while with a headquarters assignment. My focus right now is to make sure we get all we can from the Klondike program."

"Me, too," Elizabeth laughed. "So, what is next? Where do you go after this?"

Sandra shrugged. "I really don't know. I have had a couple of pretty stressful tours. Maybe it's time for a cushy assignment to Paris on the cocktail party circuit."

"Paris? Sounds perfect! I'll come visit often!"

"Nah. I want to be the first female head of the Agency's Directorate of Operations, and the path there is through the armpits of the world."

"Armpits of the world?"

"Yeah, you know. The dirtbag belt. The way to get to the top at the Agency is by going where the problems are and then succeeding beyond their wildest dreams. Like the Marines. Run toward the sound of gunfire."

"You sound like you know what you want."

"I do. At work and at home," Sandra smiled.

Traffic eased a bit as they made their way down Constitution Avenue toward Seventeenth Street.

"I moved here three years ago," said Sandra. "I saved a shitload of money when I was deployed, with my housing covered. I got a salary boost for serving in combat zones. I was able to buy a row house here."

They took R Street east until they got to Fourteenth Street and headed north. They passed a dozen French, Ethiopian, and Middle Eastern restaurants tucked between trendy shops bustling with a young crowd.

"The 'hood is rather bohemian. A real mix of people. You know the suburbs are mostly white bread, the city is rye bread," Sandra laughed. "It was a tough area after the riots. It's been gentrified but not tamed."

They turned right onto Corcoran Street and Victorian Era row houses on the narrow one-way street. The leaves on the gingko trees along the narrow street had turned yellow and the fallen leaves provided a golden carpet on the sidewalks.

"You're right," said Elizabeth. "Not much parking."

"It's insane," said Sandra." People are afraid to use their cars and lose the parking space."

"How are your neighbors?"

"The best on the planet. Everyone looks out for each other. Great parties and we all know each other well. I have a converted carriage house behind the house off of the alleyway. When they built these homes, they had carriage houses in the back for the horses and carriages. Mine is a garage now."

"Here you are in 2016 living in a neighborhood blending the nineteenth and twenty-first centuries," Elizabeth said admiringly.

Sandra pulled into the alley and her Tesla automatically activated the garage door opener. A security door rose revealing a two-car garage with one of the bays piled with boxes and bins.

"The neighborhood is mostly safe," Sandra said. "But we have our share of break-ins and robberies."

Tova pressed his nose against the car window and let out a long, muffled groan. "Let me explore this place," he seemed to be whining.

Sandra looked at the dog drool drippings running down her window and wondered what she was doing with this dog in her car.

Elizabeth found a Kleenex in her purse and began cleaning the window.

"Oh, leave it, I'll get a wipe later," Sandra said.

"Okay, I'll take Tova into the alley and see if he wants to do his business."

"Meet you in the kitchen."

***

Most of the row houses were walled-off from the alley by tall fences and garage doors. *Like Fort Apache*, thought Elizabeth.

Tova tensed up and froze when he sensed a movement in the alley. Elizabeth peered into the shadows and saw a large rat scurrying away.

"Tova, we aren't in Kansas anymore," she said.

They walked to the end of the alley with Tova enjoying the smells of the new area. Elizabeth had to keep him on a short leash as he made multiple attempts to pick up fast food wrappers, empty beer cans, and condoms scattered on the ground.

"Leave it, Tova," Elizabeth commanded multiple times. "Drop it! That's gross," she complained.

He did his business while Elizabeth admired the architecture of the restored homes. They returned to Sandra's and, after passing through Sandra's garage, Elizabeth found and pressed the button to close the door.

Sandra had changed into skinny jeans and a beige cashmere turtleneck and was working in the kitchen. Tova sniffed loudly and danced under the cheese tray.

"What a beautiful kitchen." Elizabeth snagged a piece of cheddar. "I'd never have thought the place would be so spacious."

"The house was gutted and renovated in 2011. I'm the second owner since the redo and am, for the most part, happy with it. Old houses have quirks."

Sandra pulled a bottle of wine and two glasses from her wine rack. Elizabeth picked up the cheese and cracker platter.

"Let's go into the living room," Sandra said. The living room had a fireplace with an elegant marble hearth and mantle.

"I've never seen a gas-lit chandelier before," Elizabeth said. "And I love the Victorian furniture."

She walked to the expansive bay window overlooking Corcoran Street and said, "Radiators? I have never been in a home with radiators."

"Logan Circle is an historic district, so we have to preserve the fronts of the houses as they were in the late 1890s, but we can modernize the interiors as much as we want. The developer chose a mix of old and new."

"But radiators? In 2016?"

"Yes, I love the warmth from them. No drafty cold blown air that reeks of carbon management adherence."

"You have a beautiful home," Elizabeth said admiringly.

Tova sprawled near the warming fireplace, and Elizabeth and Sandra sat on curved high back sofa by the radiator. In the quiet, Elizabeth admired the exquisite decorative plasterwork on the high ceilings.

Sandra noticed the long blonde hairs from Tova already showing on her hardwood floors.

"I have been thinking about our next steps regarding the *bashka*," Sandra said.

"Can we discuss this here? Outside of the vault, outside a SCIF?"

"Of course, Agency folks use cones of silence all the time. We just need to be a bit circumspect," Sandra said.

"Got it."

"You know, watch our words," she went on. "We need to go straight to the DCI with this. This is so explosive; we really don't want to deal with any intermediaries."

"But how do a case officer and a WINPAC analyst cut through the bureaucracy to speak directly to the head of the CIA?" Elizabeth asked.

"I've been in briefings with the director on matters regarding the K program," said Sandra. "I know his EXEC, Keisha Reilly, well enough to ask for a private meeting. I'll tell her I've learned something for his ears only that cannot be pre-briefed or written down. I can't promise anything, but I think she'll have no choice but to facilitate the meeting."

"I've already talked to my boss, Frank, but it was to complain about you," Elizabeth said. "I've already exhausted my options."

"I got this, let me see what I can do. Hungry?" Sandra asked.

Elizabeth nodded, "What's the plan?"

"Let's get dinner started." Sandra stood and headed for the kitchen.

Tova jumped up and followed Sandra toward the back of the house.

"How about pasta and salad? I have fresh tomatoes, garlic, and broccoli with some wonderful hand-pulled pasta from Domingo's. And a caprese salad? I have fresh basil on the windowsill and tomatoes on the vine in the fridge."

"Sounds delicious! What can I do to help?" Elizabeth asked.

They prepared the dinner, served their plates, and carried them into the dining room with Tova under foot.

"So, how come you live here all by yourself? You haven't found a soulmate to join you?" Elizabeth asked.

"Some near misses, but it's been challenging for me to be a part of someone else's life if they do not work at the Agency."

"I have never really had a near miss." Elizabeth smiled.

Over dinner, they discussed world politics and sports.

"I loved fencing at Cal Tech," Elizabeth said. "It's a sport that rewards speed, agility, and mental acuity. You need all three to defeat an opponent. And I loved being able to take someone out—you know, take them with a foil!"

Sandra smiled. "And I loved lacrosse for the same reason. I got to pummel my opponents with my stick!"

They listened to Motown on the soundtrack from *The Big Chill* while they washed the dishes and cleaned up the kitchen. Tova lay on the kitchen floor, making sure he was in their way, so they had to step over him often. Elizabeth looked at the clock on the microwave. Already after eleven, she had a 0700 stand-up, no car, and was a little drunk.

Sandra took her hand. "Stay tonight. I'll get you back tomorrow morning to your hotel so you can change and get into the office on time."

"No, I can Uber," Elizabeth protested.

"Of course not, please stay," Sandra said.

Tova went to the back door and signaled he was anxious.

"I need to take Tova out. Are you sure you are okay with us both staying?" Elizabeth asked.

"As long as he doesn't snore," Sandra answered. "Or you, either." She gave Elizabeth a peck on the cheek.

CHAPTER 10

Thursday, October 27, 2016

The alarm buzzed at 0530, and Elizabeth slowly and reluctantly woke up. Although they had gotten to bed at a reasonable time, they had not gotten much sleep.

"Good morning," Elizabeth said as she rolled over. "What a special evening."

Sandra kissed Elizabeth on the nose. "Are you really sure you've gotta be in at seven?" She began one of her signature neck massages.

"Yeah, I really do, regretfully," Elizabeth smiled and pulled Sandra closer. "Thank you for dinner. And... everything. I liked the everything. A lot. And you need to follow up with the director's EXEC."

"Mmmmmm." Sandra really didn't want to get up. Tova began stirring and put his paws up on the bed.

"Hey, boy," Elizabeth said. Tova, thinking this was an invitation, jumped up on the bed and demanded attention from them both.

Sandra sat up. "Tova, you and your hair are not welcome in the bed! Down!"

They then both got up, showered, and drove to McLean in time for Elizabeth to change clothes, feed Tova, and get to the morning Cloud Spinner meeting. On the way, they continued their conversation from the previous evening.

"I'll call the director's EXEC this morning and see what it takes to get him the details of the *bashka*," Sandra said.

"Please let me know how it goes as soon as you can," Elizabeth said.

"Of course! And, hey—there's a Washington Caps home game tonight, against the Flyers. Wanna go?" Sandra asked. "I'll check out StubHub and see if I can score some decent seats."

"That sounds great!" Elizabeth was excited. "I've never seen Ovechkin play. A fellow ex-Russian."

"Cool! The game starts at seven thirty. We can Uber from the house and get a late dinner after the game." Sandra touched Elizabeth's arm. "Plan to stay, please. I'll get home early and clean out the other parking space for you, so you have a place to park."

"And Tova, too?" Elizabeth asked. "I know his hair and drool—"

"Of course, Tova's welcome too," Sandra lied.

***

The seven o'clock stand-up conference room was crowded. Something was going on.

Frank started speaking with no introduction to his topic. "It looks like they really did it earlier today. An end-to-end test from Turyatam to the Kamchatka Peninsula with multiple passes over the impact area. Over 18,000 kilometers of range. They can hit anywhere in the US! Four thousand kilometers further than our predicted upper range. The goddamn vehicle did a one-eighty over the Bering Sea, then flew back west and circled the impact zone twice before its terminal engagement. Extraordinary range."

The room was abuzz. The test was expected to be successful, but every performance metric the CIA had predicted had been exceeded.

Elizabeth had read about this happening in previous intelligence assessments of emerging weapons systems. The IC would move from stating its assessment of maximum range to maximum *demonstrated* range, implying they had no realistic idea what its ultimate capability actually was. The analysts would just be in a mode of reporting what they had "seen" versus what they predicted. Policy makers and the organizations responsible for developing counter systems thought the Agency was worthless in such circumstances.

"The Russians are constrained by the same laws of physics we are, so, we backload it. We plug in the capabilities they've demonstrated and let that tell us how to modify our models," Elizabeth said.

"Good idea, Elizabeth. Let's get back at noon and report. A few months ago, when Putin bragged about Russia having a new class of weapons, we thought it was bluster and bullshit. The son of a bitch was not lying," Frank asserted.

The team in the conference room gathered in small groups, reviewed the data, and plotted in multicolor detail on many large video monitors.

"Look," Tom said. "Here is the separation event for the post boost vehicle. Nominal booster telemetry, but the bastards have encrypted the HGV system data. And, if you look at their press reports from earlier today, they are actually bragging about the Avangard test in Russian media. We lose the HGV after separation, but the vehicle is detectable as it re-enters the atmosphere and gets hot."

He continued. "We can merge the Doppler on the encrypted data stream from the vehicle and the infrared signatures and get a more precise flight profile. We'll also get a better handle on the velocities to feed the thermal predictions."

"Sounds good," Frank said.

"I'll have it in an hour," Tom said.

"Typical ballistic trajectories would have an impact in Kamchatka in just over twenty minutes, but here we detect a series of maneuvers somewhere between sixty to ninety kilometers altitude at over MACH 5. The HGV completed multiple evasive maneuvers and impacted the target area after a total flight time of thirty-two minutes. And the Doppler shows it made approximately two complete rotations at an altitude above thirty kilometers before impact."

"Where did it get the energy to go so far with such maneuverability?" John asked.

"This demonstrated capability is astounding," Bernice said. "We really don't know what it's capable of, but for damn sure MDA's missile defense systems won't be effective. And our ability to predict impact points after launch? Worthless."

"Our models of a waverider system don't show this combination of range and maneuverability," John said. "How can we be this far off?"

Bernice continued, "Hyper glide vehicles fly on top of the atmosphere. Then they skip! Like a rock on a lake's surface. They come down a little, touch a very thin atmosphere at hypersonic speeds, and skip. This extends their range and makes them extremely maneuverable to evade defensive systems and go after moving targets. A game changer. A real twenty-first-century weapon."

***

Sandra's office was a cramped, windowless refuge on the third floor of the B corridor. She was thankful her security requirements necessitated her having a single room with a door. She could do her job with some degree of privacy, but some days, the isolation was tedious.

"Good morning, Sheila," she said to the secretary.

"Good morning, Sandra. You're in early. And, it looks like you had a busy night."

"Ouch," Sandra laughed. "Do I really look that bad? Don't answer. Would you mind going down to the cafeteria and grabbing a fruit bowl and cup of coffee for me? Here's five bucks."

"Of course, anything else?"

"Nope—I'll be behind a closed door, so give a knock when you get back."

***

Sandra logged into the Directorate of Operations global database of known or suspected foreign intelligence officials. The system was used throughout the DO and was extremely comprehensive. The transliteration of Cyrillic to English was at times more art form than science, but the search algorithms were pretty good at looking at most of the possibilities. She entered the name Elizabeth mentioned: "Petrov, Alexi." Hundreds of entries. She knew Elizabeth and her grandfather immigrated to the United States in 1998, so she limited the search to include individuals in Russia in 1997 and in the US in 1998.

"Bingo."

The file was thin. *Alexi Vicktor Petrov, born in Moscow in 1941, graduate of the Moscow Institute of Physics and Technology State University, MIPT doctorate in physics in 1970.*

"The apple doesn't fall from the tree," Sandra muttered.

Served in the KGB from 1971 until 1997 in the Operations and Technology Directorate, working as a lead scientist for

Russian intelligence. The directorate was responsible for technical collection system developments fielded by the GRU and the KGB to collect information on the US. Sandra had been briefed on and trained how to counter many of the systems used to spy on Americans by the once-KGB now FSB, and had a healthy respect for their capabilities. It appeared that he had never served outside of the USSR.

Married in 1972, divorced in 1976, one son, Vicktor, born in 1964. Vicktor married in 1985, and had two children: one daughter, Yelizaveta—Elizabeth—and a son, Fedor, born in 1989.

With Alexi's background, Sandra was surprised that the US would allow him into the country and even more surprised Russia would let him out. Before the staff meeting started in ten minutes, she wanted to call the DCI's EXEC as she had promised Elizabeth last night.

She heard a knock on her door.

"Here's your fruit bowl and coffee, and a little change," said Sheila.

"Oh, thank you, Sheila. I have a call to make and then will be out for the staff meeting," Sandra said. "Can you get me Keisha Riley's secure number?"

"Of course, I have it right here, let me dial it for you," Sheila said. "It's ringing."

Sandra picked up the secure phone in her office quickly and heard a familiar voice. "Keisha Riley here."

"Good morning, Keisha. Sandra Friedman. Remember me from the briefings last month in 5F43?"

"Of course, I remember you. Quite a project you have going on over there."

"Do you have a few minutes? I want to bring something to your attention that I think your boss needs to see. Can you meet me in 5F43 this morning?" Sandra asked.

"Nothing open until 1200—will that work?"

"See you then."

Sandra closed her eyes and considered how she would raise the issue to Keisha. She knew she was playing with fire. Just like Daedalus, she would need to make sure her wings did not melt when she approached the sun. Daedalus survived, but his son, Icarus, flew too close to the sun and fell to his death.

***

Sandra recognized Keisha immediately as she walked down the corridor towards the vault: tall, dark, close-cropped natural hair, bright red lipstick, and an impressive leather pencil skirt.

"Thank you for making time on such short notice." Sandra held the door open.

"No problem at all," said Keisha, walking into the vault. "I try to keep thirty minutes of my day open in case I can get to the cafeteria for something to eat."

Keisha had been the DCI's EXEC for just over a year. She held a doctorate in psychology from Northwestern University and had been in practice in Detroit for a few years focusing on troubled youth in the inner cities. After 9/11, she applied to the CIA and was immediately hired to support the Agency Psy-Ops teams working to break the suspected Al Qaeda captives at CIA black sites around the world. The sites were established in friendly countries that didn't care what the CIA did to its captives. Keisha was an enthusiastic supporter of enhanced interrogation techniques. She became adept at waterboarding and putting the captives in stress positions for extended periods of time. Hearing them scream gave her a sense of delivering appropriate justice. While she was brought in to help break down the captives, what she excelled at was counseling the CIA employees who were devastated by the repeated torture they were forced to practice on the helpless detainees. She saw that most Agency employees were too weak or too empathetic to participate in prolonged torture. She, on the other hand, was not. Her skills in this area brought her to the attention of Agency management, and they accelerated her career. Now, she was the director's EXEC, and Keisha had evolved her responsibilities from more than a chief of staff. She set priorities and guided her boss both inside the building and with the rest of the IC. She had become a de facto deputy, and everyone recognized it.

"The boss is traveling overseas for a couple of days, so I have a little more control of my day. What's going on?" Keisha asked.

"We've located some extraordinary Klondike collects," said Sandra. "Incriminating discussions between Moscow leadership—including Putin—of their plans to blackmail a prominent American."

"You know we really don't care about this kind of dirt."

"Even if it is Putin discussing the Republican nominee for the presidency?"

"Really? Why would the Russians care about that loser?" Keisha asked.

"They have videos of him with women and tapes of him offering bribes to Putin's ministers. They don't think he'll win, so they have placed a cyber warfare unit to help with his campaign effort. They think with their help, he might win."

"I just can't see that happening," Keisha opined.

"They want him to be our next president. They refer to him as Putin's *bashka*, Putin's chump," Sandra continued.

"The boss will want to know more about this," Keisha said. "Can you put a file together of all of the collects you think he should hear? I'll get them transcribed, and if he agrees, we'll meet."

"Sounds like a plan," Sandra replied. "I'll put together the file today. Can you ask the transcriber to keep a copy of the conversations in the Klondike database for future reference?"

Keisha answered, "Of course. I'll get back to you sometime next week with the boss's thoughts."

***

Elizabeth spent the rest of the day consumed in thought about the new information regarding the Russian test. The Monte Carlo runs pointed to a curious correlation that did not make sense. If she varied the thermal control efficiency of the HGV across the entire range of possibilities, she could see that this could not explain the range or maneuverability they saw in the telemetry and IR data. If she used traditional thermal protection models and limited the HGV to stress limits associated with a titanium lifting body, the only variable she could use to fit the measured data was payload mass. The only way the NGV could fly as far and as fast as confirmed in the test data was for the payload mass to be zero. She stared at the plots again and concluded the only way they could achieve this performance is if the HGV did not carry any payload at all. *Why do a final pre-production test with no payload?* she wondered.

She remembered Polichuk telling Davidov they needed one last full-up system test that would convince everyone the Avangard system was ready to be deployed.

"Could they have faked the test?" she said aloud.

Her phone rang.

"Hey, Elizabeth," Sandra said, "I snuck out of work early and am already home. I took Tova out, and he was happy for the break." She decided not to mention that she spent an hour vacuuming up the dog hair.

"Thank you for taking care of him. I know he's happier getting some time outside."

"Leave work and join us," Sandra said. "We can get a run in before the hockey game tonight."

"Sorry, I am really jammed right now, new test results to think about," she said. "I'll be at the house by six forty-five, promise!"

"Understood, see you then," Sandra replied. "I have to tell you about my meeting with the director's EXEC, but it can wait 'til I see you."

Elizabeth continued reviewing the results by herself until she left for the day and joined Sandra and Tova in the city.

***

Elizabeth had never been to a professional hockey game. For the full two and a half hours, she was mesmerized. Everything else in her life felt temporarily put on hold. Cheering for the Caps, getting a little rowdy when a couple of fights broke out on the ice, and watching Ovechkin score a goal and get an assist in the 3-0 shutout of the Flyers made for a great evening.

"Let's find somewhere for a late dinner," Sandra said as they walked out of the Capital One Arena. "I know the perfect place." Sandra grabbed Elizabeth by the hand and led her across the street to Clyde's.

"Clyde's has the best crab cakes in the city and is always hopping, full of energy, especially after a Caps win."

"Sounds great!" said Elizabeth.

At the front door, Sandra asked the hostess for a private booth for two.

She smiled warmly. "Of course. Is upstairs okay?"

"Of course."

"Follow me," the hostess said.

***

They settled into their booth and ordered a nice prosecco.

Elizabeth immediately homed in on work. "So, I've been dying to hear about your meeting today. How did it go with the DCI's EXEC?"

"I met with Keisha Reilly and told her about the audio records. She asked me to put a file of them together so the DCI's translator could translate them. The DCI is out of the country, so she said she'd get back with me next week after he reviews the files."

"I hope he knows what to do next."

They ordered crab cakes and raw oysters and replayed the hockey game with a group of cute guys at the booths near theirs, their thoughts of a private dinner pleasantly dashed. After they finished their dinners and said goodbye to a couple of heartbroken young men, they took an Uber back to Corcoran Street.

***

Under Sandra's goose down duvet, the sheets were cool, but the fire kept the room warm. The bed warmed quickly as they made love.

***

Elizabeth just made it into the conference room in time and saw the room was almost full. All of the seats at the table and most of the chairs lining the walls were taken.

Frank started. "Thank you, everyone, for your hard work and long hours. We think we've got some things cleared up, but others, well, not so much. We've spent almost a year underestimating these guys, and now they come out with a test which not only appears to be successful but trashes our earlier estimates of what their new toys can do. Anyone have any ideas of how they have done this? The NIE is due in eight weeks, and we still don't know the full capabilities or limitations of the Avangard."

Many eyes turned toward Elizabeth. They knew she had access to a unique data source—and knew she could bring a system engineering perspective to the problem. The CIA was going to have to admit to the rest of the IC, to Congress, and to the new administration that they had no idea how the Russians had achieved this remarkable and unexpected performance.

"I ran over 10,000 Monte Carlo runs, testing our range of estimates on material stresses, thermodynamics, and payload masses. The payload mass has to be zero to meet the performance numbers we saw. Zero!"

"You're saying they tested their weapons delivery system without a weapon mass simulator on board?" Frank looked annoyed. "That makes no sense at all!"

"I am saying a zero-payload mass assumption fits the data, and nothing else does," Elizabeth replied. "The bastards may be gaming their own leadership and us."

The Klondike data made it clear the ministers were under extreme pressure to run a successful test. Putin was notoriously intolerant of people who caused him embarrassment.

"Imagine they are under severe cost and schedule constraints and have to accelerate a test program," she explained. "They don't want to be part of another failed military initiative, so they put together a 'show test.' It's not real." She saw a lot of confused faces. She tried again. "Like how the Japanese get married in Japan but create the illusion of a more elaborate, exotic wedding in Guam? They even hire guests to come. They create a complete story with flowers, dresses, music, staged photos, and a fake minister, creating an illusion for others to see and enjoy through pictures and video tapes."

"You think this last test was done to mislead us?" Frank asked.

"I think this last test was staged to mislead the Russian leadership. If we get snookered, too, all the better."

"Is there any way to know for sure?" Frank asked.

"Not with the data we have," Elizabeth replied.

"Anyone else have any ideas? No? Let's think about this over the weekend, get back together, and discuss on Monday morning."

CHAPTER 11

Saturday, October 29, 2016 to Sunday, October 30, 2016

Logan Circle

Sandra and Elizabeth had a wonderful weekend in the city. On Saturday, they shopped for fresh fruits and vegetables at the farmer's market at Dupont Circle, took Tova on a long walk in Rock Creek Park, and enjoyed the chilly October air at an outdoor café on Fourteenth Street for dinner. They slept in late on Sunday and made a dinner of grilled swordfish. Sandra was a Weber grill fanatic.

She had a grill in the back of her row house, sheltered from the worst of the winds. She told Elizabeth, "I grill year-round—meats, fishes, vegetables, everything. Food cooked over a fire outdoors is primal. It is what humans are meant to do."

On Sunday, as Elizabeth was packing her suitcase and gathering Tova's things, Sandra walked up behind her and held her tight.

"I really enjoyed being with you this weekend. I have an idea. Move out of the hotel and join me here. Having you here would make me very happy."

"That's just crazy," Elizabeth giggled. And then saw that Sandra looked serious. "We really don't know each other yet, and I don't really think I am ready for a long-term relationship."

Sandra answered, "Well, I am a person of action. Consider this. I have two unoccupied bedrooms plus a sofa bed in the basement. You've been living in a hotel with your dog. For way too long!"

Elizabeth opened her mouth to respond, but Sandra continued. "And if it doesn't work out, it's not like you're breaking a lease. You can just move back into the hotel."

"Are you sure?" Elizabeth asked, thinking out loud. "I really would like to spend more time with you. I like being in the city and getting Tova out of that hotel, but I don't want to intrude."

"Intrude?" Sandra said skeptically. "I really love your company, and that fur ball has worn me down." She ruffled Tova's ears.

"Okay, if you're really sure, we'll give it a try," Elizabeth said.

"Then how about tomorrow I come by the hotel after work and help you move your things?" Sandra offered.

"Help me move?" Elizabeth smiled. "Everything I own fits in my Toyota."

"Hah! I understand. Then I will see you tomorrow after work. Here's a key and a spare garage door opener."

Elizabeth loaded her suitcase and Tova into her car and drove back to the hotel. She used the time in the car to catch up with her grandfather.

"*Dedushka*, how are you doing tonight?" she asked. "I miss you."

"Yelizaveta, I miss you, too."

"Sorry for not calling for a couple of days. I have been busy and distracted."

"Well, I am happy to hear your voice," he said. "How are things there? Are you making progress on your project? Will you be home soon?"

Elizabeth heard some stress in his voice. "Yes, the project is going well, and we are on track to finish it by the end of the year. I could be home in December if we get the report completed a little early."

"Oh, that would be wonderful," he said. "How was your weekend?"

"A lot of fun. I stayed away from the office for once and stayed with a friend from work in downtown DC. You would like her."

"I am so glad you are making friends there. Perhaps someday, I'll meet her."

"I'd like that," Elizabeth said, wondering if she should add more detail. She decided now was not the moment.

They finished their conversation as Elizabeth pulled into the Residence Inn parking lot. Tova recognized his old home and whined to get out.

CHAPTER 12

Monday, October 31, 2016

OHB

The position of the director of the Central Intelligence Agency, the DCI, had reported directly to the president for more than fifty years until the events of September 9, 2011. After the terrorist attacks, a bipartisan commission reviewed how the Intelligence Community had failed the nation and what corrective actions should be taken. The study produced a broad consensus that critical elements of the IC had not worked together effectively, resulting in gaps in the knowledge of the threat and an ineffective coordinated IC response. The assessment concluded that the organizational structure of the IC was ineffective in understanding and communicating a holistic view of the external threats to the nation and managing the responses to the threats in a coherent way.

A new position was established: the director of National Intelligence, the DNI, who oversaw thousands of staff in the new organization with a menacing bureaucracy. The intent was that the DNI and his or her minions would bring order to the chaos. However, twelve years after the position was created, the DNI remained superfluous to and ignored by the president, the NSC, and Congress. The DCI, with direct access to unique intelligence and analysts, still swung a big stick.

***

James Plummer had been the DCI for almost eight years and was brought into the job by the current president. He had extensive experience in the military, in industry, as a US house representative, and as an ambassador to China. He liked the DCI job, and his years in politics allowed him to understand the players on the Hill, in the executive branch, and in foreign intelligence agencies, as well as the president and his cabinet. Plummer was proud of the job he had done and uncertain about his future with the upcoming election. When she was elected, he did not think he would be asked to stay in the position. She would probably want a clean start.

"Keisha, I am so glad to be back!" James bellowed from his office. "Why I spend any time with those sick Saudi bastards is just beyond me! Mirrors and smoke, smoke and mirrors. The only real thing in the Kingdom is the complete lack of finding a good bottle of scotch on economy. Thanks for putting a bottle in my luggage."

He stared at the large pile of papers on his desk. "So. What disasters have I missed on my trip to the desert?"

Keisha was glad to see him back and in good spirits. She walked into his office and selected a folder from the pile.

"Same old, same old. But you'll be interested in seeing this. One of our case officers working the Klondike program found a series of conversations you should read. I met with her last week, was a bit skeptical about her conclusions, but then had your translator transcribe conversations between a number of key Russian leadership, including Putin."

"Yeah, I'm usually interested in what Putin is saying," he responded.

"They've got a *bashka*, a chump, in Putin's pocket. A US businessman they caught in a honey pot and on tape bribing Russian officials."

Plummer looked unimpressed. "Oh, who cares? Another US businessman doing what he needs to do to be successful in Russia."

"You'll care. He's the Republican presidential candidate."

Now Plummer looked interested. "You have got to be kidding me! The Russians have a grip on the Republican candidate? Well, thank God he won't be elected. She has this thing sewed up."

Keisha shook her head. "I have the transcripts from a number of conversations here and I really think you ought—"

"No need to read," Plummer interrupted. "I really don't care. I need to focus on getting ready for her transition team. I think we should plan to be meeting with them starting as early as next week, after the celebrations are over and they realize they have to begin governing."

***

"Hey Sandra, Keisha here."

"Great to hear from you. I was getting anxious about the subject we discussed."

"No need to be anxious. I reviewed the issue with the boss, and he was really not interested. He is confident she will win and the *bashka*—the chump—is just a temporary distraction."

Sandra's voice dropped. "Really? Did he read the transcripts? I saw the files the translator put onto the server in the vault, and they looked accurate to me."

"He did not. He was mostly disinterested, like I said. He has way too many real problems to deal with right now. Hypothetical problems like this have to take a number—like number 498," she laughed. "So, thank you for your diligence and bringing this forward, but you should get back to your real job now."

"Okay, thanks for getting back to me," Sandra felt deflated. She had nurtured a hope that this Klondike find might attract senior management's attention and springboard her career.

***

Elizabeth and Sandra made plans to meet in the vault at the end of the day.

Sandra arrived first and opened the door, signed the log, and disarmed the alarm. She logged on to the system and saw new files had been added to the registry, both from WH and DC sources. She put her headphones on and began listening to the conversations. First up was a collect between Putin and Polichuk from earlier that day. It really was amazing that she could be listening to a conversation that had occurred between the president of Russia and his minister of defense only hours before.

The conversation was muffled, and her Russian wasn't anywhere near as good as Elizabeth's, particularly when applied to these recordings that teetered on the edge of interpretability. The auto-translate function did not work at all.

With the headphones on, she did not hear Elizabeth enter the room. It wasn't until Sandra saw Elizabeth's shadow crossing the wall did she turn and smile.

"You're just in time, Elizabeth! Putin and Polichuk are discussing Cloud Spinner and the *bashka*. I can't quite make out what they are saying, though. It's a really shitty recording."

"Let me put some headphones on and see if I can help." Elizabeth adjusted the equalizer to match her hearing response.

"Well, Sergei! You said you had news for me, what is it?" Putin asked.

"Vlad, actually a lot of good news. First—the Avangard test was a great success! The team actually pulled it off!" Polichuk's voice was boisterous.

"We demonstrated compatibility with the new launcher, a flight range of over 18,000 kilometers and extraordinary maneuverability. We are confident this system will render the latest version of the US missile defense systems impotent," Polichuk bragged. "We are years ahead of them with this system. Their hundreds of billions of dollars in investments in their terminal defense systems are now worthless."

"We have done to them what they did to us when they surprised us with their stealth aircraft," Putin observed. "They will want to negotiate away our advantage. When the new administration reaches out, we'll tell them to go fuck themselves."

"Speaking of the new administration..." Polichuk said. "Their election is next week."

"And the Americans have a choice between dumb and dumber," Putin laughed.

"The cyber team you authorized has made great progress," Polichuk said. "Our efforts to corrupt their election are going well. We have saturated millions of voters in key swing states with anti-Democratic messages. We have attacked her personally. Her health, her position on gun rights and health care. We won't know the effectiveness until next week, but we have learned how to covertly meddle in their election. Their antiquated system of electing their president, their electoral college, made it easy. And cheap. We focused our efforts in only eleven battle ground states."

"Any sense of how the election will go?" Putin asked.

"Not really," Polichuk answered. "But we have seen our malicious postings be replicated and reposted by millions. So, we know our campaign of lies has been heard. We actually don't have any way, yet, of knowing if will be effective. But we are doubling down on our efforts this last week of their campaigns."

"It seems likely we will be dealing with the first female US president, and the bashka will be back to give us more money to build his hotel, restaurants, and condos," Putin predicted. "Let's meet on Wednesday morning after the election. The results will be complete, and we can decide what to do next."

Elizabeth took her headphones off and relayed the conversation to Sandra.

"Unreal! Those SOBs are really focused on her. I don't think they care so much about her losing as they do him winning."

Sandra said, "Let's go home. Tova needs out, and we'll have a lot of trick-or-treaters. The neighbors always dress up and party in the street. It's a fun night."

"Deal," Elizabeth said. "I'm beat."

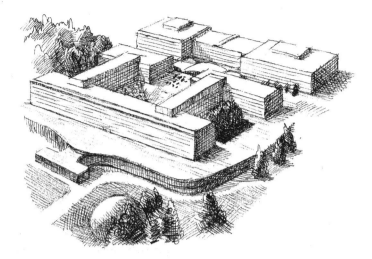

CHAPTER 13

Tuesday, November 1, 2016

Corcoran Street

After a fun Halloween evening on Corcoran Street, roaming and meeting neighbors in the 'hood, Elizabeth devoted the next evening to moving into Sandra's house. She had a few suitcases of clothes, a lot of books, a laptop computer, and framed pictures of her grandfather. She had really never accumulated many things and was content to live her life simply.

Sandra had a very large walk-in closet, one half for her clothes and the other half for her shoes. She walked Elizabeth into the closet.

"Hey, I am going to move many of these shoes down the hall to the other bedroom closet. It's empty. You can hang your clothes in here."

"Wow, I have never actually seen this many shoes before! Well, other than at a shoe store," Elizabeth said admiringly.

"It's a weakness and a passion of mine. What size do you wear?" Sandra asked.

"Usually an eight," Elizabeth answered.

"Perfect. These are almost all either seven-and-a-half or eights. Here's one of my many favorite pairs, they're eights. Try them on, and see how they fit."

Elizabeth took the shoes from Sandra and, while admiring them, looked down at her sensible flats. "Even if they fit, I'm not sure I could walk in these," she said, smiling. "But I do love to see you in them. I can always tell when you are close by from the sound they make."

"Oh, come on, try them on! Once we get you in proper shoes, I'm gonna work on other parts of your wardrobe."

"Hey, what's wrong with my wardrobe?" Elizabeth protested.

"Nothing, if you like California geek," Sandra laughed. "Try them on!"

Elizabeth sat down on the bed and slipped on the Jimmy Choo red stilettos. They fit, but she had never been in four-inch heels before, and she walked awkwardly across the room.

"How do you do it?" she asked. "Walk in these and look elegant at the same time?"

Sandra replied, "Years of practice, sweetie, many years of practice."

Sandra moved towards Elizabeth as though to help her walk but instead, gently lowered her onto the bed, kissed her, and reached down to slip the heels off.

"You don't need these right now," she said. "And I don't think you need these either," as she unbuttoned Elizabeth's pants. They made love and forgot about the distractions at work for an evening.

CHAPTER·14

Monday, November 7, 2016 to Tuesday, November 8, 2016

OHB, Logan Circle

"Hey, are you voting tomorrow?"

"Of course. I registered in Virginia when I moved from California and will vote there—even though technically I guess I am now a resident of DC," Elizabeth answered.

"Not really. You aren't officially a resident until you unpack all of your bags. I plan to vote here in the District tomorrow after work," Sandra said.

"I'll vote around lunchtime at the fire station on Old Chain Bridge Road," Elizabeth replied. "I think my vote will actually count; Virginia seems like it remains in play."

"I don't see anything else in the Klondike files of note. Let's go home," Sandra said.

***

After a day's work and voting on Tuesday, Sandra and Elizabeth met early in the evening on Corcoran Street and sat at a bar, drinking beer and eating oysters while watching election results. Many neighbors gathered to celebrate the Democrats keeping the White House and the first female presidential victory.

The District of Columbia in general, and the Logan Circle neighborhood in particular, were as blue as any voting area in the country. The voters swung to the Democratic candidate by margins of 70 to 80 percent. To the crowds gathered in the bars and restaurants clustered around Fourteenth Street, the outcome seemed to be a *fait accompli*. As the polls closed and results began coming in, the rooms began to fall silent.

"Are you fucking kidding me?" Sandra put her head in her hands and moaned. "He is actually leading the electoral college vote! Florida, Wisconsin, Pennsylvania..."

"Well, the numbers are close—maybe absentee votes will change things?" Elizabeth offered.

"Can't imagine this is happening," Sandra shook her head.

By 11 p.m. EST, it was over.

"The son of a bitch did it," Sandra said, looking miserable. "They both did it, and they deserve each other. The *bashka* and Putin will make quite a pair."

"What will the DCI do now?" Elizabeth asked. "He can't ignore this."

"I'll try again," Sandra said. "I'll call Keisha tomorrow and tell her of the latest recording."

"This just sucks! Let's go back to the house and get some rest. I think we have a busy day tomorrow," Elizabeth replied.

"What a sad day for the country," Sandra said.

CHAPTER 15

Wednesday, November 9, 2016
OHB

The 0700 stand-up was a complete waste of time. The recent Russian Avangard test was suddenly a faded memory, and all discussion focused on the surprise president-elect. Elizabeth left early to go to 5F43 and see if there were any new intercepts.

***

Putin sounded jubilant. "We have that prick by his balls, we have my bashka by the balls! We did it!"

Davidov's voice sounded jubilant, too. "Not only do we have him by the balls, we know how to influence elections in the US. She won the popular vote by almost four million votes, but the bashka won the electoral college vote by only eighty. And they call themselves a democracy! Only four states made the difference, less than 100,000 votes out of over 140 million cast. We applied pressure at the right time in the right places!"

"Do the Americans know?" Putin asked. "Have we left any fingerprints?"

"Of course not," Davidov said. "They're too incompetent to understand our actions. Even if they suspected, they wouldn't believe we could or would do this. They've meddled in so many elections throughout the world over the years, they think it is their right to do so, and now they've had it done to them. Poetic justice! So, what do we do next?"

"Easy," Putin said. "I will reach out through an intermediary, to someone on their transition team, and ask for a private call to congratulate the new president. I will tell him then that he's my bashka and that I will be expecting some decisions favorable to us after he takes office in January. The first will be to get rid of those restrictions they put in place after our little adventure in Ukraine in 2014."

Davidov replied, "Maybe we should reach out and communicate this message to one of his children, or someone in his inner circle. Vlad—we need to be more subtle. You can put the squeeze on when you meet in person. Phone calls with you are sure to be monitored."

Putin conceded. "You're right. Let's get to his incoming national security advisor and make it clear to him we have his boss by the balls. Once we see the bashka bend, then we'll really have our way with him."

***

Elizabeth took her headphones off. She had not really cried in many, many years. She cried now. The combined impact of knowing a psychopath had been elected president of the United States and that he was about to be blackmailed by the Russians was overwhelming. She was eager to see Sandra and find out what the DCI's plan was and how she could help.

***

The day after the election, DCI Plummer reached out to the president-elect's transition team. He was told the president-elect was really not interested in meeting with the DCI any time soon. Plummer's team had met with both presidential candidates on a number of occasions in the months before the election to keep them both up to date on emerging international issues. She had always been engaged in the briefings, but the president-elect—disinterested. Plummer had been told that the president-elect learned about critical foreign events only through interaction with his family, loyal staff, and Fox News.

Plummer called Keisha into his office. "Get me those Klondike transcripts you mentioned. I want to see what Putin has on this guy."

"Will do," she said. "I'll have them bagged and brought to your office in fifteen minutes."

Plummer stared out of his seventh-floor office at the grey tree line surrounding the Agency compound. Winter was coming to Washington.

Keisha soon appeared with a two-inch-thick binder of Klondike transcripts. "I have not had time to highlight any of the pages, so you'll have to pore through the details, but I am confident you'll come to the same conclusions I have."

After one look at the thick binder, Plummer yelled to his admin, "Clear my calendar for a couple of hours! I don't want to be interrupted!"

James Plummer was a complicated man. While he had never aspired to be the director of the CIA, his loyalty to the current president and background in national security made him a logical choice to take on the job early in the president's first term. It had taken Plummer a while to understand the limitations and the power of the position. Despite having relatively minor financial accountabilities—his budget was smaller than all of the cabinet secretaries—his influence was major, behind only those of the secretaries of defense and state. He was a fixer. If the president had a problem, he fixed it. Sometimes with finesse, sometimes with brute force.

He grew up in Philadelphia, the oldest in a large Catholic family of seven children. He had five brothers and the youngest, a baby sister on whom he doted. His father was a drunk who couldn't keep a job and regularly beat James' mother. Until one day, when a twelve-year-old James said, "No. Lay a hand on her again, I'll break your arm."

Plummer did have to break his father's arm—with a baseball bat. When his father realized that the next time would be even worse, he abandoned the family.

At thirteen, Plummer taught himself how to go from being a compassionate older brother and mother's son to an enforcer. Because he was stocky, he was recruited to join his school's wrestling team, but he was offended by all of the limitations of organized wrestling. Instead, he became an enforcer. An enforcer with his siblings, his teachers, his mom, and his classmates. This skill helped him in every step of his career. It wasn't that he was amoral. He understood right from wrong. He also understood that sometimes, for the greater good, someone had to get hurt.

Growing up in downtown Philadelphia also taught James practical lessons about life. He was fond of saying, "we don't lock screen doors in Philly." You either had iron-barred doors or you came to accept that people who wanted to break in were coming in. He didn't believe in facades. He believed in hard truths backed up by succinct actions.

Right now, these Russian recordings provided him with an edge. An edge in Washington was worth a lot. In fact, it was worth everything. When the experienced players acquired an advantage over others, they used it. James thought carefully about how he would use his edge.

He began reading the transcripts in chronological order. Keisha had included only discussions regarding the *bashka* and how the Russian leadership was preparing to blackmail the president-elect. Plummer was shocked at just how stupid the *bashka* was. His public tweets and campaign rallies made it clear that he was an idiot. But this Russian business? Crazy.

***

After a couple of hours of digesting the transcripts, he called Keisha to join him. He put his feet on the desk and said, "Okay, I think I have the picture. He's pond scum, and they have him?"

"Agreed," Keisha said. They raised their eyebrows at each other in disbelief. "The Russians are planning their next moves with him."

"I already reached out to his transition team and asked for an introductory meeting, and they gave me the Heisman. Said he has all the intel he needs right now. What an idiot!"

"Did you see?" Keisha asked. "Putin plans to reach out to him and squeeze him soon."

"Yes. I need to get on his calendar before then," Plummer sighed. "It pains me to do this, but I'll ask the national security advisor to touch base with his counterpart in the transition team about an 'ears only' issue for the president-elect. It will raise the NSA's concerns because he'll want to know what I am going in with, but he'll be too afraid to say no. I may get a call from the president asking what's going on. I have no intention of telling him his successor is a criminal and vulnerable to being blackmailed by Putin. Well, yet."

"I agree sir," she said. "What can I do to help?"

"Lock down access to the Klondike material and the transcripts. Nobody new gets access to the logs and the files."

"Will be done in fifteen minutes. I'll get it locked down."

CHAPTER 16

Monday, November 14, 2016
New York City

Plummer's meeting with the president-elect was not going to be easy. He had numerous moat dragons in place—individuals skilled in the art of keeping people away from him and in managing his view of the world. The *bashka* said he knew who he needed to see and did not take counsel from those he did not wish to see. He claimed to be a stable genius. Fortunately, the current national security adviser was able to break through the moat and get Plummer fifteen minutes on the newly elected president's calendar.

Plummer's security detail drove him to New York City for the meeting in the *bashka*'s office tower. The first time his mother saw his security team, rather than being impressed with the agents charged with keeping her son safe, she told him, "I feel so sorry for all of those fine young people."

Plummer asked why, thinking it must be the long hours, the risk to their personal safety, or the time away from their family.

"Oh no, Jimmy. I feel so bad seeing so many young people with hearing problems," she said.

"Hearing problems?" an incredulous Plummer replied.

"Yes, they're all wearing hearing aids," she observed.

He had complete trust and confidence in these young people with hearing problems. He and his security detail arrived at the president-elect's office in about the time it would have taken to fly, and he was able to get some work from his car during the trip.

***

Plummer did not bring many supporting materials with him—just a few simple hand-written notes to help him cover the material he needed to discuss. He arrived early and was told the president-elect was running more than two hours behind schedule and perhaps would not be able to see him at all today.

"That's just bullshit, the president-elect needs to meet with me," Plummer said.

He was willing to wait for as long as needed. He didn't like being stiff-armed, not when he had something to say and had made it clear he needed to see the president-elect that day.

"I don't think you'll survive long if I don't see the president-elect today," Plummer said to a toadie who appeared repeatedly with a clipboard. "What is your name?" he asked.

Finally, after a three-hour wait in a room outside of the *bashka's* office, Plummer was called in. The room was filled with transition team members and family. They seemed curiously amused that the director of the CIA was here to tell them something he thought was important.

The president-elect was a large man. He greeted Plummer like an old friend, reaching out his hand to extend a welcoming shake. *Weird*, Plummer thought. *He really does have small hands and truly orangish hair. And for God's sake, it matches his skin.*

"Welcome to the White House North," he said. "I am pleased to see you again, James. I understand you have an issue of great importance to discuss with me."

Plummer was surprised. The president-elect had seemed completely disinterested in Plummer and the discussion of Kurdish allies supporting US interests in Syria when they met during the campaign.

"I do, sir, but this issue arises from the most sensitive of sources and is for your ears only. I really don't think it is appropriate to discuss such material with all of these people here."

"Oh, that's not an issue for me," said the president-elect. "See, I intend to change how Washington operates, and I think it should start now. I'd like for my team to hear what you have to say."

"I understand sir, and if I might make a suggestion? How about I discuss these issues with you in private and only after you've heard them do you decide whether you think it's wise to share with your family and staff? It would be completely your decision, of course."

***

If the president-elect said no, Plummer decided he would just get up and leave, letting the *bashka* dangle in the breeze.

The *bashka* considered. "I can make that work. Everyone? Clear the room."

As the room emptied, Plummer sat in the chair across from the seated president-elect.

The *bashka* jokingly said, "Where is your pile of PowerPoint charts? Don't tell me you have come to talk to me without a stack of PowerPoint slides! Why do you need a private meeting where my staff and family are being asked to step outside? What is it you want from me?"

"No PowerPoint slides, nothing to ask of you. I'm actually here to tell you what the Russians are saying about you, sir. And, I am here to help you."

"Oh, this should be interesting—more fake news!"

"Actually, sir, I think you should consider this real news. The source of this information is unassailable."

"Bullshit! It isn't real unless I say it is real," the *bashka* said.

Plummer kept talking. "We have audio tapes of conversations among key members of the Politburo, from inside the Kremlin and other key locations. In one very troubling discussion, the Russian prime minister, Putin, is told by his minister of finance, Davidov, whom you know well—"

"I don't know who you are talking about," the *bashka* said, crossing his arms.

"Sir, they claim to have video tapes and audio tapes of you offering bribes to Russian officials and having sex with Moscow whores," Plummer said. They have transcripts and irrefutable evidence—videos—your attempts to sway your Red Square hotel project approval process."

The *bashka* sat back in his chair and smiled. No sign of the slightest concern or worry. Plummer wondered if he was thinking about the nameless women he fucked in Moscow.

Plummer saw his advantage and kept driving his points. "They are planning to blackmail you. They are planning to make demands of you."

"How do you know? And what do they want?' the president-elect asked.

Plummer put both elbows on the table and leaned forward, "The day after the election results, I heard them discussing their plans for you. Putin ordered an intermediary to contact your team and tell you he would be reaching out to let you know what he needed. First on his list was removing the sanctions dating back to his invasion of the Crimea in 2014."

"They already have," the president-elect said.

"Already have what?" Plummer asked.

"They have already reached out to me," the *bashka* replied.

"Fucking A!" Plummer exclaimed. "They got to you before I could get on your calendar! Insane, just goddamn insane. Who was it?"

"My incoming national security advisor. He got a congratulatory call from their ambassador to the US and was invited to meet for coffee. Kislyak made it clear they were prepared to release sensitive files if I didn't take some concrete steps to relieve pressure on them," he said nervously.

"Forget the embarrassing porn star tapes for now. We know they have you implicated in the middle of a bribery scheme to move your Red Square project forward, and..."

"Ohhhh... those were not really bribes. Those were just regular business expenses to get government lackeys to do their jobs. No one will be able to prove anything."

Plummer shook his head. "But you see, sir, they actually were not regular business expenses. They were clear violations of the Foreign Corrupt Practices Act. Each violation carries a twenty-year sentence in a federal penitentiary. We have the account numbers, dates, and transaction amounts for all of your bribes."

The *bashka* just smiled. "But—my attorney general would never pursue this, so nothing will ever happen to me. I have a get-out-of-jail-free card. No one will ever know, or care."

"No, sir, I'm afraid you still don't understand. The *current* attorney general will certainly care, and he is in the job for the next two months. There is hard proof that you personally bribed foreign government officials. How could you have been so stupid?"

"The Russians would deal only with me," the president-elect explained. "It was necessary to deal at the top to get it done quickly. You know, time is really money. I knew I was safe from their anti-bribery laws, but it never occurred to me you would be bugging our conversations. How did you do it?"

Plummer ignored the president-elect's question. "They also plan to nationalize your project after it was completed. They are planning to blackmail you."

Suddenly, the president-elect looked dejected. He slouched back in his chair and clasped his hands together, as if in prayer. Plummer saw that the president-elect felt unsure about what to do next and realized he could not ask his family for advice as he faced his first international crisis. In a meek voice, he asked, "What do we do now?"

Plummer liked that he said those words and said them with meekness. "We have a couple of months before you are inaugurated to figure out the best path forward. For now, we need them to think you are all in and ready to accommodate their every need."

"Who else knows this at the CIA?" the *bashka* asked.

"Only a few hundred employees are aware of how we learned this information, and only a few dozen have access to the raw data. And only a handful of us know about your exchange with Putin."

"You need to protect me and get rid of the raw data. Get rid of the tapes," the *bashka* pleaded.

"I can do that for you, sir, but then I need you to do something for me."

"Anything."

"I need access to you. If I need to talk to you, you need to take my call. You don't keep me waiting, and your family and minions stay out of the picture."

"I can make that work. Here's my private number. I'll put you on the priority list. You'll be able to reach me at any time."

"Okay, let me get back to Langley and plot the next steps for us to take. I'll get back with you in a few days."

"Okay, call when you have something."

Plummer stood up and briskly walked towards the door. Upon opening the door, the crowd gathered outside the office rushed in. It was like running with the bulls in Pamplona. Only this time, the bulls were coming straight at him, and it felt like he was about to be stampeded by the president-elect's sycophants and family. He hoped this was not a foreshadowing of things to come.

CHAPTER 17

Tuesday, November 15, 2016

OHB, Logan Circle, and JV's

Plummer's security team changed shifts at midnight. The new shift brought his morning reading packages with them so he could begin the day with an up-to-the-hour understanding of the issues the CIA was confronting. The security team was stationed at his elegant house in Alexandria, Virginia when he was at home. Being a senior public servant in Washington usually meant living in a nice but compact home outside the Beltway. Plummer, on the other hand, had made excellent individual stock investments whose values had soared over the decades. He was able to buy a home typically associated with law firm partners on K Street who billed over $1,000 per hour. His neighbors enjoyed his presence in the neighborhood but looked forward to the day that his security details would no longer be present, either in their vehicles or his yard.

Plummer typically woke up at 5:30 a.m. and, after making a cup of strong coffee, would begin reading the materials delivered by his security detail.

The files were sorted geographically, with the usual suspects occupying the front of the book: Russia, China, Iran, North Korea, and Cuba. Today's reports started with a number of reports from spies within the Cuban government.

For all of his time at the CIA, Plummer never understood the almost sixty years of the United States' fixation on Cuba. A dirt poor, third-world country that presented no risk to the United States yet occupied a place in the grave threats part of the American psyche. It had been this way for decades and until recently, he had no idea why. Two years earlier, when he spoke at an NSC deputies meeting about the apparent insanity of US foreign policy regarding Cuba, he was berated by one of the political hacks in the room.

"Keeping a focus on Cuba is all about Florida's electoral college votes. So shut the fuck up about Cuba not being a threat!"

Plummer came to understand that political theater required him squander limited IC resources to curry favor with the Cuban American community in a swing state. So, that morning, he read reports from spies inside the Cuban government reporting on the challenges Cuba continued to face. Cuba. He moved on to the other highlights and saw nothing alarming, then settled back to think about his next steps with the president-elect.

Being a Washington insider was both an asset and a liability. After working more than thirty years in Washington, Plummer knew he had become an insider when he was invited to join a small dinner discussion group that called itself the Cockroaches. The Cockroaches wore distinctive gold lapel pins. The fifty-some members aligned themselves with the resilient insect that could theoretically survive anything, including a nuclear war.

Presidents come and presidents go, but the Cockroaches—elected, appointed, or career members of the House, Senate, Judiciary, and administration—survived. They met monthly at the Capitol Hill Club or the Monocle Restaurant, depending on the size of the group and how rowdy the conversation might be. Plummer became a regular and enjoyed the spirited discussions about world affairs and politics conducted under the Chatham House Rule: Freely use the information shared, but never name the source. He could voice his opinion on the issues of the day, learn from others, and not be quoted.

His years with the group gave him a good sense of where Washington actually was and where it was going. This perspective shaped his thinking on what his next steps with the president-elect would be.

He had choices. Do nothing, help the president-elect out of his jam with the Russians, or take the obvious violations of laws to the Department of Justice.

The Russians planned to use what they knew about the president-elect to benefit the Russian position in the world. This was unacceptable. If Plummer helped the president-elect with the Russians, he would gain an edge with him. He could use his influence with the president-elect to protect the Agency from budget cuts and administrative interventions, should they arise, and, if necessary, protect key elements of the Cockroaches from the psychopath. It was a high-risk gamble. Covering up a federal crime, too, but what the fuck? He needed to closely monitor the Russians while he was having his way with the president-elect. He could not imagine that their interests would overlap.

Plummer decided on a path forward and concluded he needed to move quickly. He would need to see the president-elect again soon. But first, he needed to clean up a few things at the Agency.

***

From his car, Plummer phoned Keisha. She was in her Kia plug-in-hybrid on the George Washington Parkway.

"Good morning, Kee, I need to see you first thing this morning," he said. "What time will you be in?"

She looked at her watch. It was 6:22 a.m. "I'm ten minutes out."

"Good, I am right behind you. Let's meet in the special vault."

"Okay. See you there in a few."

The DCI's three-car motorcade, armored black Chevy Suburbans traveling in close formation, exited the George Washington Parkway on to the Headquarters compound while the security officers held up employee traffic so the motorcade could enter without stopping or slowing down. Since 1993, when five CIA employees in multiple cars were shot while waiting at a stoplight on Dolly Madison Avenue to turn into CIA Headquarters, the Agency had been very cautious about having the DCI's vehicles slow down or stop as they entered the facility. The shooter, Mir Aimal Kansi, was subsequentially captured in Pakistan, repatriated to the US, and executed in Virginia.

After passing through armed guards and vehicle barriers, the DCI's car pulled into the garage under the OHB. Normally, Plummer took a private elevator, which opened directly to his office. Only this morning, he would have to go via more public routes to get to the Klondike vault.

He enjoyed walking the halls and taking the two flights of stairs from his office to the fifth floor to meet Keisha. He had fans.

"Good morning, sir!" said a cheerful employee in the stairwell. "Thank you for supporting our Agency and protecting us from those idiots on the Hill."

"We'll be sorry to see you leave with the new administration coming in," another said. "It has been great having you here for the last seven years!"

He arrived at 5F43 and found Keisha opening the vault. They entered together, and while she disarmed the security system, he entered the glass room.

She followed and took a chair across from him. She had her ever-present yellow pad open to take notes.

Plummer planned to tell her some of his conversation with the *bashka*, just not all of it.

"I got fifteen minutes with him in New York. He was completely surrounded by sycophants. He loves to be admired. I got his people to leave the room and told him about the recordings and Putin's plans for him. It was a difficult conversation for him to hear. He knows he is screwed."

"What did he say?" Keisha asked.

"He asked for my help," Plummer answered.

"Help with whom? The Russians? The Department of Justice?"

"I am not sure he cares about the Russians. I told him he was in violation of the Foreign Corrupt Practices Act and that he faces twenty years per violation. The idiot said it was just the cost of doing business overseas. He may be president-elect, but he knows the current president and attorney general would kneecap him if they could. They have the next sixty days to act," Plummer replied.

"And you said...?" Keisha asked.

"I said I would help him. I told him he didn't need to worry about the Russians until he was actually sworn in. I didn't say it, but he understood that we have incontrovertible evidence that he bribed foreign officials."

"How can I help?" Keisha asked.

"I need to restrict the access analysts and translators currently have to Klondike—severely. Only the few people who actually are working regularly on the intercepts can keep access. I know the auto translation function leaves a lot to be desired, but no more new accesses," Plummer directed.

"I stopped all new access yesterday. I'll scrub the list today and get rid of most of the others. There are only seventeen analysts who have access to the raw data," Keisha said.

"Good. And get the woman who found these audio files, Friedman, off the access list. I want her reassigned. To a new job where she has nothing whatsoever to do with this program."

"How about if we put her in an assignment somewhere far from Langley? You know, put her on ice but tell her it is a big promotion?" Keisha asked.

"Good idea. Call the DDO and tell him she is a rising star I am taking an interest in. I want her in Moscow next year to fill the critical role that he and I spoke about recently," Plummer said.

"I know the job you are thinking about," Keisha said. "She can probably pull it off."

"Simmons will think I have lost my mind but tell him to do it. Get her out of DC, trained up for the new job, and to Moscow soon."

"Will do," Keisha said.

"And I want to meet with Friedman."

"I'll get her here just after lunch."

"And lastly—is it possible to erase the files of them discussing the *bashka*?" Plummer asked.

Keisha shook her head. "Not really. Everything we do is backed up securely, and there would be a record of the attempt to erase. I will erase the written transcripts and shred the written files you have read. No one will re-find the original audio files. It was a fluke Friedman found them in the first place."

"Jim?" Keisha followed him to the door. "What do you think the next DCI will do when he or she learns of this?"

"Next DCI?" Plummer held the door open for his EXEC. "I am the next DCI."

***

Plummer placed a call to the *bashka*'s private phone and was surprised to hear him answer immediately.

"Good morning, sir," Plummer said. "I was able to take the steps we talked about yesterday. I need to see you soon to discuss some additional issues I know you will be interested in hearing about."

"Of course. Just like we agreed, I will make time to see you when you think it is necessary. Join me in New York this afternoon."

"Traveling to New York today wouldn't be convenient for me," Plummer said. He enjoyed telling the *bashka* when and where they would be meeting. "I know you will be in DC tomorrow. Let's meet then."

"Of course," the *bashka* said. "Let's meet first thing in the morning at my hotel on Pennsylvania Avenue for breakfast. It is the best hotel in DC, you know. The best. Everyone says so."

"I will need to go by Langley first, so let's plan on meeting at 0930?" Plummer asked.

"I look forward to seeing you then," the *bashka* said.

***

Whenever Keisha received orders from Plummer, she enjoyed using his authority to get things done. On occasion, she overstepped his directions, knowing he would have her back and support her. Simmons, the CIA's deputy director for operations, was a weakling, and she was looking forward to talking to him and watching him squirm.

He answered on the second ring. "Simmons."

"Hi Ted, it's Keisha. Jim needs your help arranging an assignment for Sandra Friedman. He wants her to take on the key role in Moscow that you and he spoke about last week."

Ted sounded surprised. "I've already been working this. And Sandra was not on my short list."

"Look, Tom..."

"It's Ted..."

"Whatever. Ted, the decision has been made. We need you to get the wheels in motion as soon as possible."

"I don't like this," he protested. "I don't like it at all. Sandra is not ready for this kind of role, and I think you know it."

"I don't need to tell you, Ted, that in our line of work, we do things every day we don't like. I don't need you to like this. The boss needs you do your fucking job and get Sandra Friedman to Moscow as soon as possible. Are we clear?"

"Crystal," replied Ted.

***

Sandra arrived early to the DCI's office. While she sat impatiently waiting, she wondered what it must be like to be the head spy at the CIA. He knew *everything*. She had never had a one-on-one meeting with Jim Plummer before. Had she finally been noticed and was up for a promotion or special assignment? She was filled with anticipation and ready to accept any opportunity presented to her if it meant she could advance her career. Even if it meant leaving DC and Elizabeth.

The door to Plummer's office opened.

"Sandra Friedman—what a pleasure it is to finally meet you."

She responded, "Sir, it is truly an honor to be invited to meet with you." She shook his outstretched hand and noticed how firm his grip was.

"Can I get you anything to drink? Water, coffee, tea?"

"Water would be great. Thank you."

Plummer called to his administrative assistant to get Sandra some water, and then shut the door and invited her to sit on the couch in his office.

"I really hate having discussions from behind my desk." Plummer sat across from Sandra in a well-worn leather chair that didn't look particularly comfortable.

"Sandra, I'm going to cut to the chase. I have been keeping up with your work on the Klondike program. The WINPAC NIE appears to be on schedule, and the DDI is thrilled with the support he has been getting—in particular, with the support you are providing. You have managed to bring the science and technology geeks, the DO case officers, and the WINPAC analysts together to do some truly groundbreaking activity."

Sandra felt humbled. "Thank you, sir. It is truly a privilege to be working on such an important mission."

Plummer smiled. "You have proven you are ready for something bigger. I'd like you to go to Moscow for a special assignment."

"I am honored you would think of me. What makes me qualified?"

"You have had a number of successful overseas assignments, you've demonstrated that you can anticipate unacceptable outcomes and develop alternative paths, and you are ambitious, unconditionally committed and, frankly, beautiful."

She shifted on the sofa and thought carefully about what to say next. She took a breath. "Thank you. With respect, what does this assignment have to do with my physical appearance?"

"We need you to go to Moscow and get close to a male source," said Plummer. "Let's just say he favors beautiful blondes."

"But I'm not a blonde," Sandra said, and immediately regretted saying such a stupid thing.

Plummer grinned. "We'll help you with your hair color. I need to know you are up for the challenge of getting close to this target."

"Do you mean I might have to get intimate with him?"

Plummer nodded and appreciated her candor. "Quite possibly. Whatever it takes to get close to him and stay close to him. To trust you and confide in you. He's in the FSB, and I won't tell you his name now—you'll learn the specifics later in your training, but he is young and rising in the organization.

Our current case officer handling him has to return the US, and we need a replacement for her soon. You know how hard—and dangerous—it is to penetrate the FSB."

Sandra made a decision. "I will get it done, sir."

"I knew I could count on you, Sandra. This assignment could be career-changing for you. Details will be provided to you soon. Very soon. We need you to leave for Moscow in less than three months. Take care of anything personal you need to as soon as you can."

"Will do, sir. Thank you for this extraordinary opportunity. I won't let you down."

"I need you to see the DDO this afternoon. He is expecting to see you after you leave here," Plummer said.

"I'll head right there," Sandra said.

Plummer stood and shook her hand. He held her gaze and nodded curtly. "I'm counting on you, Sandra."

***

Unlike Plummer, Simmons stayed behind his desk and motioned for Sandra to take a seat. Memorabilia from his earlier exploits decorated his walls and shelves: photos of him on horseback in the Afghan mountains, photos of him receiving awards from Obama and George W., and a badly damaged AK-47 in a case on his credenza. *Like a hunter's trophy room*, she thought. Heads on the wall.

Sandra opened. "The director sent me. The DCI tells me you have chosen me to take a critical assignment in Moscow."

Simmons grimaced. "That's not how I would characterize the process," Simmons said, not meeting her gaze. "Let's say you were chosen without a lot of input from me."

Sandra felt very uncomfortable as he looked up and stared at her.

"In fact, I had no input into your selection."

Sandra stated emphatically, "I told the DCI I would do what was necessary to get the job done. I make the same commitment to you."

Simmons stood and walked towards her. "This is one of the highest potential, highest risk assignments at the Agency. You will be managing an asset who is currently in the FSB. He is giving us extraordinary intelligence—not for money, but out of a sense of loyalty to the US. He is temperamental, trusts no one except his handler, and we believe will only produce information if he is close to his case officer. Unfortunately, she has to return to the States. We need you to replace her and keep the asset performing and safe."

"You know I have been tested before and have succeeded."

"Your life and his will be on the line," Simmons said somberly.

He really doesn't trust me yet, Sandra realized. She needed to do something about that right now or watch this Moscow opportunity evaporate. She leaned forward in her chair.

"Permission to speak frankly, sir?"

Simmons was standing with his right hand on the glass case containing the AK and his left hand on his hip. Considered. Nodded.

"This decision should have been yours to make and it sounds like it got made for you. That can't feel right. You should not have been disrespected that way, and I am sorry I was the instrument for that disrespect."

Something in Simmons eyes started to shift.

Sandra continued. "I'm not your first choice. I hear that. I don't know how or why I got foisted onto you, but I can tell you this: I will make it my mission to deliver the goods for you, sir."

Simmons inclined his head slightly. Sandra took that as a yes.

"When do I leave, sir, and how long will I be gone?"

Simmons crossed the room and sat on the sofa. He was in. "You'll be retrained on our most modern systems: disguise, communications, surveillance evasion. We'll brush up your Russian language skills. You'll be sent, as soon as you can leave, to a very small training facility. You'll be the only one in training there."

"What's the location?" she asked.

"You'll find out shortly before you travel there. Your current status as a NOC will help, though. This is not an openly identified US government facility."

"I'll need a few weeks to get things arranged here. I have a roommate, so I won't have to worry about renting my house in DC. And I'll need to finish up some loose ends here on the Klondike activities."

"No need," Simmons said. "We are zero-baselining access to the control system, scrubbing the list with steel wool. We're eliminating everyone who's not critically needed. As of this morning, you've been removed from the access list and won't be able to access the vault."

Sandra was disappointed she would never meet with Elizabeth in Their Room again. The room had a special place in her memory. But she wasn't overly concerned.

"Understood," Sandra said. "I'm glad I was able to help the program for as long as I did."

"In addition to your training, you'll be integrated into a commercial company to learn your 'day' job. Having a credible job at a commercial company will be critical to your success in Moscow."

"Makes sense."

He flipped over a tablet on his desk and made a few clicks, opening his calendar. "Let's plan on you starting the training program Monday," he said. "Three weeks from today."

"I'll make that work, sir," Sandra replied.

"We'll see if you have what it takes," Simmons replied.

***

Elizabeth entered the vault combination, but the door to 5F43 did not open. She noted new initials on the door log. A "KR" and another set of initials on the sheet that were scrawled and not legible. She tried three more times, gave up, and returned to her office to call the Security Ops Center.

"Gordon. This is Elizabeth Petrov, in WINPAC-Cloud Spinner. You may not remember me—you helped me out when I didn't sign the security log for 5F43?"

"Of course, I remember you," he said affably. "What's going on?"

"I was going to work in the vault and just tried to open 5F43 but was unable to unlock the vault. I don't think I have forgotten the combination."

"Let me look at the vault log. What's your badge number?"

"PS 258."

After a minute, he replied. "It looks like the combination to the vault has been changed, but you're still on the access list. I apologize for the inconvenience. We are required to change the combinations randomly and frequently, which forces us to revalidate the access list. Come to 1K20 and I'll give you the new combination."

* * *

Elizabeth made her way to the Security Operations Center where Gordon was waiting for her. He was cute but probably only twenty-seven or so. He seemed way too eager to help.

"I have an eyes-only envelope for you with the new combination," he said. "I could have come up and opened the vault, but I'm really only supposed to do that in the case of an emergency. And you didn't sound like you were in distress." He smiled.

She smiled back. "Thank you so much." She opened the envelope, noted the new combination, and handed him back the envelope. He immediately slid it into a shredder near his chair and asked, "You sure you have the number memorized?"

She smiled again. "I have a gift for remembering things."

"I am terrible at remembering things," he laughed. "Particularly numbers, passwords, and names."

"I used to be, too," Elizabeth said. "Then I read a really helpful book on improving my memory—*Moonwalking with Einstein*—and, voila! Now have quite a knack for remembering many things I could not have before."

Gordon grinned, walked from behind the counter, and said, "Sounds like a book I need to read."

Elizabeth could sense him checking her out.

"Thanks for your help today, Gordon," Elizabeth said as she turned to go back to the vault.

"Hey! Um... Elizabeth..." Elizabeth appreciated that he didn't call her "Liz" as most everyone else did around here. "I couldn't help but notice when I opened your file that today's your birthday. Happy Birthday!"

"Thank you. I guess I shouldn't be surprised that everyone in this place knows everything."

"The big three-zero!" he smiled broadly. "Any birthday divisible by five is a reason to celebrate, and turning thirty is momentous! I turned thirty last year but don't remember much of it," he laughed.

"Sounds like an unmemorable kind of memorable evening," she laughed.

"Hey," he said, "I have an idea. A group of us from the Agency get together every Tuesday at a local bar called JV's in Falls Church, just a few miles from here. They've been in business for almost seventy years, and tonight is open-mic night. You should stop by tonight, and we'll celebrate your thirty orbits around the sun."

"Oh, I don't want to intrude, and I was planning to be in the vault this evening."

"Never! Let me tell you about the place. JV's motto is 'Ageless Charm Without Yuppie Bastardization.'"

"Yuppies? Are there still yuppies around?" she asked, smiling.

"They have live music every night and good food. They close at 2 a.m. and cater to music lovers and dancers of all ages. I play in a band that mostly does old covers. Come listen tonight? Everyone is a lot of fun, and I know they'd love to meet you."

"Sounds fun, Gordon, it really does," she said.

"Any time after nine! The place'll be rockin'!" *He did have a cute grin*, she thought.

"You know, I'll try to be there."

"Anytime, PS 258," he said. "See? I may not need the memory book, after all."

***

Elizabeth returned to the vault, dialed the new combination, entered and disarmed the alarm system, and added her name to the log. She was disappointed to see no new activity. She scrolled around the data, hoping that new clues might miraculously surface. The folder that Sandra had prepared for the DCI, the folder containing all the transcripts of the *bashka* conversations, was missing. Gone.

She worked until five o'clock, reviewing dozens of conversations of Davidov and Polichuk but found nothing new about the Avangard systems or the *bashka*. Although it was early to knock off, since there were no new transcripts, she secured the vault and walked to the parking lot to drive home. On the way to her car, she recognized Keisha exiting the OHB. Sandra had sent Elizabeth a link to a photo of Keisha. Keisha opened the door of a car parked just outside the Northeast Entrance.

Must be nice to be the DCI's EXEC, thought Elizabeth. *Scored a prime parking location for sure.*

The drive home was fast tonight. When she came into the kitchen, she smelled the aroma of a wonderful dinner and saw Tova sprawled in the hallway. He ran to her and shook his body so she would know how much he missed her. She stroked his ears and then gave him a back rub, just at his tail. His favorite.

"Hey boy, settle down," she murmured. "I missed you, too."

Sandra set down her paring knife, washed her hands, and gave Elizabeth a warm hug and lingering kiss. "Welcome home," she said.

"Smells terrific," Elizabeth said. "Middle Eastern?"

"Moroccan, just like you would have if you were settling in for dinner at an oasis in the Sahara. I spent three months in Casablanca and learned a thing or two—about food and love. Chicken tagine with almonds and apricots."

"Since I'm the birthday girl, may I make a suggestion?" Elizabeth asked. "I was invited to join some Agency folks at a bar in Falls Church. Live music, good food. Join me there after dinner?"

Sandra shook her head. "I'd love to celebrate with you. But my NOC status pretty much dictates that I don't socialize too much with open Agency personnel. If you want to go solo after dinner, I don't mind at all, honest."

"Let's eat, dinner's ready."

Sandra waited until Elizabeth took her first bite. "Good?"

"Fabulous!"

"Keep eating. I have news. Simmons asked to see me today and gave me a new assignment. A big new assignment."

Elizabeth smiled and lifted her glass. "Wow! A toast!"

Sandra's eyes were sparkling. "I'll be running toward the sound of gunfire! Moscow! I'll be handling a critical source there."

Even though Elizabeth was new to the Agency, she knew an assignment to Moscow in a leadership role was a plum assignment, and a role like this was one future Senior Intelligence Service officers coveted.

"Oh my God! This is huge!" Elizabeth set down her glass, half-stood in her chair, and delivered a kiss on Sandra's forehead. "I am so proud of you, Sandra. Truly. Congratulations!"

"Thank you, Elizabeth." Sandra was beaming. "All day, I've been looking forward to telling you."

"When do you leave?"

"That's the hard part." Sandra covered Elizabeth's hand in hers. "In three weeks, I head out to training. I'll be gone before Christmas. After that, Moscow, but I don't know when, precisely."

"Where's training?"

"Don't know. Somewhere out of the region."

"You really deserve this, and I know you'll do a terrific job," Elizabeth said. "Instead of seeing you in Paris, I guess I'll have to go to Moscow."

"Or we'll meet halfway. Paris!" Sandra beamed.

"Cheers to meeting in Paris," Elizabeth toasted.

"Cheers," Sandra responded. As she raised her glass to her lips, she reflected on how this had all come to be by taking advantage of the work Elizabeth had done and by hiding Elizabeth's role from the DCI. *It was worth it*, thought Sandra. *Elizabeth would sometime have her day, but not today.*

"I was debriefed from Klondike, and apparently many others were, too," Sandra said. "They said they don't need me there anymore. Now I won't be able to help you with the intercepts and Cloud Spinner."

"I'll miss working with you," Elizabeth said, while clearing the table. "I bet that's why the combination to 5F43 was changed today. I still got in, though."

"Don't tell me," Sandra said. "I am debriefed, and we both need to pass our next poly!"

They laughed.

"I saw Keisha today when I was leaving. What happened with her?"

"The DCI met with the *bashka* in New York City," Sandra said. "I don't know the plan, but I know they met. I would speculate they'll turn Putin's moves around on him. By knowing what he wants from the *bashka*, we'll learn about Russian intelligence priorities."

"I am so relieved to know the DCI took this on. I was worried," Elizabeth admitted.

"Me too," Sandra agreed.

***

The Uber slowed down and turned into a nondescript strip mall housing a nail salon, a Vietnamese restaurant, and an ice cream shop. Elizabeth's first thought was that the address was wrong, but when she opened the car door, she heard the music.

She paid the three-dollar cover—"For the bands," she was told—and headed in. A small, crowded dance floor in front of the band had a mix of a young and old crowd. Aged booths on the right, stand-up tables on the left, bar in the middle. Everyone was clearly enjoying themselves, dancing and swaying to the music. A large woman was standing on a small stage, microphone in hand, belting out Aretha Franklin's *R-E-S-P-E-C-T*. She was backed up by keyboards, guitars, and some brass. Elizabeth spotted Gordon, standing with a group on the far side of the restaurant. He noticed her immediately, walked over, and said, "I was sure hoping you'd be here."

"Wow, this place looks like a lot of fun," she said. "They're really open until 2 a.m.?"

"Yeah, a lot of retirees are here most nights. They don't have to get up and go to work like the rest of us. I don't start until four tomorrow, so I can be here late."

"Well, I have to be in the office at 0700, so I suspect you'll be here a lot later than me," she answered.

"Then I need to get you on the dance floor quickly," Gordon said.

He took her purse off her shoulder and hung it from the stool, grabbed her hand, and led her onto the dance floor. Before she could protest, they were dancing to the music, a slowish version of Hendrix's "Hey Joe."

After the song was over, he said, "We're on stage next." Gordon and his buddies performed two songs, part of a rotation on open-mic night where local talent could take the stage. Gordon played lead guitar and sang with a pianist, bass player, and drummer. *They were very talented, she thought, and clearly enjoyed playing to the friendly crowd.* She couldn't resist when they played a cover of Semisonic's "Closing Time" and got up and started dancing. She was quickly joined by a grizzly old, retired Marine who just couldn't stand the idea of such a pretty woman dancing by herself. They had a fun time, and Gordon's band reveled in the crowd's reaction to their music.

Time went quickly and before she knew it, 11 p.m. came, and she knew it was time to call it a night. Before she left, many of the open-mic musicians gathered on the small stage while JV's proprietor, Lorraine, the daughter of the restaurant and bar's founder, came out of the kitchen and stood next to Elizabeth.

"Happy Birthday, dear. Here is a piece of our famous carrot cake," Lorraine said. "With a candle, of course!"

The band played, and the rest of the crowd joined Lorraine in singing a rousing version of "Happy Birthday" and cheered when Elizabeth blew out the candle.

"Yummy, this is delicious," Elizabeth said. "Here, there's plenty for everyone to have a bite."

"Oh no, dear, I have a whole carrot cake in the kitchen, and everyone at JV's is going to get a piece to celebrate your thirtieth birthday!"

Elizabeth looked at Gordon, saw his smile, and realized he had organized the impromptu celebration. She gave him a hug and a kiss on his lips.

"Thank you for the best thirtieth birthday party ever. And I remember all of mine!" she smiled.

"Hey there, beautiful," he said, "It was my pleasure to celebrate with you. Perhaps I can see you again?"

Elizabeth felt conflicted. But in three weeks, she'd be single again. "I think that would be nice."

"Here's my cell phone number, 555-876-5309. If you can remember it, call me," she said as she walked towards the door. "It'd be fun to see you again."

CHAPTER 18

Wednesday, November 16, 2016
Bashka's *Hotel, Washington, DC*

Plummer's security detail drove him to the *bashka*'s hotel on Pennsylvania Avenue where they were met by the president-elect's security entourage. The president-elect's presence in the hotel was a total clusterfuck for the city. The avenue and street blockages had completely disrupted DC traffic, which was actually hard to screw up further. Still, the *bashka* had done it.

Plummer finally got to the hotel lobby from the underground garage and made his way to the elevator to take him to the president-elect's suite. He exited the elevator and saw the same gaggle of sycophants surrounding the *bashka* that he had seen in New York City. *If only they knew what a total loser this guy was and how close he was to heading to a federal penitentiary,* Plummer thought.

The *bashka* greeted him warmly and invited him into a small anteroom off of the major office area. The anteroom was festooned in pictures of the *bashka* playing golf, at a podium, cutting a ribbon, getting on a private jet, with a buxom young woman. *He obviously liked pictures of himself,* Plummer thought.

"I ordered you breakfast," the president-elect said, indicating a table with two place settings, steaming coffee, and an omelet, toast, bacon, and hash browns. "Not sure what you like. I have already eaten breakfast, but I ordered another for myself, too!"

"Smells great, but I think I'll just have some coffee."

"Oh shit, never drink the stuff. Makes me too edgy."

Plummer noticed the Diet Coke on the table and figured out where the *bashka*'s caffeine came from.

The *bashka* stood up from his chair and walked around the table to stand next to Plummer. He put his hand on Plummer's shoulder and said, "I knew I could trust you; I saw right away you would be loyal to me. Loyalty is very important to me, you know."

Plummer nodded. "I value loyalty, too. Here's what I've done for you, sir. I have restricted all new access to the audio files and reassigned the individual who discovered your conversations in Moscow."

"Good. I'm glad to hear."

"I looked into erasing the audio files of these conversations and learned that's not possible. They are already backed up. The act of trying to erase them will attract unnecessary attention that you don't want," Plummer said.

The *bashka* frowned. "Well, that's unacceptable." He crossed his arms over his girth. "I think after I'm sworn in, I can order for them to be erased."

"I don't think so, sir. I plan to stay on as the DCI, and those files are my insurance policy with you. You will be announcing shortly that I will be continuing as the director of the CIA. I know you will be criticized for this, but you have no choice. I will safeguard these files for you and me for as long as we have a positive relationship, but only as long as we do."

"So, exactly what do you want?'

"I will be your DCI until I tell you I am not."

"Who the hell do you think you are, telling me what I am going to do?" the *bashka* bellowed.

"I am the guy standing between you and spending twenty years in a federal pen for FCPA violations," Plummer said evenly.

"You can't blackmail me..."

"Here are the terms of our deal. You keep me on as your DCI, and that keeps me in the best position to protect you. You'll need to support the budgets I request and nominate the candidates I suggest for Director of National Intelligence, the National Security Agency, the National Reconnaissance Office, and the National Geospatial Intelligence Agency."

Plummer picked up his fork and began eating his omelet. The *bashka*'s face was turning reddish, becoming a closer match to his hair.

Plummer picked up a piece of the thick-sliced applewood smoked bacon and bit off a piece. "You'll do this, or I take what I know to the attorney general."

The *bashka* slumped in his chair. Plummer continued. "And, I will help you deal with the Russians now and even help you win a second term, sir. You have an army of appointed positions to hire in the next few weeks. Take mine off your list. It's the smart move."

The room was quiet, the food was growing cold, and the drinks were untouched. The *bashka* reached his hand out across the table and said, "Deal! You know I wrote a book on making deals, and you and I have a deal. I usually like when I make a deal, to screw the other guy, but in this case, I think we are both getting what we need. I am going to like working with you. I hear you are a fixer."

"Yes, Mr. President-elect," Plummer replied. "I will be your fixer."

Plummer stood up from the table and started towards the door.

The *bashka* sat slumped in his chair and bellowed, "Don't get used to this, you know, upping me in a deal. We'll be together for a long time, and I will be calling on you to help me fix some things," the president-elect said. "That's my nickname for you, Mr. Fixit."

"You know, Putin has a nickname for you too," Plummer said.

"Really? I like the guy. What does he call me?" the president-elect asked.

"He calls you *bashka*," Plummer answered.

"*Bashka*. What's that mean? Should I ask him when I speak with him?"

"Please don't. He'll know we are intercepting his conversations."

"But what does it mean?" the *bashka* asked.

"Google Russian translator, b-a-s-h-k-a," Plummer said as he opened the door to leave.

As he exited the room and the president-elect's sycophants began rushing in, he heard him call out, "Someone Google the translation for *bashka*, b-a-s-h-k-a."

Plummer was glad he was not in the room when the *bashka* got the response.

Putin's chump.

***

Sandra would be in Moscow without diplomatic immunity, so it was critical she not be caught. Her tradecraft skills had to be perfect, so she spent most of day reviewing training procedures, including FSB tracking techniques. Although this was a closely held assignment, her colleagues in the Operations

Directorate learned of her upcoming posting to Moscow and were surprised to hear that she had been selected.

No one actually said anything negative to her, but some of her closer friends told her what they were hearing.

"Over her head..."

"There are a dozen better candidates than her for this critical post."

"She must be fucking Plummer."

"She might be able to do it, but in ten years."

She had just learned she would be moving to Texas for training. Her NOC position was to work for an oil company with a large presence in Russia with offices in Moscow and drilling operations in Siberia. She would never enter the US Embassy in Moscow; her cover assignment would be as an IT specialist for the oil company. *Christ*, she thought, *an IT specialist. How do they come up with this stuff?*

***

Elizabeth's day was consumed by Cloud Spinner. The team was continuing to analyze the most recent test data, and her initial estimates were gaining traction amongst even the most skeptical parts of the team. While they were getting the physics-based modeling refined, they were also fusing multiple data sources to create a more accurate assessment of the flight. The accelerations, decelerations, and flight profile estimates were now trustworthy—what the Agency called "high in confidence." Now, the primary challenge was to understand why the Russians would conduct a test like this and what it meant about the effectiveness of the hypersonic system.

Elizabeth led the conversation with the Cloud Spinner team in the conference room. She stood at the whiteboard with a red marker in hand.

"Let's put in one column everything we know and how we know it," she started. "Then, we'll start a second column of what we think it means and why. First, we know there have been eleven flight tests of the Avangard system."

Heads nodded in agreement.

"And, we know that there have been four test failures, and the last five tests were successful."

No one added anything.

"We have multiple measurements from the boost phase, glide phase, and re-entry phase from the last three tests that allow us to create a flight profile with great precision."

"And no one knows how the hell they're doing it," added a voice in the room.

"Stop—let's just write down what we know."

A team member who had been at the Agency for many years said, "In the press, Putin brags about the program being a game changer."

Elizabeth wrote his thoughts on the board and added, "We have a report that the Ministry of Defense was behind schedule and under cost and schedule pressures to complete the program."

She stared at the whiteboard. It was the size of the entire wall. She didn't understand how anyone could be an engineer or scientist and not have a large whiteboard in their office. She continued adding the team's thoughts to the wall, then changed pen colors and said, "What do we take from these facts?"

The room became more engaged.

"During the last fifty years," one team member said, "we have never seen them go to production and deployment of a new ballistic weapon system without making at least twenty tests and repeating at least six successful tests of the same configuration. So, we can conclude that this means there will be many more tests."

He was immediately challenged, "Putin said they would deploy this year. He didn't say they would deploy after six successful tests of the same configuration!"

"Yeah, but they'd never stop testing and deploy an immature system. This is a critical part of their deterrence program. If it doesn't work, it doesn't deter."

"Bullshit. They would deploy early if they had no more time and no more money."

Elizabeth smiled as she watched most of the team add to the discussion. *No silent dissension here*, she thought. After fifteen minutes of debate, they reached her conclusion.

"Senior Russian officials need the program to look successful," she summarized. "They could've doctored the test so that, to the external observer, it appears ready to deploy, even though it really can't achieve the range and maneuverability claims that have been made."

"So, you think they're gaming us with this?"

"No, I think they're gaming Putin!" Elizabeth answered. "They create a Potemkin village, a fake. They pull off a test they claim is a fully functional test, but they leave the warhead mass off. They demonstrate phenomenal range and maneuverability numbers, never mind there are no weapons on board, then pass the test, and everyone is happy."

Frank, who had joined the meeting late, was standing at the door and asked, "Anyone else have a better idea?"

The room was silent.

"Okay," he said. "Let's adjust our estimate based on this supposition. We'll add the mass to the HGV of a W-40 class warhead and estimate max range and maneuverability with the updated mass."

Tom said, "If we do that, it'll show their system sucks. It'll almost be ballistic—really no advantage at all."

Frank nodded. "I know. Do it. Let's review the results at tomorrow's stand-up. And Elizabeth, can I see you for a minute in my office?"

***

He shut his office door and said in a hushed voice, "You know the answer to this—don't you?"

She sat and said, "I actually don't. I know that the Ministry of Defense is under tremendous pressure and the Ministry of Finance would fund only one more test. There is a lot of money to be made for their defense industry when they go to production, just like here."

"You think they would screw with Putin and his cronies?" Frank asked.

"For big money? Of course, just like in the US," Elizabeth said.

Frank liked her. She had been at the Agency less than six months but had already made a terrific difference and was leading the team. They would get the NIE done on schedule, and it would show the Russians have to deal with the same laws of physics as Americans do.

"Are you still getting the additional materials on Avangard from the activity you got read into?"

She shook her head. "Not as often as before, but it did provide us some solid information. I'm planning to spend some time on the other activity this afternoon. Perhaps I'll learn more," she said.

"Understood. Let me know if you do."

башка

[baška]

Chump

CHAPTER 19

Thursday, November 17, 2016

OHB

Elizabeth attended the 0700 stand-up and then headed to the vault, curious to see if there was anything new from the Klondike intercepts. She was sorry she would not be meeting Sandra there any longer. She was on her own now. As she unlocked the vault, she saw that the room had been opened multiple times by "KR." Keisha had been spending time in the vault in recent days. Elizabeth wondered why.

She entered the glass room, logged on to the system, and saw there had been recent files added to the database. She put the headphones on and started with the most recent intercept. While it was loading, she thought back to that first time she and Sandra had been together. Was it only three weeks ago?

She did not even bother reviewing the badly translated transcript of the conversations—waste of time. A new conversation she just opened was between Putin and Davidov earlier that day. Moscow being eight hours ahead of Washington was so convenient. She could catch up on the most recent discussions without having to be in the office at crazy hours. And, she loved the efficiency of the system: intercept, exfiltration, and transmission to Langley. A conversation in the Kremlin that day to her ears in only a few hours. *Klondike was real gold*, she thought.

"*Vlad, we have a problem*," *Davidov said.*

"*We always have problems. So what?*" *Putin replied.*

"*We got to the* bashka's *national security guy, Gershwin, on his transition team and told him to expect some guidance from you. He was taken aback by the message, but we know your message got to the* bashka," *Davidov answered.*

"*How do we know?*" *Putin asked.*

"*We have his office in New York and his hotel in Washington, DC compromised with audio equipment. The moron has no idea how vulnerable he is*," *Davidov added.*

"*He will eventually, I suspect—but in the meantime, what's the problem?*" *Putin asked.*

"*Plummer has found out about us. He warned the* bashka *about us coming after him. The CIA has somehow compromised us. They have audio of our conversations about him.*"

Putin showed exasperation. "*Not possible. The CIA recorded us talking? Where? When?*"

"*Well, maybe they don't*", *Davidov said.* "*But Plummer claimed they have. He may be lying to the* bashka, *maybe not. If true, we don't know how... yet, or when or where, but Plummer told the* bashka *he has heard us, you and me.*"

"*So, we are listening to them, and they are listening to us? What a world,*" *said Putin.*

"*We sweep all of our offices every day for bugs but have not detected any for quite some time. The* bashka *does not check for electronic bugging devices in his personal offices or hotel rooms. We have compromised a couple of individuals in his cleaning crews in his buildings and hotels, and they install our bugs. The funniest thing is, we are reusing equipment we found from the FBI, so if it is found, he'll blame the FBI!" Davidov said.*

"So, the director of the CIA found out we have the bashka by the balls. What has he decided to do? Send us a nasty letter?" Putin laughed.

"Maybe place travel and financial restrictions on us? Strangely, Plummer seemed far less interested in taking us on than on taking advantage of the bashka himself," Davidov said.

"So, what are they doing about it?"

"The bashka or Plummer?"

"Both," Putin said.

"The bashka is a pussy looking for help. Plummer, on the other hand, has made his own demands of the bashka, threatening to expose him and have him jailed if he doesn't cooperate. He got to him before we did."

Putin laughed and said, "We both have him by the balls. We'll each grab one and squeeze together!"

"Yes—he's everyone's bashka, it seems," said Davidov.

"If they collected earlier discussions, can they be intercepting this one?" Putin asked.

"No, impossible," Davidov said. "We are working on where they have penetrated us, and when we find the scum, I will personally put a bullet in his head."

"After I do," Putin said.

Elizabeth was startled. The DCI was blackmailing the president-elect, the Russians were planning to blackmail the president-elect, and Klondike had been compromised—or at least, it was on the way to becoming compromised. She needed to talk to Sandra and let her know what was going on. She really needed to talk to her. But more than that, she needed to talk about this with her grandfather.

***

The drive into the city was torturous. There had been an accident on the GW Parkway heading into the city from headquarters, and after she had gotten on the Parkway, there were really no options but to slog through the mess. While the house at Logan Circle was charming, the commute to it was painful compared to her short drive to the hotel in McLean. She eventually made it past the crash site and then quickly into the city and up Fourteenth Street to Sandra's row house. The weather was getting cooler in the evenings and the number of sidewalk diners was dropping dramatically. Winter was coming to DC.

She arrived at Sandra's and was greeted by a very happy yellow lab. Tova could not restrain himself and his whole body wiggled as she gave him his usual big ear and tummy rubs. *The aroma was amazing again*, Elizabeth thought.

"Sandra, you're a great cook. No, you're a chef," she called out from the carriage house. "I've never eaten this well! You are spoiling me. And Tova. Is that chili?"

"Yes, my special Afghan chili, straight from a small village outside of Kabul—except I use turkey instead of goat!"

"Thank you," Elizabeth said. They met in the kitchen and hugged.

Sandra had already poured two glasses of a nice Merlot for them. "Let's go sit by the fire while the chili simmers."

"How was your day?" Elizabeth asked.

"Oh, I just goofed off. Got my training assignment location, though. Looks like three months in Texas and then off to Moscow in April. How about you? Any progress today?"

Elizabeth stared into her wine glass. She did not know where to start about the day's discoveries. She took a sip and said, "I think we are fucked."

"What's going on?" Sandra asked.

"I listened to a Klondike file between Putin and Davidov this afternoon. The audio was collected earlier today and was just the two of them in a conversation at the Kremlin."

"And...?" Sandra asked.

"Davidov told Putin that Plummer had dirt on the *bashka*, and it's our dirt! They said Plummer was blackmailing the *bashka*. His blackmail is based on the transcriptions from Klondike I found. That son of a bitch Plummer took the Klondike intercepts we had about the *bashka* and is using them to blackmail the president-elect. He isn't doing right!"

"Impossible," Sandra said. "Plummer would never do that! He would have alerted the president-elect about his vulnerabilities and used the Agency to turn this to the CIA's advantage."

"Not what's happening. Davidov described their audio intercept capabilities in both the *bashka*'s office in New York City and in his hotel. They've been listening to his transition planning and also his conversations with Plummer. The Russians have learned that we know of their dirt on the *bashka* and are trying to find out how we got it. Plummer and the Russians are both planning to manipulate the *bashka*!"

They both sat silently for what seemed a long time. Sandra stared into the fireplace, and Elizabeth stroked Tova's neck and ears as he sat by her side.

Elizabeth broke the silence. "We need to get to the DCI. We need to hear what he is saying and not just rely on the Russians. We need to know exactly what he's up to."

Sandra said nothing. She continued staring into the fireplace.

"Did you hear me?" Elizabeth asked. "We need to take on Plummer. We need to take him on and take him down."

"We can't take on the DCI," Sandra said. "That's just crazy."

"We use Klondike, we monitor his conversations," Elizabeth said.

Sandra shook her head. "How in the world do we do it? He doesn't wear a Fitbit and doesn't drive a car."

Elizabeth was undeterred. "We get to Keisha's key fob. She drives to work every day, and we could activate her key fob.

She is clearly close to him, and he's probably discussing his plans with her."

"You think you can activate her key fob? Have you ever done this? I know the answer to that: no!"

"I have an idea. I'll activate my key fob and make sure the vehicle identification number access process works. Test run."

Finally, Sandra responded. "Nothing good can happen from bugging the DCI, but I don't have an alternative or better idea."

"Okay!" Elizabeth said. "So, tomorrow morning, I'll use the Klondike VIN auto-activation system to initialize my key fob and see if the sorting and search algorithms find it and if the system starts recording my discussions. If it works, I will somehow get Keisha's VIN. She parks in the Northeast Parking lot near the entrance. I've seen her car. We may not have Plummer, but we'll have his executive officer."

"Before you take those steps, let's first make sure it works with you and that you can limit other analyst's access to your data collects on the server before you go after Keisha," Sandra said.

"Agreed. This is some serious shit we've gotten into," Elizabeth said.

"Yes, but we are not screwed—they are," Sandra said sharply. "Let's eat, the chili smells good, and I am hungry."

***

Dinner was delightful. They talked about Sandra's upcoming move to Moscow and Elizabeth's upcoming decision.

"It's been an amazing six months," Elizabeth said, "but I think I am going to return to JPL after Cloud Spinner is finished. I am conflicted, though."

Sandra reached across the table and took Elizabeth's hand. "You're a natural here, Elizabeth. You'd have a great career. I'm confident we'd work together again and see each other more often if you stayed at the Agency."

"You're right—and I relish the idea of seeing more of you," Elizabeth replied. "We'll figure it out together."

They cleaned the dishes and headed to bed early, exhausted and uncertain about the days to come.

CHAPTER 20

Friday, November 18, 2016

OHB

The next morning, Elizabeth attended the 0700 stand-up and, as soon as she could, returned to 5F43 to log in to the system. She went into the administrator's section of the software and found key fob activation. She entered the VIN for her Toyota and was pleased to see an icon appear that implied someone had a sense of humor: lightning bolts flashed. She had left her key fob in her cubicle, so she could not test it in the vault. But she'd have it with her when she went back to her office and joined the Cloud Spinner team.

She returned to her cubicle and placed her purse with her key fob on her desk. John appeared and wanted to talk about the most recent test of a dummy warhead of essentially zero mass. The test results converged with the analytical modeling.

"Liz, I think you are on to something," he said. "The Russians are definitely gaming the system. I miss the old days when we allowed sharing of telemetry results under the SALT I and SALT II Treaties and even exchanged data tapes of ICBM weapons testing under the START treaty. Transparency worked—until it didn't."

"I had no idea," Elizabeth said. "Once, we enabled each other?"

"I can quote the language from the START II Treaty: 'Each party is free to use various methods of transmitting telemetric information during testing, including its encryption, except that, in accordance with the provisions of paragraph three of Article XV of the Treaty, neither party shall engage in deliberate denial of telemetric information, such as through the use of telemetry encryption, whenever such denial impedes verification of compliance with the provisions of the Treaty.'"

"Freak!" Elizabeth exclaimed.

"Yeah, I guess I am," he smiled. "Anyone who has been doing this shit for thirty-eight years... well, would be a freak. You know, the Ruskies successfully tested their first ICBM in August 1957 using a modified R-7 as the booster, more than a year before the US tested a similar system. Never, never underestimate them."

"I suspect we have done some test manipulation, too," Elizabeth said. "I remember a critical Missile Defense Agency test of a warhead interceptor that was structured to guarantee success. We wanted the Russians to think we had a system that worked in difficult geometries when it only worked with a straight-on shot."

"Yep," John said. "We have all cheated more than once."

***

Back in the vault, it took only a few minutes to find conversations from her key fob. They were geotagged from her phone metadata, time tagged, and labeled "unknown female speaker number one" and "unknown male speaker number one." All she had to do was enter a simple seventeen-figure alphanumeric code and her key fob became a snooping device— thereafter, her conversations were recorded and archived. She checked the auto-translation system and reviewed the transcript. It was almost perfect. Obviously, the system worked better with English than Russian. *The CIA's Siri needs to spend more time learning Russian*, she thought.

She listened to the audio file and found the quality very good, also. Her key fob had been in her purse sitting on her desktop, so not very far away from her conversation with John. No wonder they referred to the DS&T at the CIA as the Wizards of Langley. The sons of bitches could do anything!

She knew there were cameras throughout the Agency's parking lots. Truth was stranger than fiction, and breaking and entering in the CIA lot was a commonplace problem. She had been told to not leave anything of value in sight on her car seats because of the problem with car thefts. Since the cars were parked in a controlled area behind high fences that was equipped with motion detectors and ground pressure monitors, it stood to reason that the cars were being broken into by current employees. Didn't these people undergo background check and polys? Then she thought of her own circumstances and smiled. Maybe they do hire some sketchy people.

On the way to her Toyota, Elizabeth walked past Keisha's car. The VIN number can be found in several locations on a car. The easiest was the dashboard in front of the driver's seat. But she could not stop and stare or take a photo or copy down the number with pen and paper. She would have to locate, see, and remember the VIN number from a quick glance at the dashboard. What could go wrong?

She left her office while it was still light enough to read the VIN and took a long route through the OHB to the exit closest to Keisha's car, through the historical museum on the ground floor, past exhibits and displays of both Russian and CIA artifacts of the Cold War era. Coat button cameras, poison-tipped umbrellas, briefcases with secret compartments, covert writing pens, and encrypted communication systems, all from the 1960s, 1970s, and 1980s. She wondered how long before the Klondike program systems were housed in an unclassified display case.

She exited the Northeast Entrance and proceeded to the parking space where she'd seen Keisha a few days before. Her car was there, and Elizabeth nonchalantly strolled towards the front of it. Following the skills she learned in the book she had recommended to Gordon, she cleared her mind and focused. She created a memory palace, a method of loci taught by the ancient Greeks, in her mind. She glanced down at the dashboard and—the VIN was clearly visible. Got it!

After reaching her own car, she recorded the number she had so quickly memorized: JTDKARFU6G3503712. The VIN of every car sold in North America was a seventeen-figure alphanumeric code that included car manufacturer, car attributes, model year, plant code, and serial number. She would go to the vault in the morning and activate the recording and geotagging capabilities of Keisha's key fob.

Fuck it, she thought. *I'm right here. Why wait until morning? Do it now!*

She walked back to the OHB and the vault. She saw that no one had been in since the last time she was there. The room seemed unusually warm. Or maybe it was just her. She logged on to the system, went to the activation page, and deactivated her Toyota key fob. And then, as she had done with her own VIN, she entered Keisha's VIN. Lightning flashes. The system recognized the VIN and set up a file structure to begin accumulating audio records. Elizabeth smiled and wondered if this was what a spider felt after spinning its web to capture its prey.

She secured the vault and left the building. As she walked toward her car, she saw that Keisha's car was gone. *Keisha's not working too late tonight*, she thought.

***

The drive to Sandra's place was easy tonight, and she was greeted by a happy Sandra and a very happy Tova. They walked to the Tabard Inn, between Sixteenth and Seventeenth on N Street, where they could catch some live music and have a quiet dinner.

"What do you think we'll get from Keisha?" Sandra asked on the walk back home.

"Truthfully, I've no idea," Elizabeth said. "We know what Plummer is up to, but I have no idea if she is a part of his plans."

"The Klondike activation system seems to have worked. I'll check the files on Monday. I hope I remembered the VIN correctly and that Keisha's conversations are being recorded," Elizabeth said. "If not, I may be listening to some random person in DC."

"We crossed a line—a big line—today," Sandra said, unlocking her door.

"Feels that way already," Elizabeth said.

"It's bedtime, but I don't know if I can sleep. Let's get naked!"

Elizabeth smiled and took Sandra's hand. "Let's go upstairs."

CHAPTER 21

Monday, November 21, 2016 to Tuesday, November 22, 2016

OHB

Elizabeth left for the office very early the next Monday morning, as she wanted to review both Keisha's files and the most recent Klondike source data. Even though she arrived early, she still had to park in what employees called the "north forty," the section of the lot furthest from the building. With the expansion of the headquarters in 1994 and the compacting of more employees into the buildings than originally intended, parking was inconvenient. On her half-mile walk to the Northeast Entrance, Elizabeth walked past thousands of empty parking spaces assigned to carpools, shift workers, and Agency seniors. She did not care to take the shuttle for lazy people.

She'd rather walk in the rain. *Gotta get in my ten thousand steps a day*, she thought.

"I knew this walk would suck," she said out loud to no one in particular.

The morning stand-up was lightly attended and covered the same ground they had been plowing recently: Frank had committed to completing the first draft of the NIE quickly and getting it to the chairman of the National Intelligence Council by the end of December, so they had fewer than five weeks until "pens down." Elizabeth learned that the first draft would be circulated throughout the Intelligence Community and the Department of Defense for review and comments. It was at this time, she was told, that the sharp knives would be unsheathed.

It would be impossible to present an intelligence assessment of this magnitude without pissing off one or more agencies, companies, or departments. There would be apologists, like those in the State Department, who would try to create a narrative of the US overstating either the capabilities or intentions, or both, of the Russians with this new weapon system. There would be those in the military who would claim the Russian capabilities were actually understated. The US Air Force and Navy budgets depended on portraying the Russians as "ten feet tall," and both military branches would fiercely lobby for new systems to both counter the Avangard systems and build systems of the same type for the Navy and Air Force. And, of course, the debate would be incomplete without the US defense industry and its gaggle of lobbyists forcefully arguing for new defense expenditures because of the new threat. *Welcome to the political underbelly of Washington*, she thought. Pasadena was a distant, pleasant memory.

***

She was relieved that no one had been in 5F43 since she had been there last Friday.

She recognized that she was violating many laws. Conducting unauthorized wiretaps on US citizens was criminal conduct. But, she rationalized, the end justifies the means. If monitoring Keisha could provide the necessary data that proved Plummer's criminal behavior, then it was worth the risk.

She went to the files from Keisha's key fob from the weekend. There were many conversations. The auto-translation function continued to work much better with English than Russian, so she was able to quickly scan the transcripts and saw nothing of interest from Keisha's evening. She learned Keisha had a sister with three children, and Keisha doted on her nieces and nephew. Elizabeth was surprised Keisha spent most of Sunday at church and had a wonderful voice. But nothing about Plummer. She then went to the *bashka* files and saw it was a slow news weekend there, too.

After a few minutes, she concluded that her day would be best spent working on final sections of the Cloud Spinner report. If she could get out of work a little early, she'd take Tova for a long walk before it got dark.

***

The next morning, Elizabeth returned to 5F43 and saw new audio files from Keisha's key fob. She scanned the transcripts and could not believe what she was reading. She quickly went to the audio recording to listen for herself.

"We have a couple of hours before my wife and kids will be home," Plummer said. "It's been way too long since we've been together."

"Let's not waste a moment," Keisha murmured. "I want you, all of you."

Elizabeth forwarded quickly past the sounds of their lovemaking. Loud, raucous sounds.

She was thankful the vocoder algorithms in the key fob filtered out television, radio, and background audio. She wished it filtered out lovemaking. She finally got to a place in the file where the DCI and Keisha were speaking in full sentences.

"I told the president-elect I was going to be his DCI for as long as I wanted to be. I and only I will decide when I was done. And then I told him that it would be me making key nomination selections for the other Senate-confirmed positions in the Intelligence Community," Plummer said.

"What did he think about that?' Keisha asked.

"Very little. He was pissed," Plummer said. "I also told him that he would be supportive of my budget requests."

"And..."

"At the end, we made a deal."

"Unbelievable!" Keisha said. "You had your way with him!"

"Like I am going to have my way with you again right now."

More noises Elizabeth wished she could skip over.

She couldn't believe it. Keisha was fucking her boss. Not that this was all that unusual at the Agency. Every water cooler conversation seemed to be about who was bedding whom. *Hey,* she thought, *I'm doing it, too.*

This worked for their cause, actually. Keisha and Plummer in bed together made great opportunities to get more information on the *bashka* from their pillow talk. Unfortunately, outside of the bedroom, the DCI was likely to be discrete because his security detail was never far away, and Elizabeth was certain they were trying to keep their tryst a secret.

She forwarded through a longer section of irrelevant audio before she landed on a more interesting discussion.

Plummer was speaking. "More good news. That analyst Sandra Friedman? Well, she is packing up to head to Texas for training before leaving for Moscow in the spring. She's taking a position with an oil drilling company for her cover. I hope she can adapt to the people there and the business. Simmons is moving forward with my plan for her, but that asshole plans to stop her move as soon as I am gone from the job, I know it. I can't wait until he hears I have been chosen to stay with the new administration. First thing I do, get rid of that lame son of a bitch!"

"You aren't really going to send her to Moscow, are you?" Keisha asked. "We just needed her out of the way."

"Moscow is out of the way. When I made a deal with the president-elect, I told him we'd restrict new access to Klondike and make sure his secrets would not be found by anyone else."

"Think about this. She may be more dangerous in Moscow, knowing Putin was manipulating his *bashka*," Keisha said.

"Fair enough. If you can think of something else to do with her, let me know. I'm okay with her leaving for Texas and being cut off from here."

Elizabeth listened with disgust. Sandra received the Moscow assignment not because she had earned it, but because the DCI wanted her out of the way. He told the *bashka* that he would take steps to limit exposure and damage from the *bashka*'s incriminating actions and Sandra was being dealt with promptly. Even though it seemed like Sandra would be keeping the assignment, the DCI had a low opinion of her value. Should she tell Sandra of this discovery? It might devastate Sandra's self-worth and confidence.

It was also clear that the DCI had no interest in going to the justice department and having the attorney general confront the president-elect with his crimes. Seemed like a lot of people would come out of this ahead: The president-elect becomes president, the DCI keeps his job, the Russians have their *bashka*, Sandra gets her plum assignment. The only ones screwed over are the American people.

There was no obvious next step, yet the consequences of doing nothing seemed tragic. Then she decided to do what she had always done when confronted with a problem with seemingly no solution. She needed to see and talk to her grandfather. While she called him almost every day since she had left Pasadena, she had never mentioned Klondike, the *bashka*, the DCI, or Sandra.

She would return to California and tell him everything. He would know what she should do.

***

"I have to deal with an emergency at home," Elizabeth told Frank.

He looked concerned. "I am sorry to hear that, Elizabeth. If there is anything I can do to help, please let me know."

"Oh, thank you, Frank. It's my grandfather. I need to see him. I should only be away from the office for only two or three days," Elizabeth said.

"Okay, but hopefully you'll be back quickly," he replied. "It's all hands on deck until we meet this NEI deadline."

***

She drove to Sandra's on autopilot, her mind racing and replaying the day's, the week's, and last three month's events. She was not stressed but focused—very focused. Times like this required her full attention; it was times like this when she was at her best.

Sandra and Tova were out for a walk. She found a note on the back door giving Elizabeth the route and an invitation to meet. She saw they had only been gone for ten minutes, so she would quickly change clothes and catch up with them. They wouldn't have gone far yet, as Tova loved to sniff every building corner and lamppost. He was in no hurry to do his business because he had learned that on some days, the sooner he pooped and peed, the shorter his walks were. He learned to hold it for a long time and enjoyed long walks on many days.

She left the house, jogging towards Dupont Circle. She found them on Connecticut Avenue.

Tova saw Elizabeth first and immediately pulled so hard on the leash that Sandra could hardly restrain him. She held on, but when she recognized Elizabeth, Sandra let go of his leash and Tova bounded down the block, rushing past pedestrians on the sidewalk. When he got to Elizabeth, he leapt up and embraced her while barking wildly.

Sandra, laughing, caught up and gave Elizabeth a hug and a kiss. "We're so glad you found us!" Sandra said.

"I'm so glad you let me know where you were," Elizabeth said. "I needed to see you both." She ruffled Tova's ears. "We have a lot to discuss tonight."

"When we get back, let's order some Chinese."

"Sounds great," Elizabeth said.

They finished their carryout in front of the fireplace. Next to them, Tova slowly turned himself like a roasting marshmallow, carefully sleeping on one side and then the other, making sure neither got too hot from the flames and the warming hearth.

"Keisha's key fob worked, and I heard a very troubling conversation." Elizabeth said. "Keisha's fucking Plummer. She is fucking her boss!"

"Well, maybe he is fucking her!" Sandra replied. "You don't know who's zooming who, do you?"

"Of course not. I was just surprised," Elizabeth said.

"Oh, so what," Sandra said. "Everyone is fucking someone else at the Agency."

"The two discussed the *bashka*, and the son of bitch is getting away with it. Plummer keeps his job and isn't doing anything about the criminal acts of the *bashka*."

"That is really disappointing to hear," Sandra sighed. "But I am not really surprised."

"And to keep the *bashka* happy, they are sending you to Moscow. Plummer said your assignment is a sham. They just needed you gone."

"What do you mean my assignment's a sham?" Sandra spit out.

"I didn't say it was a sham, I said *Plummer* said it was a sham," Elizabeth said. "He did it at the *bashka*'s request to limit people's access to Klondike and to send you far from here. They don't want you anywhere near Washington right now. Plummer said Simmons thinks you are underqualified and plans to reassign you as soon as he can."

"Well, that was true," Sandra admitted. "But I already met with Simmons and dealt with his concerns."

"Don't worry. Since Plummer essentially blackmailed his way into remaining DCI for the next administration, you'll still be on your way to Moscow."

Sandra smiled. "You know? It's fine, honey. It sounds like office politics to me. I know many others who have benefited from insider moves to accelerate their career. As long I am still going to Texas for my training and heading to the assignment Moscow in April, I really don't care."

"*I* care," said Elizabeth. "These are despicable people. They lie, they cheat, they disparage, they manipulate—"

"They do whatever it takes, just like I do," Sandra interrupted.

"But you don't blackmail people and manipulate colleagues—"

"I'd do what it takes to get the job done," Sandra emphasized.

"Why do you think they are worried about getting you out of the way but not me? I still have access."

Sandra shifted in her seat and looked away. "I didn't tell them."

"Tell them what?" Elizabeth asked.

"About you," Sandra replied. "About you discovering the audio files of the *bashka*. They think it was all me."

"Why didn't you tell them? We've been a team on this." Elizabeth reached over to touch Sandra's arm.

"I thought it was more important to make sure Plummer got the data and took it seriously, and I thought if it came from a more senior officer, that would make it more likely," Sandra replied curtly.

Elizabeth patted her leg, summonsing Tova to come closer. "Sure, yeah, sure. And you wanted to make sure you got all of the credit for this. All the credit."

"Honey, no." Sandra reached out her hand. "You've been here only a few months. You're so smart and skilled, you'll have plenty of chances to shine. And you still have access to the Klondike data."

"And what do we do about the *bashka*, then?" Elizabeth asked.

Sandra put her hands on Elizabeth's back and began slowly rubbing her neck. "I don't know, I really don't know."

They sat silently for another long time. Tova rolled over. Elizabeth did not respond to Sandra's touch.

"Let's go to bed," Sandra said.

"I'll be up later. I have a lot to think about. I am going to take a couple of days off to go back to California and see my grandfather. Can I leave Tova here with you? I know you're packing and getting ready to go and everything, but I need the favor."

"Of course," said Sandra. "How long will you be gone?"

"I'll call now and see what flights look like. I should be back no later than Friday, maybe Thursday for Thanksgiving," Elizabeth said. "Frank needs me back to work on Cloud Spinner."

Sandra left Elizabeth and Tova sitting in the glow of the fireplace.

Elizabeth was surprised at Sandra's reactions. Sandra was obviously not trying to fix the world. Her professional future looked good, her star was rising, and she did not much care about anything other than herself right now. *That includes me, too*, Elizabeth thought.

She went online and found a flight from Dulles to LAX leaving at 0730 and getting in at 1030 PST. She would take an Uber to Pasadena and surprise her grandfather. She finished her reservation, got her seat assignments, and decided it was time for bed.

Sandra was sound asleep. Elizabeth and Tova went down the hall to the guest bedroom.

CHAPTER 22

Wednesday, November 23, 2016

Pasadena

M*ooooo*, she thought, *we are just cattle*. After arriving at the United terminal in Los Angeles, she observed that Terminal 7 at LAX was third-world—few amenities and always filthy. *Why should our airports be so bad?* she wondered.

The drive from LAX to Pasadena was tortuous at this time of day, but her Uber driver was funny and a good companion on the ride. Five stars and a tip for him! He was an actor waiting to be discovered in LA—who wasn't? Until his big break, driving worked well to pay the bills, he said. Plus, he enjoyed meeting people and networking. Elizabeth thought, *I could never be an Uber driver. Too many people to deal with.* She arrived at her house and walked up the brick sidewalk to the front door.

She smelled freshly cut grass. A slight breeze carried the scent of the next-door camellias. She missed Pasadena.

She unlocked the door and cracked it ajar. "*Dedushka*, it's Yelizaveta! *Dedushka*, are you home?"

His surprised voice echoed from his bedroom.

"Yes, yes! Give me a minute. What are you doing here? Why didn't you tell me you were coming?" her grandfather answered. "Give me a moment, I'll be right out."

"I wanted to surprise you," she said.

"You did, you did!" He entered the living room wearing his pajamas and a robe. Elizabeth hugged him for a very long time. She noticed a tear on his cheek.

"I should have called," Elizabeth apologized. "You were still in bed, *dedushka*, it's after noon. Are you sick?"

"Please, make us some tea, and we'll catch up. I'll go get dressed."

Elizabeth went to the kitchen and put a kettle of water on. She selected an assortment of tea bags. She went to the cabinet that held the tea tray, took it out, and placed it on the marble counter. She set sugar, spoons, teacups, and saucers on the tray. The pot whistled. She poured a kettle full of hot water into a thermos bottle and took the tray into the garden. The roses were still fragrant in the mild California weather, a bit late for the season, but lovely, nonetheless. *Like everyone*, she thought.

She sat on a bench and enjoyed being home. The ripening buds on the trellis were giving rise to new blooms and fragrances.

She was worried about her grandfather.

He entered the garden and walked to her quickly. She stood and held him for what seemed a very long time. "You are looking well, *dedushka*, and moving well, too," she said. "I am so happy to be here, to see you."

He sat on the bench, and she sat next to him. "What kind of tea today?"

She knew the answer. His first cup of tea every day was always strong black tea with sugar. A lot of sugar.

"Black tea, please," he answered.

She poured the hot water and put a teabag into his cup. He would add the sugar. After she placed his tea in front of him, she poured her own cup. They sat silently, watching the tea steep and enjoying the ambiance of the garden and the afternoon's blue sky.

"So, things are going well for you?" he queried.

"Oh yes, *dedushka*, things are, well, okay. I am doing well, and Tova is doing well, too," Elizabeth said.

"Yes, when a dog is well, all is well," he replied. "So, where is Tova now? In a kennel? I miss him."

"No, Tova is staying with a friend in DC," she replied.

"Ahhh. I am glad to hear you have a friend in DC. I was worried you would not make friends easily, particularly at the CIA."

"She works there too, and I am living at her house in downtown Washington," Elizabeth said.

"Very nice, I am happy to hear," her grandfather said. "Washington is a nice city."

They sipped their tea slowly. Her grandfather knew she was there because things were not going well, and he was going to wait until she brought up the issue.

"Tell me why you are still in bed this late. Were you out late last night?" she smiled.

"Oh, just a late morning for me, I am fine. But I am slowing down a bit, and I can be very lazy some days."

"I have not been getting a lot of sleep lately," she said. "Late nights and early mornings for me. Dealing with some very troubling things".

Her grandfather sat back in his chair. "That was a delicious cup of tea. Perhaps I can have another?"

Elizabeth smiled. "Of course. And I will, too."

While she poured the second cup, she said, "I have big issues to deal with, and I am here for your help, your advice."

"Tell me how I can help."

"*Dedushka*, I am going to tell you everything, everything that has happened to me over the last three months. I will be violating many security protocols to do this, but you need to understand the complete picture."

"Of course," he nodded. "The entire picture is usually necessary to deal with complex problems." He had aged a great deal since she left in July. He had not shaved for a few days and needed a haircut. His skin color seemed greyer, and he was not sitting as upright in his chair as she remembered. He was much older.

Elizabeth told him of the Cloud Spinner project, her co-workers, the analysis in production, the ambiguous intelligence reports, the Klondike Program. He interrupted her when she when she told him about Klondike. He marveled at the technological prowess of the United States.

"The things this country can do," he said. "The marvelous things."

She told him about the Russian conversations about the *bashka*, about Putin's plan to blackmail the president-elect, about Plummer's treachery. She avoided telling him too much about Sandra, only that she had a hand in bringing the *bashka*'s crimes to the attention of the DCI. He listened quietly until she completed her chronology and let the moment settle.

"*Dedushka*. No one is honorable. No one is patriotic. They protect themselves, not the country. What should I do?" she asked. "What can I do?"

He reached out and took her hands. "I used to work for the KGB. From Breznev to Andropov to Chernenko to Gorbachev. I have seen despicable behavior. I worked in a swamp of amoral creatures, who did everything they could to assure their friends and family a better life while screwing my country. This is why I left."

"You worked for the KGB? "a startled Elizabeth asked. "Why didn't you ever tell me?"

"The past is the past and not worth discussing most days. I was trying to make a new life for us here and didn't want my past to complicate our new beginning. I almost told you that day when you were visited by the men from the CIA, but I didn't think you knowing this would help."

"The polygrapher asked me about you!" Elizabeth said. "He asked if you had been in the KGB and whether you were in contact with people in Russia."

"See, it was best you didn't know," he murmured.

"So, what should I do?" she asked again.

"For many people, it is difficult to maintain a moral compass when working in such an environment. The fact that you are troubled by the events you told me about gives me hope," he said.

"Of course, I'm troubled," Elizabeth said.

"Troubled enough to risk your job? Your friend who watches Tova? Your *dedushka*?" he asked. "This is as bad as I ever saw in Moscow, with the corrupt leadership of the Soviet Union. It is clear what men like this in power do."

"Maybe I should go to Congress."

"Why do you assume they have integrity?" he asked. "They are part of the problem. You can count on no one, you can trust no one. You have to take actions that assure success with a minimum of others helping, because anyone you seek help from will have leverage on you, too. Be in control."

"How do I get control?" she asked.

"Make a physical copy of the tapes, the financial transactions, all the incriminating details, and back them up, so if something happens to you—or to me—the scum will be exposed," he said.

"But *dedushka*, why would anything happen to you?"

"I know how these men operate. They will do anything to keep their power and money."

"If I get caught, they will prosecute me," she said. "But I don't have anything else to fear."

"This is the only way," Alexi went on. "Gather hard, irrefutable evidence. Then, you go to the press."

"But I cannot risk Klondike for this," she said.

"You have to risk Klondike. And yourself. And me. The country is at stake."

Again, they sat silently for a time.

"Would you come back to Washington with me? I would love to have you near me again, and you could be a tourist in the beautiful city," Elizabeth asked. "And I don't want you here alone for Thanksgiving. I'm a little worried about you."

"I'd like that," he said. "When should we leave?"

"Let's fly back tomorrow, Thanksgiving Day. The flights won't be crowded at all; I should be able to get us seats."

"If you'd like me to be closer to you, I'd love to," he said. "And I miss Tova."

"And—I need to tell you one more thing about Washington, a real secret," Elizabeth said.

"A real secret?" he took her hand again. "Haven't you already told me all your secrets?"

"No, there's one more. It's about Sandra, well actually about Sandra and me. We have become very close—we are lovers. I need to know you are okay with this before you come to Washington with me."

He rose and embraced Elizabeth, "Of course I am okay—I am more than okay! I am happy you have found someone. I am happy for you—and for her! I look forward to meeting your Sandra."

"Oh, *dedushka*, thank you," she said.

"So, tell me all about her," he said.

They talked for the next hour about Sandra, things to do and see in DC, and what to pack for the trip back East. Winter was coming.

***

After their conversation, Elizabeth went to her old room, changed clothes, lay on her bed, and grabbed her phone. She wanted to check in with Sandra before she made plans for her grandfather to fly back to DC with her.

"Friedman here."

"Good morning, Sandra."

"Oh, hi, sweetie! Everything okay?"

"The flight to LA was uneventful: one takeoff, one landing."

"Perfect. What's going on?" Sandra asked.

"I've talked with my grandfather about everything, and I'm a little worried about him being here all alone. I asked him to come visit me in Washington," Elizabeth said. "He's agreed."

"Oh, that is wonderful news!" Sandra said. "I'd really like to meet him. Will he get here before I leave for training in Texas?"

"We're planning for him to fly back with me tomorrow. We'll get an early flight and land in plenty of time for Thanksgiving dinner," Elizabeth said. "I'll find him a nice hotel close by—there is a Hilton just a few blocks from your place."

"Oh, don't be crazy," Sandra said. "He's welcome to stay at my house. I have two extra bedrooms."

"I don't want to impose," Elizabeth said. "First me and Tova, now my grandfather! He'll be fine at a hotel for a couple of weeks."

"Nope, I've made up my mind, he stays with us. Oh—unless him seeing us together would be a problem?"

"I told him all about us," Elizabeth said. "He is happy for us and eager to meet you."

CHAPTER 23

Thursday, November 24, 2016
Logan Circle

Elizabeth and Alexi flew back to DC on an uncrowded Thanksgiving Day flight. They took a cab from Dulles, and when they arrived at the row house, they were greeted by a very happy yellow lab. There was a note from Sandra on the refrigerator saying she had gone for a long run through Rock Creek Park and would be home before dark. Tova rejoiced at being reunited with Elizabeth's grandfather. His tail wagged and his body shook while Alexi rubbed his ears.

Alexi was tired from the flight and the long day. Elizabeth settled him in one of the spare bedrooms to take a nap.

The weather was nice, and Elizabeth decided to take Tova to Logan Circle to play on the grass and chase squirrels. They walked down Thirteenth Street and crossed at the light to the grassy circle.

Logan Circle was in the center of the intersection of Thirteenth and P Streets and Vermont and Rhode Island Avenues. The circle was an artifact of the design and layout of the District of Columbia by Pierre L'Enfant, combining north and south streets and diagonal avenues to provide defensible strong points in case of attacks on the city. While most of the city's twenty-two traffic circles were dominated by commercial buildings, Logan Circle was the last one to remain completely residential. The circumference of the circle was lined with beautiful three and four-story Victorian homes and row houses, and in the center stood a large, bronze statue of General John A. Logan atop a steed. Originally, the circle had been named Iowa Circle but was renamed in 1930 to honor General Logan, who earned his place by commanding Union troops during the Civil War seventy years earlier. In 1853, he earned an additional, regrettable place in history as a leader of the Illinois General Assembly that oversaw the passing of the state's infamous "Black Law," limiting the immigration of African Americans into the state.

Tova was unimpressed with the history of the park but always found smelly grass to roll in and plenty of squirrels to chase. Elizabeth and Tova played until the sun began to get low on the horizon, and then they headed back to Sandra's.

Sandra was a sweaty mess after a ten-mile run. She was still cooling down when she greeted Elizabeth in the kitchen with a hug and a kiss.

"So, how was La-La Land? The flight? Your grandfather? "Sandra asked.

"Oh, the flight was not so bad. Being back made me remember how different Pasadena is from DC." Elizabeth replied. "And my grandfather is great. He's in the lower guest room resting a bit from a long day."

"How is his health?" Sandra asked.

"He says he's fine, but he just doesn't seem to have his normal energy. He was still in bed at noon when I arrived home," Elizabeth said.

"Hey, I sleep 'til noon some days," Sandra giggled.

"Yeah, but only after you have been out drinking all night. I hope he's okay. He did give me some advice that you and I should talk about."

"Let me get showered, and we'll talk with glasses of wine in our hands. I put a turkey on the Weber a few hours ago to smoke. It should be ready in an hour."

"I'll wake him when we get Thanksgiving dinner ready. I'm sure he'll be hungry," Elizabeth said.

"Oh, and I haven't fed Tova yet," Sandra said.

"Okay, I'll feed the bottomless stomach."

Tova was happy to have his kibble and the few snacks Elizabeth could scrounge from the refrigerator. Tonight, for the three of them, it would be a small smoked turkey, a spinach salad, and some iron skillet corn bread. Sandra came downstairs into the kitchen as Elizabeth was frying bacon to garnish the salad and pouring the corn bread mix into the skillet.

They sat in the living room with one of Sandra's favorite wines, Prisoner Red.

"I'm so glad to have you back home," Sandra said. "What did he suggest?"

"Well, I told him everything," Elizabeth said.

"Everything?"

"Everything. I asked him what we should do."

"And...?" Sandra asked.

"He said we should get hard data that could not be refuted and go to the press with it, and to trust no one. He said we were dealing with people and institutions without a moral compass, and they would put everyone I knew at risk to protect themselves if I went public with my concerns."

"That is scary. He thinks you are at personal risk?"

"He thinks we all will be. He also told me he worked for the KGB when he was in Russia," Elizabeth said.

"No shit!" Sandra interrupted, feigning her amazement.

"I never knew. When we moved here, he had an export business. I never knew what he did when he lived in Moscow."

"You never asked?" Sandra asked.

"He made it clear that it was a subject he wasn't going to talk about with me. We left that world behind us, and I stopped asking."

"Well, I just thought you would be more inquisitive about your past," Sandra said. "We all like to know about our past. You know I still want to know lot more about yours!"

"So, I was born in Russia and my grandfather is a former KGB officer, but now I work for the CIA, and he is an American senior citizen. I don't think it can get more complicated than that."

"Are you going to do what he recommends?" Sandra asked.

"I think I will. Tomorrow, I'll go into the vault and make copies. Then I'll find a reporter to share them with."

"You're looking at some serious jail time if this goes bad."

"That was the question my grandfather asked: What was I willing to risk?" Elizabeth said.

Sandra brought in the turkey while Elizabeth slid the corn bread into the oven. Tova lay at their feet in the kitchen while they finished up dinner preparations.

Elizabeth woke her grandfather. "Would you come join us for dinner? Everything is ready, and Sandra really wants to meet you."

"Of course, just a little nap. I feel rested and, more importantly, hungry," he said. "What did you make for dinner?"

"Oh, nothing too special, but we love to grill, and tonight, it is a wonderful smoked turkey," Elizabeth said. "We'll have everything on the table in ten minutes."

"Perfect," he said. "I'll be down shortly."

Sandra and Elizabeth got the table set and the hot serving dishes on the trivets. Tova was at their feet waiting for any morsel that might be dropped. The aromas filled the warmed dining room, and Elizabeth heard her grandfather's footsteps coming down the stairs.

"Ohhhh, this smells wonderful," he said. "I may have my sleep disrupted by the time zone changes from California but not my appetite."

Sandra came out of the kitchen and gave him a big hug. "I am so happy to meet you. Elizabeth has told me everything about you!"

"Everything?" he laughed, "Not everything, I hope. I'm so glad to meet you, Sandra. I have heard so much about you. Thank you for befriending my Elizabeth and Tova. And, please, call me Alexi."

Sandra liked him right away. He was a gentleman who stood tall and spoke firmly. She could sense he was a man of accomplishment and pride. "Please," she said, "sit at the head of the table, and we will sit on either side."

"Oh, a thorn between two roses," he replied with a smile.

The dining room was decorated in Victorian-era furniture and wall and window treatments. While Sandra was not much of a slave to home decoration niceties, she had followed the advice of her real estate agent and decorated the home in keeping with the late 1880s. The table and chairs and dark paneling evoked the era, as did the gas-lit chandelier. The dining room table was an excellent Victorian reproduction, with ornately carved legs and richly upholstered matching chairs. Red velvet draperies tied back from the windows warmed and quieted the room.

Elizabeth brought a bottle of Grey Goose out of the freezer and set it on a silver tray with three small glasses. She poured the vodka and raised her glass.

"To my *dedushka*, my girlfriend, and my companion. *L'chayim!*" Elizabeth said.

"*L'chayim!*"

They downed the vodka and she refilled their glasses.

"And to the cause that brings us together in Washington now—draining the swamp. *Nostrovia!*" Elizabeth added.

"*Nostrovia!*"

They drank again.

Alexi said, "Please, let's eat, or I won't make it through dinner."

They enjoyed the dinner and did not speak of the cause that brought them together. The conversation took place in both languages since Sandra could keep up with much of the Russian. They spoke of international affairs and tensions and of food they all enjoyed. The conversation turned to Sandra, and Alexi asked, "So, how did you two meet?"

Sandra fidgeted in her chair. She knew Elizabeth had told Alexi about Klondike but did not know how many of the details she had shared of her involvement in the program.

"Elizabeth, tell your grandfather how we met," Sandra said redirecting the question.

"We met working on the project I told you about," Elizabeth answered. "But Sandra is leaving on a new assignment soon."

"I'm leaving the Agency," she lied, hoping Elizabeth would stay silent. "Next month. Going to a training facility in Texas for a few months, and then off to Jakarta for a couple years."

Elizabeth quickly understood. Sandra did not want Alexi knowing she was being assigned to Moscow as a NOC. "I plan to visit as often as I can. I can get some good diving in, and it's not that far from LA."

"How exciting for you. Your next big adventure, it seems," Alexi said. "I would like to hear more, but I am tired. I think it's time for me to go to bed."

They made plans for the next day and the week. Elizabeth and Sandra would be off to work, and Alexi would visit the Smithsonian Museums. He insisted he was fine by himself.

"Let's clean these dishes and go to bed," Sandra said. "It's been a long day and a long week for both of us." Tova gave a look that said, "Please let me help with those dishes." Although he was wearing Sandra down, she drew the line at letting him lick the plates. He got table scraps in his bowl.

"Good night, ladies," Alexi called out. "Don't wake me in the morning if you are getting up early. Even if you are getting up late."

CHAPTER 24

Friday, November 25, 2016

OHB

The next morning, Elizabeth woke up early and quietly left the house after taking Tova out for a short break. Sandra would take him for a longer walk before she went to work. On the drive to the Agency, she decided what her next step would be. She would risk it all. She would download the Klondike data that morning onto her iPhone. After that, she would get it to a reporter. Right now, it was time to get the unassailable data captured.

The traffic was terrible on the GW Parkway. A fatal accident caused her to miss the 0700 meeting. Frank would not be happy with her. He knew she had returned from California, and with the pressure on the team to complete the NIE in December, every missed opportunity for collaboration caused him angst. She decided to go straight to the Klondike vault and, in complete violation of the Agency's protocols and her oath to honor security regulations, carried her iPhone into the OHB and then into the secure vault.

She used the voice recording function on her iPhone to capture key Klondike conversations. Putin, Davidov, and Polichuk discussing the *bashka* and his bribery of Russian officials. She photographed computer displays showing the accounts where money had been transferred and the time and dates of the wire transfers. She recorded the conversations that Keisha had with Plummer. She worked most of the day collecting incriminating audio files, transcripts, and image files of computer screenshots. She felt dirty doing it but still believed that it was the best path forward. She understood the personal risk she was taking—life in a federal penitentiary. Now that she was a criminal and a renegade CIA employee, the next step was to make contact with a reporter at the *Post*. As she finished duplicating the records and encrypting them on her iPhone, she took a deep breath and looked around.

The glass room was cold and silent except for the hum of the electronics. It really was a heartless place of digital records, plastic, glass, and metal. It had only ever been alive when she and Sandra were there working and enjoying each other's company.

Security routinely screened devices at the many Agency entrances to detect wireless communications systems going into or out of the building, so she would turn her phone off before she exited the vault and keep the phone off until she was in her car. She was thankful the RF shielding afforded by the vault also prevented the Office of Security from detecting that her iPhone was turned on inside the glass room.

Once outside the building, she would send the encrypted Klondike files from her phone to multiple email addresses and, from there, copy them to USB drives and secure them in multiple locations.

She captured the entire sorry story of the Russians, Plummer, and the *bashka* in less than one gigabyte. Elizabeth left the vault and walked towards the nearest exit to the parking lot. She walked quickly to her car and locked her iPhone in the glove compartment without ever turning it on. She felt relieved as she returned to her office. She had done it.

***

She stopped by her cubicle to check in with the team and see the progress they were making. A large note on her chair read "See me ASAP—Frank." She went straight to his office, stuck her head in his door, and saw him at his computer.

"Frank, you wanted to see me?"

"Welcome back," he said. "How's your grandfather?"

"He's okay, thanks for asking," she replied. "He flew back with me yesterday, so I will be keeping a closer eye on him. It was great to see him in Pasadena, but I'm really happy to have him back for a couple of weeks. Probably through the holidays."

"Bah, humbug. The holidays. Just what we need to interrupt the NIE getting done," Frank said. "But it is almost ready and going into final review."

"Your note?" Elizabeth asked.

"Hey, I am really glad he is okay. I was worried about you, Liz," he said. "A little worried. It looks like your Cloud Spinner analysis was on the mark! The Ruskie SOBs have definitely been pulling some kind of game to obfuscate the overall performance of the Avangard system, but it looks like it was directed at their leadership as much as at us. Every analytical data point and every observable we have takes us to the same conclusion. They have gone operational with a system that carries no warhead!"

Elizabeth smiled and walked to his desk. "We can't feel too sanctimonious about this, Frank. I know you're aware that we have done similar things in the US, and after a number of military and contracting hoaxes, Congress established the Office of Operational Test and Evaluation. It's not a perfect solution to corrupt practices but constrains the worst of behaviors. Maybe Russia doesn't have an OOTE."

"You're right, of course," Frank said. "Even so, this NIE is going to be very controversial. The hawks will dismiss our work and want to proceed with new systems to detect and defend against the Avangard system. They won't believe us when we tell them it doesn't really work. There are a lot of people and organizations in this country who want the Russians to be ten feet tall."

"Well, caution and concern on our side may not be such a bad idea," Elizabeth said. "The Russians may have an upgrade available soon to their initial deployment, and that really would be a threat. And given how long we take to develop our counter-systems, we should get started now."

"Not for us to decide," Frank said. "We produce accurate intelligence assessments and the policy makers make decisions."

"Sometimes pretty dumb ones," Elizabeth offered. "We're just a piece of the process, I get it. But a big piece."

"I just wanted to thank you and tell you how critical all of your work has been to the team."

"You're welcome. It's been a good four and a half months," Elizabeth said.

"I know you're committed to staying with the Agency through completing the NIE, but I want you to know you should consider a career here. Stay a few years," he said. "I can think of many areas where we could use you."

"I'll give it some thought, but you know I want to get back to JPL and my research," she replied.

"I know. But let me get back to you with some specific opportunities I think you should consider?" he said.

"Okay, I'll consider them," Elizabeth lied.

***

She returned to the vault to look for more intercepts. The login sheet indicated the vault had been opened by three people whose initials Elizabeth did not recognize.

She first searched for new conversations of Putin and his ministers discussing the *bashka* but found none. Then she searched for conversations between Keisha and Plummer. There were many. She found one of Plummer talking to Keisha in her office.

"Kee, I am not so sure I have all the loose ends tied up with Friedman. Yeah, she is heading to Texas and then Moscow, but I'm worried she knows too much."

"What are you thinking we should do, Jim?"

"I know it's risky and may not be completely effective, but I want you to arrange to move the bashka *files into a system that only I and people I personally approve can access. And make sure the IT folks you use to do this don't speak Russian."*

"Will do," Keisha replied. *"This may take a day or two."*

"As soon as you can, please. And I want the access list to Klondike scrubbed again. If an analyst hasn't accessed the system in the last two weeks, take them off the network. I want to personally approve anyone who is briefed into the program and has access to the raw collects."

"There'll be some bitching about that," she said.

"I don't care. Have them call me if they don't like it," Plummer said.

"Good move, darling. You know they'll be afraid to."

"Back to Friedman. Any thoughts?" he asked.

"Perhaps she should be dealt with permanently," Keisha said slowly.

His pause was a lengthy one. *"Permanently?"* he asked.

"Well, eliminate the problem so we don't have to worry about it in the future."

"Never," he answered.

Elizabeth gasped; Keisha had just suggested killing Sandra.

CHAPTER 25

Monday, November 28, 2016

OHB

Keisha opened the outer door of the vault, logged into the Klondike system, and accessed the system administrator files. From there, she could see all activity on the system and lock down all future access without a sysadmin approval. There were only three sysadmins on the system: herself, the DCI, and the watch officer in the Office of Security. With a few keystrokes, future access to the network would be extremely limited. She had not yet quite figured out how to isolate the files of Putin discussing the president-elect, but she would deal with that later. Now, she wanted to severely limit the access to the Klondike System as directed, so she looked at the data logs to see who had actually been on the system in recent weeks.

For many CIA employees, the number of accesses and clearances to programs across the IC was a badge of honor, whether or not they were ever used. Like how the highest point on a fire hydrant a male dog can lift his leg to establish the pecking order. Usually, not being briefed into a program didn't necessarily mean you were out; it meant you weren't in. Access to the Klondike program meant you were in.

There had been two activations in the last two weeks. One for a 2011 Toyota Corolla and one for a 2016 Kia plug-in hybrid. Both here in the US, both initiated by someone named Elizabeth Petrov.

"Who the hell is Elizabeth Petrov?" she murmured. And why was she activating these two key fobs? She checked the license plate numbers of the cars.

"No fucking way!" she yelled, which echoed in the glass room. "No fucking way!"

Elizabeth Petrov, whoever that was, had activated Keisha's key fob and had been monitoring her for the last ten days. *This cannot have happened*, she thought. *We have protections against this!* She thought through the internal controls she knew about and realized that the initial safeguards had been eliminated so that immediate activations could be made in case of an emergency or an imminent threat. Petrov—and whoever else she might be working with or for—had taken control of the Klondike System and used it against Keisha.

She located transcripts associated with intercepted conversations and many hours of audio files. She tried to open the folder. Denied.

"Bullshit!" she said aloud. "I am a fucking system administrator, and I should be able to access everything!"

Keisha thought back to Kubrick's classic movie *2001: A Space Odyssey* and Hal. Computers should not have to be negotiated with.

After the Snowden releases of classified materials, the US Intelligence Community changed how files could be accessed and maintained. If a user deemed the files to be sensitive and for restricted viewing, a single sysadmin could no longer access them without the user's permission. It would take two sysadmins to log in and open restricted files. Apparently, Petrov was hiding her trail.

Keisha could see two recent accesses; she could see the VIN numbers of the cars; she could see the geographic regions where they had been activated, but she could not see the files or transcripts. "This is just bullshit!" she said again to the acoustically dampened walls.

She needed to get Plummer down here as soon as possible, so they could satisfy the two-sysadmin issue and see the files. Elizabeth Petrov, whoever she was, knew what she was doing.

***

"I need to see him; this is an emergency. Now!"

The secretary immediately rang Plummer's phone. "Director Plummer, Keisha is here and says it is an emergency."

"Send her in," he calmly replied.

"Get the personnel file on a current employee, Elizabeth Petrov," Keisha barked to Plummer's assistant. "The boss will want it ASAP!"

***

Keisha entered the sprawling office. Plummer looked up from his laptop.

"What's going on?" he asked.

"I was just in the vault following up on those KLO actions you gave me..."

"Great, thanks for getting right on it," Plummer said.

"After accessing the sysadmin database, I found two recent key fob activations that were not done per our approved protocol."

"When?" Plummer interrupted.

"Some employee named Elizabeth Petrov activated my goddamn key fob ten days ago."

Plummer looked stunned.

"That means that my—our—conversations at home have been recorded for nearly two weeks."

"Who the hell is Elizabeth Petrov?" Plummer asked. "And what did we say in the last ten days?"

"I don't know the answer to either of those two questions, but we will soon. I asked Sheila to pull Petrov's file. I need you to join me in 5F43, where we can open the transcripts and audio files collected from my key fob and find out. Elizabeth Petrov protected them from single sysadmin access. Fuck Snowden!"

Plummer looked distressed, "Where is your key fob now?"

"It's in my purse in my office. I think it's still active," Keisha said.

"We have to assume it is," Plummer said.

"She can't know we have found out about her. We need to immediately deny her access to KLO and not have her suspect why until we have our next steps sorted out."

"Understood," Keisha said.

"Let's go—Sheila, we're heading to 5F43," he said, as they exited his office.

They raced down two floors and walked briskly to F corridor.

***

Before they entered the glass room, they heard a knock on the exterior door. It was Sheila with the personnel file for Elizabeth Petrov. Keisha opened the vault door.

"Thank you, Sheila, your timing was perfect," Keisha said. "Thank you for being so diligent."

Plummer added, "You can head home; I won't be returning to my office to work this evening. Please let security know I'll meet them in the garage in a while."

"Certainly," Sheila replied. "See you tomorrow morning." As she walked away, she wondered about the DCI and Keisha in that isolated room.

Keisha logged in first, and then Plummer did. Keisha was able to open the files containing transcripts of the many files.

They both read the transcripts in stunned silence. It could not have been worse. Petrov knew everything.

"Who the hell is Elizabeth Petrov," he repeated. Plummer grabbed the file from Keisha and read aloud: "Joined the Agency four months ago. Recruited out of JPL. Born in Moscow—what the fuck?—in 1986 and moved to the US with her grandfather in 1989. Fluent in Russian, working on the Cloud Spinner NIE in WINPAC. Busted her polygraph but WINPAC overruled it. I'll never allow that again."

"What?" Keisha asked.

"WINPAC to waive security requirements for new hires," he said. "They fucked this up. And look, her goddamn grandfather was in the KGB. Have we lost our minds?"

They went back to reviewing transcripts of their meetings and others Elizabeth had placed in a folder.

Plummer gasped when he saw the transcript of Putin learning that Plummer and the president-elect had made a deal. Putin had the hotel anteroom bugged and was monitoring the president-elect's conversations. Plummer recoiled at the thought that his visit to the president-elect was likely listened to by the Russians. He, the director of the CIA, might be responsible for revealing the Klondike program to the Russians.

"The FSB will be trying to find out how we got their conversations," Plummer said. "We need to shut the KLO program down in Russia immediately. We need to deactivate the key fobs and Fitbits. We can't have the FSB suspecting the devices and detecting abnormal transmissions from them.

They are smart enough to eventually figure it out unless we act now."

Keisha said, "I can do it right now from this terminal."

"Do it!" Plummer ordered. "Then we'll figure out what to do about that woman."

Keisha's fingers flew over the keyboard. She focused on the terminal for a few minutes and then announced, "There, it's done. All key fobs and Fitbits in Russia are no longer intercepting audio and will no longer be transmitting Bluetooth data out. If the S&T guys are right, with the modified RF output disabled, even a physical inspection of the innards of those things won't reveal their full functionality."

"Good. We can get those things reactivated later when there is less paranoia," Plummer said.

They scanned the rest of the intercepts from Keisha's key fob and realized they were fortunate that most of their conversations took place without being close to the device. But too many had been.

"She knows about us," Plummer observed.

"She appears to have activated your key fob to understand more about me and the president-elect," Plummer observed.

"I'm surprised I haven't heard from her to make some demands on me. I wonder what she wants?"

Keisha added, "I need to let someone at the FBI know the president-elect is being bugged. I won't say how we know, just that we know."

"Oh, yeah, good idea. Give them a call now. I'm going to go back to my office. I'll take Petrov's folder. Come to my office after your call," Plummer said.

***

Keisha entered his office thirty minutes later with the FBI report. "They weren't a bit surprised when I told them about the bugs. They said the president-elect doesn't trust the FBI to sweep for electronics in his home or meeting areas. Says he wants to wait until *his* director can oversee the Bureau's work".

"What an idiot," Plummer said. "He must think we're all out to get him."

"He may be right about that," Keisha observed.

"The Bureau is going to tell him they have evidence that some of his conversations have been compromised and then find the bugs and show him," Keisha explained. "That should help him decide which side the Bureau is on."

Plummer said, "Go home. I have an idea how to deal with this."

CHAPTER 26

Monday, November 28, 2016 to
Tuesday, November 29, 2016

OHB

Plummer knew his options were limited. He had originally thought that Friedman was operating on her own, so simply sending her to Moscow would clear his path. After learning that she was working with Petrov, the WINPAC analyst who was listening to and translating raw Klondike intercepts about the president-elect, Putin and his cronies, and now him and Keisha, Plummer knew he was in trouble. As he sat in his office looking over the grey, leafless trees painted purple and mauve by the setting sun, he pondered his options, in no particular order: resign, claim he had been set up and fight, or eliminate the threat.

Getting Friedman out of the way would no longer be enough. He had to eliminate the threat from Petrov. Completely eliminate it. Friedman seemed like a person willing to broker a deal. She wanted to advance her career and advance US interests abroad. And she seemed to be a team player. Petrov, on the other hand, was a rookie whose motivations and ties to the Russian intelligence service he did not yet understand.

He had learned over his many years in the intelligence business that there were very few people who could be trusted. Maybe no one. But he was going to have to reach out for some help.

He looked at the world time zone monitor on his wall and saw it was just after 2 a.m. in Riyadh. He would go home and wait six hours before placing a secure call to Yousef, the young, energetic leader of the GDI, the Saudi organization responsible for intelligence and operations. Plummer needed help from Yousef and was willing to reciprocate to keep the score even. Plummer knew a few things Yousef would appreciate learning and could—more or less—trust him to keep a secret.

Plummer left for home and went to bed early. He told his wife, Lisa, that he had a telecon scheduled just after midnight and would sleep in his SCIF so as not to wake her when he took the call. Having a fully certified SCIF, a sensitive compartmented information facility, in his house was unusual for a DCI. The SCIF provided secure document storage as well as space to hold meetings at the highest classification levels without worrying about being monitored. To avoid requiring a full-time staff member to guard the home SCIF from intrusion, the Agency had constructed a secret room that was accessible only from behind the elevator shaft in Plummer's home, hidden so it was almost impossible to find. It was right out of an old *Get Smart* television show. To start the process of entering the SCIF, he had to push the up and down buttons on the elevator door in the correct sequence at the ground floor elevator entrance. This would cause the elevator to rise and the elevator shaft door to open. With the elevator above, he could enter the empty shaft and approach a panel that looked like an electrical panel. Even though it was festooned with a "Danger High Voltage" sign, it was really the location of the SCIF access biometric scanner. Plummer would then have his retina scanned, enter a code indicating he was not under duress, and a hidden door would open. From his home office, he could safely conduct any sensitive business.

Plummer's alarm went off just before midnight. He wanted to talk to Yousef early in his day, before the young leader became distracted by his calendar.

His SCIF was equipped with a communication suite that allowed him to talk securely with not only the US Intelligence and Defense Communities but specific international intelligence officials. Yousef's office was equipped with a system that the US had installed during the first Gulf War. It had been updated and maintained ever since so the Americans and the Saudis could coordinate their response to the threats they both faced in the region—primarily the Iranians.

The GDI leader's phone rang many times before it was finally answered.

"Hello, hello," a male voice answered. The encryption and low-speed digitization made it difficult to recognize voices. "This is Yousef Khan. Who's calling?"

Plummer knew the phone would show his name on the secure phone caller ID but understood that Yousef would want to confirm it was Plummer on the phone.

"Yousef, Jim Plummer here. I hope I am not disturbing you. Do you have a few minutes to talk?"

"Yes, yes, of course. Jim, it is never a problem or disruption to talk to you. How have you been? How are Lisa and your family?" Yousef asked.

"Oh, they are well. Thank you for asking. And Fatima and those beautiful children of yours?" Plummer asked.

"Everyone is fine," Yousef replied. "I am entering the challenging years with my teenagers; I'll be calling you for advice soon."

Plummer and Yousef had met a number of times in covert locations with other allies to coordinate intelligence activities around the globe. Although Plummer liked Yousef and thought of him as a pragmatist rather than an idealist, Plummer detested the Saudi's royal family: corrupt, amoral, and not to be trusted. Like Plummer, Yousef could be counted on to fix hard problems. Over cigars and fine double malts, they came to know each other and each other's family and background.

"To what do I owe the pleasure of this call?" Yousef asked. "And thank you again for joining us here in Riyadh last month."

"I'll be brief. And direct. Is there anyone else on the call with you?" Plummer asked.

"Of course not, Jim. You know I'd never do that."

"I know, I know," Plummer said. "But as Reagan said, trust but verify. I could use a favor to help with a little problem I have. Actually, a big problem."

"What sort of problem?" Yousef asked.

"Two of my employees have gone rogue, and if they aren't stopped, they'll threaten many people and institutions. I don't have the resources at hand to quickly, discretely deal with it. I would really appreciate your help."

"Are you seeking a permanent solution to your problem?" Yousef asked.

"Yes," Plummer said. There it was. "A quick, permanent solution to my problem."

"How quickly do you need this done?"

"As soon as possible."

"Where is your problem located?"

"Ten blocks from the White House. I was hoping you might be able to arrange an accident. An accident that won't be discovered," Plummer said.

"I understand," Yousef said. "Tell me their names and give me some time to do a little research, and I'll get back to you."

"Their names are Elizabeth Petrov and Sandra Friedman. They live together, at 1318 Corcoran Street, in a row house owned by Friedman. I know I'm asking a lot, but you remember the call you made to me after your little problem in Dubai?"

"The Yemenis. You helped me, Jim."

"Help me with this, Yousef, and I am in your debt," Plummer promised. "I do understand if you can't do me a favor on this one, Yousef, I really do. We all have our own operational issues."

"Jim, if I can help you, I will. Let me look into this today. I'll call you back at your office number at 8 p.m. my time tomorrow," Yousef said.

"Thank you, Yousef. Would you use this number, though, please? It's my home secure line. Safer," Plummer said.

"Before we go, Jim, I need to ask. Has this been approved at the top?"

"Yousef, I'll be honest with you, especially for a favor like this one. This has not been approved. The boss shouldn't know that my problem ever existed."

"I understand, Jim. This is a matter between you and me, and the stakes are high. We don't carry out many ops in the US."

"I know, my friend," Plummer answered. "I know."

***

This is how the international intelligence business operates between countries. When you need a black operation done, when you need a favor, you don't go to your own people. Instead, you bring in an outside agency that is completely dissociated from the problem. Perfect deniability and no lasting harm. The Saudi GDI and the CIA had traded favors many times over their decades of cooperation. They had mutual respect for each other's capabilities and understood each other's limitations.

Plummer knew the GDI could handle the problem but did not know if they would. He needed a backup plan, too.

***

He awoke after a restless night and got his morning briefing bag. The first thing he reviewed was the PDB, the President's Daily Brief. This was a four-to-eight-page document summarizing the intelligence issues of the day. While it was called the PDB, its distribution went far beyond the president to seniors in the administration. As a result of the broad distribution, it was watered-down bullshit. The current president was polite to the briefers who delivered the PDB and were available for his follow-up questions, but after eight years in office, he knew that if there was something momentous, the DCI, the DNI, or both would deliver it personally. Plummer scanned the PDB and saw little of note. Nothing he couldn't learn by watching thirty minutes of CNN.

He then began reading an eyes-only paper summarizing the status of critical intelligence operations around the world, prepared by the Agency. The eyes-only designation meant it could not be copied or shown to any other intelligence official. It contained a succinct summary of Agency operations, both HUMINT and TECHINT collection activities, that could become national embarrassments if discovered. All collection systems changes were nominal, but he did note that the number of Klondike monitors in use had recently increased.

"No shit," he murmured. "Talk about old intelligence."

***

Keisha met him in the office before his first morning meeting.

"I've run out of options with the problem women and moved forward with a plan," he told her. "I asked Yousef for a favor. We'll talk again today, 1 p.m. our time."

"What can I do to help?" Keisha asked.

"I'll let you know after we talk."

"Thank you for trusting me with this. I agree with your decision, Jim."

"I'm going to take the call from the SCIF in my home. Lisa will be out of the house for a few hours then. Join me there?"

"Of course," Keisha said.

"Maybe we'll have a few minutes to ourselves after the call," Plummer said.

"I'd like that," Keisha said, rubbing his shoulder.

At noon, Plummer asked his security detail to drive him home. They made good time through light traffic and arrived early. Plummer quickly set up the secure link and awaited the phone call from Yousef. Keisha arrived with sushi for lunch. The security team opened the door for her, and she walked to his SCIF.

He greeted her at the bottom of the elevator shaft and motioned her in.

"I thought you might forget to eat, so I stopped by the food court and brought you those California rolls and yellowtail that you like," Keisha said.

"You're a mind reader," Plummer said. "I'm hungry."

Keisha set the containers on the counter and opened the soy sauce packets and wasabi sauce. It was still ten minutes before the scheduled call, so they enjoyed the fresh sushi, amazingly good for CIA food court fare.

The phone rang at precisely 1 p.m. He picked up the phone and waited while the encryption system synched.

"Plummer here," he said.

"Jim. Yousef. Good day, Jim. Are you alone?"

"Of course, Yousef," he lied.

"Trust but verify, Jim, as someone told me not too long ago," he chuckled. "The activity will be completed on Thursday, Jim. I'm having to burn some very valuable assets to do this so quickly and make sure they get out before anyone realizes what happened. You need to know how big a favor this is."

"Yousef," Plummer said. "I am in your debt."

"Jim, not to be too blunt, but since the president-elect is in your debt, I suspect we'll want to leverage the debt he owes you someday soon," Yousef responded.

"Of course, Yousef, of course. I'm not surprised that you know I have leverage on the president-elect," Plummer lied. *How did they find out this is about the president-elect?* he wondered. "And truthfully, Yousef, I have not made any substantive demands of him, only to keep my job and put the Intelligence Community under my control."

"Jim, I think we'll both be able to take advantage of your leverage with the president-elect," Yousef said.

"I understand, Yousef. We are a team on this," Plummer responded. "A team."

"So, with that agreement, we'll solve your problem this Thursday. A gas explosion in their house."

"Thank you, Yousef. I don't think we should communicate directly for a couple of weeks. My EXEC, Keisha Riley, is fully aware of my request to you. If you need to follow up on anything, please call on her secure line."

"I'm glad we could come to an agreement, Jim, and fix your problem together."

Keisha sat across the desk, listening carefully to Plummer's side of the conversation.

"Yousef, I owe you for this. I look forward to the call you make in the future that allows me to return this favor."

"No return favor needed. This is just what friends do for each other," Yousef lied.

"Thank you, my friend. Goodbye."

Plummer hung up the phone and looked at Keisha. She was unbuttoning her silk blouse and moving to his couch.

"I think we should celebrate our solving this problem," she cooed.

They had sex like sixteen-year-olds, unrestrained and with passion. The moment had drawn them together in a way they never anticipated.

Keisha left the house, waved to the security detail in their cars in the driveway, and told them the DCI would be out in a few minutes.

"Thanks, Keisha," Rob said. He opened his Suburban door and motioned two of the detail to approach the front door to escort the director to his vehicle.

Keisha wondered if Rob knew or suspected how the boss had just spent his lunch hour. Then again, she didn't really care.

***

Alexi had spent very little time in Washington as a tourist, so he, Sandra, and Elizabeth devoted the weekend to exploring the city. Elizabeth and Sandra had so much fun that they decided to both call in sick and take a couple of mental health days away from the office. They all continued visiting the Smithsonian museums, monuments, and art galleries, but by Wednesday, Sandra and Elizabeth had to return to the office, even if for a short day. Nothing had been said about copying the Klondike files. It was almost as if the problem had disappeared.

***

Alexi went on his own to visit another museum, while Elizabeth and Sandra got home early and took Tova on a long run.

Tova wasn't much of a runner, but after a day in the house, he was ready to stretch his legs. They ran a loop from the Capitol Building to the Washington Monument. It was a beautiful fall day and the air was crisp. Running past the

National Gallery Art and Natural History Museum, they warmed up and moved from eight-minute miles to seven-and-a-half-minute miles. They continued past the Museum of American History toward their turn-around point. Elizabeth loved this route. It made her feel a part of American history. Tova was getting his legs, too. At the start of the run, he was a bit of a laggard, going along grudgingly. When they rounded the majestic monolith, Tova sensed they were heading back and picked up speed. Past the Hirschhorn and the Air and Space Museum, picking up the pace to less than seven minutes per mile. Elizabeth was dripping wet, or as Sandra said, "glistening," as they raced down the wide walkways. They finished on the Capitol steps and looked out over the scene that many American presidents had seen when they took the oath of office. They both looked at each other and knew what each other was thinking. The *bashka* would be standing here shortly. It was time to act.

They jogged home at a slow pace to cool down and talk.

"I have the Klondike files on my iPhone and all that's needed to bury Plummer and the president-elect," Elizabeth said. "I encrypted them and sent them to email addresses I set up that can't easily be traced directly to me. I'm ready to go to the *Post*."

"Are you sure?" Sandra asked.

They made their way north up Fourteenth Street, past Thomas Circle and into the Logan Circle neighborhood. The sidewalks were bare. The temperatures had dropped that evening, and everyone was eating and drinking indoors.

By the time they got home, they had put all of their layers back on and pulled their hands up inside their sleeves. Sandra said, "Let's take a sauna."

"Let me check on my grandfather," Elizabeth said. "If he's still asleep, I'll be right down."

Elizabeth checked on Alexi and saw that he was sound asleep. Tova curled up on the floor beside him and looked like he would soon be out. She quietly closed the bedroom door and started back down the stairs to the basement.

Shortly after closing on the row house, Sandra had a sauna installed. During an extended business trip to Finland, she'd learned the Finns did it right. Every workout or long run was followed by a hot sauna; November was her favorite time, when the sun was low on the horizon and the winter winds were beginning to blow.

It could fit three or four comfortably. Elizabeth opened the sauna door and saw Sandra though the steam, naked, reclined on the upper seat, her eyes closed. She smiled and beckoned Elizabeth in with her index finger.

"Come in and join me," Sandra whispered. Elizabeth dropped her towel at the door and joined her lover in the steam. She lay on a bench, below and to the side of Sandra, and felt the wet heat enter her body. Then she felt Sandra's hand on her back and neck, caressing her and gently massaging her. Elizabeth turned, stood, and kissed her passionately for a very long time. They made exhausting love in the steam.

After, Sandra began putting together a dinner of cheese omelets and homemade biscuits. As the biscuits were browning, Elizabeth went upstairs. "*Dedushka*, wake up," she said gently. "Dinner is ready."

"It smells wonderful," he said.

"It's just omelets and biscuits, but Sandra makes these amazing sautéed onions in a skillet with butter, salt, and pepper."

"I'll be down in five minutes," he said.

Elizabeth helped Sandra set the table. Alexi arrived and sat at the head of the table. "What a great day, " he said. "Toured every floor of the Air and Space Museum, and it wasn't crowded at all. What did you two do?"

Elizabeth jumped in before Sandra could respond. "Last Friday, I copied all of the incriminating files I talked to you about. Audio records, financial details, and transcripts of months of conversations. I encrypted them and now have them on multiple USB drives and uploaded to the cloud."

They sat in silence for a moment. "Now there is no going back," Alexi said. "You have taken an irreversible step. You have committed a crime that you—and we—can now be jailed for."

"Do you want to see the files?" Elizabeth asked.

"No, I don't need to. You've told me what they contain, and I'm confident you are correct," he replied. "It's more important we determine our next steps."

Elizabeth like that he said "we." They were now in this together.

"My plan is to reach out to the lead reporter on intelligence matters at the *Washington Post*, Robert Carlson. I'll see if he'll meet with me. I don't know him, but his reporting is balanced and accurate. He obviously has sources inside the Agency who trust him."

Alexi shook his head. "That could be a problem. What if one of his trusted sources inside the Agency is Plummer?"

Sandra sat silently during the discussion, picking at her food—clearly displeased.

"You want a reporter who doesn't owe anything to anyone at the CIA or any other intelligence agency, someone young who is aggressively pursuing his or her career, who won't be easily sidelined by senior reporters or editors. Find a reporter who writes about local overnight murders and criminal activity. It's a junior assignment. That one will be hungry."

Elizabeth said, "Great idea. I'll check the online *Post* for those kinds of stories first thing in the morning."

"Before you do that..." Sandra said. Alexi's and Elizabeth's eyes turned toward her. "I've been thinking about this. I'm worried. I think you're making a mistake."

"I thought we agreed this was the right thing to do," Elizabeth said.

"I know, honey, I know. I've thought about this a lot and think there are other paths to take that do not put the three of us in danger," Sandra answered. "I think we need to be pragmatists about this and not be the only people who put ourselves at risk. We could all go to jail for life. I now think you should go to the IC inspector general. There's a process for whistle blowing. Use that process to ensure that the right steps are taken and that people are held accountable."

Alexi was quiet, stone-faced, as he took in Sandra's words. When she finished, he spoke slowly and firmly.

"You speak of the three of us being in danger and at risk. But we are in far greater danger if we do nothing. If you follow a whistle blowing process, these people will have time to cover up their behavior and come after us. Elizabeth, you have committed criminal acts. They will come after you. I have conspired with you in the conduct of these criminal acts. They will come after me."

Elizabeth looked him the eyes. "*Dedushka*, you are not in danger. It's me."

"They will come after me to get to you," he explained. "They will be ruthless."

"I am going to the *Post* tomorrow," she said.

"Then these next steps are on you and you alone, Elizabeth," Sandra spoke loudly. "Leave me out of it."

The room was silent for a very long time.

Alexi broke the silence. "Dinner was wonderful. I'll excuse myself and go to bed."

Elizabeth looked at her very tired grandfather. "Is there anything you need right now?"

"An elevator would be nice. I overdid it today, I think." He chuckled as he walked slowly to the stairs.

Sandra walked to Elizabeth and asked, "Are we okay?"

"Of course, we are. I'm just confused over your change of heart. But I understand," Elizabeth said. "At least I think I do."

As they walked up the stairs, Sandra asked Elizabeth, "So, you'll be up and out early tomorrow?"

"Unfortunately, yes. Even though we have completed the final draft of the NIE, I plan to go in early."

Sandra said, "Okay, I've gotta go in late. I need to hang around to meet some repairmen. I got a note from Washington Gas saying they needed to test our gas meter and the gas lines inside the house. It's apparently way overdue, and these old homes need to be checked often."

"Old houses need a lot of TLC," Elizabeth opined. "Hopefully it won't take too long."

"Indeed, they do. Let's go to bed," Sandra said.

CHAPTER 27

Wednesday, November 30, 2016

Rock Creek Park

The last day had been frantic for the two Saudi GDI agents. Ibrahim was a veteran of multiple foreign assignments and had served in the GDI for more than twenty years. His current assignment in the Saudi Embassy in Washington, DC, was considered a "sunset cruise"—a quiet, final posting before retirement.

He had participated in many operations over the years, including the notable retribution for the assassination of Mahmoud al-Mabhouh in Dubai in 2010. Ten days after al-Mabhouh was found dead in his hotel room of "natural causes," the local intelligence service found conclusive evidence that al-Mabhouh had been murdered by a team of twenty-nine Israeli agents operating freely in Dubai. The Mossad's tradecraft was good, but it proved ineffective against the overwhelming array of security video cameras, cell phone surveillance and biometrics used for identification at the airport and during hotel check-in. The Mossad operation was uncovered and made public, resulting in a minor public stir and diplomatic demarches. However, since the Israelis and the Palestinians both wanted al-Mabhouh dead, the event never became an international incident.

Ibrahim had been assigned to locate and help eliminate at least one of the Israeli team who carried out the assassination. Some of the Israelis had been accurately identified and would leave the safety of Israel only under aliases with disguises. A year later, Ibrahim and his colleagues located one of the Mossad agents in Cyprus, traveling with his family. The GDI left him dead and in many pieces. An eye for an eye, the Muslims believed.

Bassem was a graduate student at Georgetown University, pursuing his MBA in international business. He served two years in the Saudi Air Force and graduated from Riyadh University before being recruited by the GDI to join the Saudi's secret service and become an undercover agent. A day ago, he had been surprised to receive the emergency activation message from his supervisor directing him to meet Ibrahim at the park for further instructions. For the two years he'd been at Georgetown, he had never received a call. He'd been told it was likely to never happen. But now it had.

The meeting at the tennis courts in Rock Creek Park was scheduled for 3 p.m. Bassem showed up early, at 2:30 p.m. He was wearing exercise clothes that could double as a tennis outfit and carrying a borrowed tennis racquet from a friend in his apartment building. He thought it was important to look the role he was supposed to be playing in case he was questioned by anyone. He sat on a bench overseeing two clay courts. A nondescript sedan entered the lot and parked. An overweight man appearing to be in his sixties got out of the car. Dressed in business clothes, he was obviously not here to play tennis. He approached Bassem and said, "Clay is not a good surface to play on in December."

Bassem responded per his instructions. "Particularly French clay."

With this exchange, they introduced themselves to each other as GDI agents. Ibrahim said, "Let's take a short walk."

"Of course," Bassem said. "I have been sitting all day and a walk would be nice."

They walked up the trail that passed next to the tennis courts and paralleled the Parkway.

"It's good to meet you, Bassem. I'm pleased to see we are preparing new young agents like you to take up the cause."

"Ibrahim, I am proud to be on an assignment with you! I'm in awe of the career you've had. You are a legend and we all know of your accomplishments."

"Thank you, but we're only as good as the success we've had in our last assignment."

"So, why am I here?" Bassem asked.

"I have received orders to carry out an operation here in Washington that will result in the deaths of two people. The mission must be accomplished by the end of tomorrow."

"I see. Stopping a Zionist plot? Or an action against the Yemenis or Iranians?"

"I only know we have orders to arrange an accident."

"Okay, but I'm confident we are doing the right thing," Bassem answered.

"The challenge won't be executing the mission; it will be not getting caught. We cannot be caught or identified. Do you understand?"

"Yes, I understand."

"I'm not sure you do," said Ibrahim. "We have to be prepared to die rather than be caught. Are you prepared to die?"

"Allahu akbar," Bassem answered.

"We will pretend to be Washington Gas employees to gain access to a local row house. The occupants are expecting a gas crew tomorrow morning. We will be playing the part of a crew to both test the meter outside the house and to pressure and leak test the lines inside the house. Once we gain access to the house, you will pretend to test the meter outside the house. It's in the front. While you are doing that, I will place an explosive device, manufactured by our technical team, on a gas line inside the house," Ibrahim said.

"I don't know anything about testing a gas meter," Bassem said. "Do you?"

"No. But you were selected because you've always figured these types of things out. You'll know way more about it than they will, anyway. Just pretend to be doing something useful while I am installing the explosive device in the house."

"I can do that," Bassem said.

"The explosive device arrives today from Riyadh. It's an operational cell phone but contains a shaped C-4 explosive in the case. It's been modified so the explosive can penetrate a gas supply line, and the imbedded steel wool in the C-4 explosive will assure a fireball of flammable incendiaries to quickly spread the fire."

"Won't they find evidence of the trigger? "Bassem asked.

"Not likely. The shards of steel wool and the C4 will be completely consumed by the inferno. The remnants of the cell phone, if they find any at all, will look like typical cell phone parts. We have used these many times around the world and never been detected. A perfect accident."

"Where will you trigger it from?" Bassem asked.

"Oh, I won't trigger it," Ibrahim said. "You will. I'll be on a flight to Riyadh tomorrow night. This is going to be all you."

"Are you sure? I've never done anything like this."

"Bassem, you are ready. I'll provide you with detailed instructions tomorrow on how to activate the device. It is designed to be very simple. After initiating the timer, you'll then go back to your apartment and return to your studies. You'll be fine. I will pick you up outside your apartment tomorrow at 0630. We will use a white van with stolen plates. I have work clothes and tools for us to wear tomorrow morning. Leave your cell phone in your apartment. There can be no record of our being in the vicinity."

"Of course," Bassem said. "See you at the northwest corner of Thirty-Sixth and N Streets tomorrow at 0630."

They walked back to the tennis court parking lot in silence. Ibrahim got into his car and left. Bassem called an Uber to take him back to his apartment. As he waited for his ride to arrive, he imagined the incredible, uplifting feeling he would have tomorrow after becoming a critical element in crippling an enemy of the Kingdom. He was unaware of any similar achievement in Washington, DC, since the Chilean secret service, under orders from Chilean President Augusto Pinochet, blew up the car of Orlando Letelier on Embassy Row on Sheridan Circle on September 21, 1976. Letelier, it was later learned, had been paid by the Cubans to bring down the Pinochet regime. Carrying out such a task in Washington would bring him notoriety at home in the GDI but would be certain to result in an extensive FBI investigation in the United States. He was concerned for a moment that he would not be leaving like Ibrahim.

CHAPTER 28

Thursday, December 1, 2016
Washington, DC

0550

Tova was a bad dog that morning. He spied an old chicken bone in the alleyway and grabbed it before Elizabeth could pull it from his jaws of steel. The neighborhood's Popeye's Chicken meant that fast food restaurant patrons tossed their leg and thigh bones on the sidewalk and in the alley with abandon. Tova's walks were filled with fried chicken treasures. He became adept at not telegraphing his interest in a chicken bone but suddenly lunging forward to pick it up before Elizabeth could restrain him. Once in his jaws, he refused to let go of the disgusting remnant until he was able to chew it into small enough pieces to swallow it. One day, when she dragged him home before he had consumed the bone, she put a dab of hot sauce on her finger and swiped it on his gums. His jaws opened wide as he spit the bone out onto the floor. His eyes seemed to say, "Please, never do that again!" Now when she walked Tova, she usually carried a small bottle of Tabasco. All she had to do was show him the bottle, and he would drop the bone. He was a smart dog and enjoyed pushing the limits.

"NO, Tova," she yelled quietly. "Those things cannot be good for you."

Tova responded by putting his ears back and giving her a look with those big brown eyes that melted away all her anger and frustration. But after three quick chews, the chicken bone was gone.

"Back to the house with you, I've gotta get to work," she said.

***

0625

At 0625, Bassem paced nervously between lampposts outside his apartment. A white Ford van stopped. From behind the wheel, Ibrahim motioned to Bassem to get in.

"Clothes, boots, and toolbelt in the back. Try everything on and make sure it all fits," Ibrahim said. "I have a hard hat, also. Adjust it for your head size."

"Got it," Bassem said. He climbed into the back of the van to change. He put on the uniform and found that it and the boots fit him well enough. He laughed out loud at the sticker on his hard hat. "Do I have to wear a fucking MAGA hard hat?" he complained.

"You'll wear what I tell you to wear," Ibrahim said. "From this moment on, we are a gas repair crew. Stay in character until we are out of the area."

They drove slowly to the corner of Fourteenth and P Streets and pulled in front of a coffee shop.

"Coffee and bagel. You?" Ibrahim asked.

"Sure. Black coffee and a plain bagel with cream cheese."

"Here's ten dollars," Ibrahim said, motioning for Bassem to go inside.

Bassem, nervously exited, looked carefully behind the van and in both directions on the sidewalk for anything amiss. He returned to the van after a few minutes, and they ate and drank in silence until Bassem asked, "So—who are we taking out?"

"It doesn't matter. Our orders are to kill the occupants of 1318 Corcoran Street in a gas explosion and have it appear to be an accident."

"Don't you want to know why we are going to kill them?" Bassem queried.

"It doesn't matter, never has. We are cogs on the gear. When we do our job, the gear turns, and Saudi Arabia is a better place," Ibrahim said.

"I guess I understand," Bassem said.

Ibrahim pulled forward and parked on the northbound part of Fourteenth, just at Corcoran Street in front of the John Wesley African Methodist Episcopal Zion Church. They would wait there until it was time to go to the row house.

***

0647

Elizabeth arrived at the stand-up in plenty of time, fifteen minutes early. The NIE was in final reviews across the Intelligence Community with comments due back in six days. The comments would be reviewed by the Cloud Spinner team and, if issues remained, adjudicated by the DNI in a cross-IC session. Usually, the multiple agencies of the IC would arrive at a consensus view, but there were occasions when different agencies would take unreconcilable positions on an NIE. Footnotes and dissenting opinions to the consensus view would be added to the final document that would be given to Congress and lawmakers a more accurate sense of the issue. Where there was broad agreement and where there were strong dissents. Policy makers hated this type of NIE with mixed interpretations—it gave them no clear, obvious path of action. The most notable example of this was the pre-Iraq War, Weapons of Mass Destruction assessment. No one read the footnotes to see that there was debate in the Intelligence Community about whether or not WMDs actually existed in Iraq. The leadership of the Pentagon, the House, and the Senate either never read or did read and disregarded the dissenting footnotes. They blindly followed the president into a war based on an NIE with nuances and uncertainty. There never were any WMDs.

The morning meeting was short as they had not received any of the expected questions and views challenging their conclusions.

"Folks, I think we gave them to the 11th, and they are going to use every day to get us their thoughts," Frank stated. "I think no news might be bad news."

Elizabeth left and went to the vault to see what was new with the *bashka* or Plummer. She noticed there had been sign-in activity over the weekend by new initials that she did not recognize. She carefully entered the combination, but the door remained locked after she engaged the inner lock and spun the dial.

She re-spun the lock to clear it before her next attempt. She entered the combination, and once again, no joy.

She slowly entered the three-number code into the vault dial and still was not admitted. Annoyed, she returned to her cubicle and called the security office. She wasn't surprised when the phone was answered with "Security Ops, Gordon Haver speaking."

"Gordon, Elizabeth Petrov. Thank you again for a wonderful birthday evening at JV's!"

"Loved seeing you there and hope you had a memorable evening," he said. "Would be fun to see you again."

"I'm surprised to find you at work this early."

"Oh, we trade shifts now and then, and I sometimes end up on days."

"I'm having trouble entering 5F43 again. Can I come to the Ops Center and get the new combination?"

"Of course, but let me check a few things first," Gordon said.

A minute later, he was back on the line. "Sorry, Elizabeth. Looks like I can't help you this time. Access to the vault is revoked. You need the DCI's specific permission. Do you have that?"

"That's unusual, I don't, but I've never needed it before. Has he delegated approval to someone I can contact?" she asked.

"File says it's gotta be the DCI."

"Thank you, Gordon," Elizabeth said.

"No problem, Ms. Petrov, badge PS 258. Let me know if there is anything more I can do."

Elizabeth sat back in her chair. What was going on? Was this just another restriction of Klondike? Had she been found? With Sandra out of the system, Elizabeth had no idea who to contact about being denied access to the vault. She would ask Sandra when she got home that evening.

She went through the motions for a couple more hours in her office but knew neither her heart nor soul were in it. She fixated on the Klondike program being closed to her now and probably forever. What should or could she read into the denial of access? Her mind wandered through the possibilities—none of them were good.

***

0802
Corcoran Street

Much to Sandra's surprise, the Washington Gas crew arrived at the house on time. Two men in uniforms wearing toolbelts and hard hats at her door, looking eager to get started.

"Good morning Ms. Friedman. We have a work order to do a meter test at your house," said the older one.

"Thank you for being on time," Sandra said. "I'm hoping to get to the office later this morning. How long do you think this will take?"

"This should only take an hour. We have to test your gas lines, meter pressure, and flow rate. If needed, we'll replace the meter. We'll then test the gas lines indoors and out. Each crew does seven or eight of these a day, so we need to be pretty efficient."

The younger one said, "While he's doing working inside the house, I'll be testing the meter outside."

"Okay, sounds good," she said. "Let me know if you need anything."

She went to the kitchen and worked on finishing the crossword. She loved the New York Times daily puzzle and viewed it as a personal challenge to complete every day's without going online and cheating. Four down's clue: "Asian wild ass," six letters. Sandra mulled the options and letter patterns before concluding it was *onager*, a word used nowhere else in the world except in crosswords and Bananagrams. She was on track to finish when she was addressed. "Ms. Friedman, I think we're done."

The older guy was standing at the kitchen door with a clipboard in his hand. "Please sign here, indicating we were here today, and you are satisfied with our work."

"Of course," Sandra said. "You guys finished up when you said you would. Not sure whether I should thank you or not, because now I have to go in."

"Fortunately, we didn't hit a snag," he said.

Ibrahim and Bassem left the row house and put their tools back in their truck. Sandra watched them drive away. Then she went back into the house to let Tova out of her bedroom and wake up Alexi.

"Good morning," Sandra said. Tova was not shy and ran into Alexi's bedroom, jumped on his bed, and gave him many face licks. He was saying "wake up," also.

Alexi woke quickly and said, "Good morning, Sandra. Good morning, Tova. I slept well last night; I think I'm getting over the three-hour time change."

"I have fresh coffee downstairs and some fruit and yogurt for your breakfast," Sandra said. "Come down and start your day."

"Oh, the coffee smells wonderful. I'll be down shortly," he said.

"Perfect. I am heading into the office soon. The repairmen just left. I kept your door closed so they wouldn't disturb your sleep," Sandra offered. "They probably never knew you were here."

"I didn't hear a thing until that mongrel attacked me," he said.

He came downstairs into the kitchen and poured himself a cup of coffee. As he spooned yogurt, fruit, and granola into a bowl, Tova was at his feet waiting for the chance to lick the carton. Sandra disapproved but knew she had lost the battle.

"So, Alexi, what's your plan today while Elizabeth and I are slaving away at work?"

"Well, I still have a lot of museums to visit. The African American Museum and the Museum of Natural History are on my list. I'm not sure I can make it through both of them completely, but I will spend most of the day at one of them, I think. Or until I get too tired," he answered.

"I think Elizabeth and I will both be home at a reasonable time. How about we go out for dinner?"

"Sounds great!" he said. "Can I ask you a personal question?"

"Of course," she said.

"I know you and Elizabeth are very good friends, but I'd like to know if she can count on you? Can she count on you in this trying time?"

"Of course she can," Sandra answered. "Always!"

Sandra left the row house and headed into the office.

***

"Good job," Ibrahim said to Bassem. "She was distracted enough while I got the explosive device attached to a gas line. They have gas chandeliers in the living room and dining room. The entire first floor with be a fireball within seconds after you detonate it."

"Why the hell are we going to kill a woman? I don't understand. Are you sure we have the right orders?"

"We do. She and her roommate must pose some critical threat to Saudi Arabia or an ally of ours. Get over it."

"I can deal with it, I'm fine," Bassem lied.

"Change back into your street clothes, and I'll drop you off in front of your apartment," Ibrahim directed. "Tonight, stake out the row house. You need to be within 100 feet of the house. Make sure you see both of them in the house and the lights out before you call this number on the burner phone."

Ibrahim handed Bassem a small piece of paper with a 202 area code number written on it.

"The device will explode 180 seconds after you call. Use the time to calmly walk away from the house. Do not run. Many homes these days have video surveillance systems that might pick up a man running down the street. After the explosion, look back—it would be abnormal not to—but continue calmly leaving the area. Don't take a cab or Uber. Walk at least as far as Dupont Circle. Then throw the phone into a sewer line."

"I understand," Bassem replied.

"I'll be on this evening's flight to Riyadh. I may be in the air when you compete the mission. Text me after you trigger the device, and I want to read your full report in the morning when I land. Use our steganography app to encode your report. Understand? Questions?" Ibrahim asked.

"I am confident. I understand exactly what to do," Bassem said.

"Good," Ibrahim said. "Perhaps we'll meet again. *Allahu akbar.*"

"*Allahu akbar,*" Bassem answered. He looked at his watch as Ibrahim drove away. 9:37 a.m. He'd plan to be back at at 8 p.m. to monitor the row house.

***

0953
OHB

Elizabeth walked purposely to Sandra's office, took the stairs, and arrived in less than five minutes. It was up one floor and down one long corridor. She rang the buzzer next to the door and, once it noisily unlocked, entered the office suite. One secretary sat in the common area; she barely looked up after opening the door for Elizabeth. She pointed to her left. Elizabeth saw Sandra sitting in a small single office surrounded by large piles of paper. What was it with these people and their piles of paper? Even Sandra, who was a neatnik at home.

***

"Hey, girlfriend, grab a chair. Welcome to my humble world for the last year and for the next couple of weeks, anyway."

"Can I close the door?"

"Of course," Sandra said. "That's why I have a private office."

"I went by the vault this morning and couldn't open the outer door. The combination has been changed."

"That's not so unusual. They change combinations all the time. Just give Security—"

"I did give them a call. I spoke to the Operations desk, a guy I've come to know, Gordon Haver. I learned they had shut down access to the vault so no one gets in without the DCI's personal approval. I'm no longer accessed. Who do I call to get re-accessed?"

Sandra gave Elizabeth a disapproving look and said, "You really shouldn't call anyone. What would you say? I need access for the Cloud Spinner NIE? That doesn't work anymore; the NIE is written and done. Or, I need access to keep monitoring the DCI and his girlfriend?"

"You know I can't do that," Elizabeth answered.

"The problem with programs like this is that since they are waived and the control system unacknowledged, anyone outside the system has no way to invite themselves back in."

"So, I just go on my way now. Move on to the next project," Elizabeth said.

"Yep. Forget you know about the program, and when you get to your next assignment, you may be re-briefed, or you may not. That is why they call it *need to know*, not *want to know*."

"That's too bad. I was hoping to keep track of Keisha and Plummer as I moved forward. This means I'll be blind," Elizabeth said.

"I really don't want to know what you mean when you say you are moving forward," Sandra said.

"You know I can't just let them get away with it," Elizabeth said. "You are too focused on your next assignment and career—"

"You know it is not that simple," Sandra said. "I just don't see this as big a problem as you do. I suggest you just drop it and focus on getting Cloud Spinner completed. Spend time with your grandfather and move on to your next assignment."

Elizabeth shook her head no.

"I'm not just going to move on to my next assignment. I'll see this through then head back to Pasadena."

***

1056
CIA parking lot

Elizabeth left Sandra's office and thought about going back to her cubicle, but instead, she left the OHB and went straight to her car. Because she couldn't wear her Fitbit in the office, she wasted a lot of uncounted steps from parking lot to office because of the Agency's very wise security policy.

She looked up the *Washington Post* online edition and found a local crime reporter and his number. She called and got his voice mail. She was reluctant to leave a message, so she hung up and decided to try again in a while. She sat in her car for another thirty minutes catching up on some Howard Stern and then called again.

"*Post* metro, Samuels speaking." The voice paused. Elizabeth did not immediately respond. "Hello, Samuels here."

"I can't tell you my name," she said. "But I have a story I want—no, need—to tell you."

"I'm having a hard time hearing you," he said. "Can you give me the gist of the story?"

"I have proof that the CIA knows that the president-elect bribed Russian officials for private business reasons and that the DCI is covering it up for his personal gain. Both the DCI and the Russians are going to blackmail the president-elect after he takes office. Actually, the DCI is already blackmailing him."

"And who are you?"

Samuels was twenty-five years old and had been at the *Post* for only two years. He had broken stories about corruption on the DC Council and had been a key contributor to one local story about the mismanagement of metro system recapitalization funds, but those were local, not national, stories. He knew he was not the right reporter to cover this lead. If it was a legit lead.

"Miss, whoever you are, you have reached Robert Samuels, and my beat at the *Post* is the metro section. You know, local stuff. Let me get you in contact with the right reporter."

"If you do, I'll never call back," said a determined Elizabeth. "I've chosen you to do this story, only you."

"Okay, okay. How do you propose to move forward? Do you have any evidence you can share with me?"

"Yes, financial records and audio files," she replied.

"I'll need to meet you, verify who you are, and know that you have access to the evidence," he said.

"Can we meet tomorrow? I have all of the data on a USB thumb drive. Bring your computer, and you can download everything."

"Sure. Where and when? And tell me who you are so I know more about you when we meet."

"You can google me. Elizabeth Petrov. Cal Tech grad and employed by JPL in Pasadena until July. I need to remain anonymous."

"Of course. You have my word."

"Meet me at the Tabard Inn on N Street at noon," she said.

"How will I recognize you?" he asked.

"I look like my pictures on Google," she said. "Just be there then."

She started her car, gripped the steering wheel, and began both her exit from the parking lot and her exit from the Agency.

***

Elizabeth ran a few errands before driving home. When she arrived, she found the house empty except for Tova, who was obviously not feeling well. He could hardly get up to meet her when she entered the house, and when she took him out, she saw that the chicken bone he had consumed earlier that day had disrupted his stomach and brought on diarrhea. She felt sorry for him. But not too sorry. Maybe now he would leave those chicken bones alone. Probably not.

She found her grandfather had returned from another day of touring DC and was taking a nap in the living room.

She let him sleep and went to the sauna to relax and plan her next steps. After soaking in the steam, she showered and went upstairs, only to fall asleep herself. She was awakened a few hours later by rumbles from Tova's very noisy stomach.

***

1646
Logan Circle

"*Dedushka*, have you had a good day?" she asked.

"Ahhhh. Yes, Yelizaveta, I had a wonderful day," he said.

"Please, tell me about it," she said.

"I changed my plans and spent the entire day at the Newseum. Toured the entire place. It was not crowded, and I was able to spend a great deal of time in all of the exhibits. It is amazing, the critical role the press has played in the development of the United States. More Americans should understand this," he said. "Can you imagine? We left a country where we were subject to a state-approved news organization, TASS! What a joke. It still is."

"*Dedushka*, I need to tell you. I talked to a reporter from the *Post* today. Like you suggested, a junior reporter. He wanted to hand me off to someone else, but I told him no. I told him it was him or no one. He agreed to meet me tomorrow at noon."

"That is the right path," he said. "Only sunshine on the criminal behavior of these people will bring an end to it. Do you want me to join you at this meeting?"

"*Dedushka*, I'd love that. Sandra's wavering, and I need you there to help me tell the story and make sure it is followed up on."

"*Da*. I will join you at noon. I am going to my room for a few minutes. Sandra thought we'd go out for dinner, and I want to change."

"And I'll take Tova out again. His stomach is bothering him."

Sandra arrived home at five thirty and found Alexi watching TV. Elizabeth had opened wine, and they were sharing a cheese tray in the living room.

"Yum," Sandra said. "I missed lunch again today and am hungry." They sat in the living room and listened to Tova's stomach rumbling above the sound of the fire in the fireplace.

"I talked to the reporter from the *Post* today," Elizabeth said. "We're meeting tomorrow."

Sandra frowned. "I told you it's best for me to not know your plans. I need to focus on my upcoming training and my assignment in Moscow."

"I'd appreciate your support or guidance," Elizabeth said.

"Support or guidance while you commit espionage against the US? Forget it. I really don't want to know what you are doing. If they catch you, they'll come after me, and I need to be able to tell them I had no idea what the fuck you were up to."

"You know, we started this, not just me."

Sandra ignored that. "I am serious. I do not want to know what you're up to. Not now, not ever."

Elizabeth spoke slowly. "Understood. It's all mine now."

After a long pause, Sandra said, "Let's go to the Logan Tavern for dinner. They've got live music tonight, and it would be fun to have a kickback evening."

"Okay, I am up for that," Elizabeth replied.

Sandra said, "Sorry to be so prickly, but you've gotta know where I stand. Let's agree to go our own way with this thing, but let's go have a good evening."

They went to dinner at the nearby pub, an early fixture in the area as the neighborhood recovered. It was overshadowed, however, by the New Vegas Lounge next door that had been serving food and the best jazz in the city for the last fifty years. Unfortunately, New Vegas wasn't open that evening. The pub dinner was nice and the music great. They finished up after eight o'clock and walked home in the brisk evening.

***

2052
Logan Circle

Walking home from the Logan Tavern, the three of them did not notice the young man watching them closely from across the street. Bassem recognized the brunette who had let him and Ibrahim into the house that morning. He was surprised to see that there were two more entering the house—an older man, moving slowly, and a tall, blonde woman who was young and fit. Bassem wondered how long it would be before they all went to bed.

Bassem watched as they entered the house. Then he walked purposefully down the sidewalk towards Fourteenth Street. He would wait for the light in the master bedroom facing Corcoran Street to go off before he called the cell phone detonator. He felt vulnerable being on the sidewalk for so long, where it was cold and easy to be seen, but he had no other option. When the lights went out, the firestorm would begin.

Alexi called out, "Good night, ladies! Thank you for a wonderful evening of food, drink, and music!" He closed the door to his room on the second level.

"Good night," they called back.

He cracked his window to let in the cool December air for a peaceful sleep. He turned out the light.

Sandra undressed and was in the bathroom when Elizabeth noticed Tova making signs that he wanted out. Elizabeth said, "I'm taking Tova. He is still struggling with a chicken bone he ate this morning."

"Okay, poor baby. Come back quickly and get naked with me. I'll have the bed warmed up for us," Sandra replied. "I'm turning the lights out and the fireplace on. See you in a few."

As Elizabeth exited the bedroom with Tova, she turned the hall lights off and quietly went down the stairs as to not disturb Alexi.

When Bassem saw the master bedroom light go off, he pulled out the burner cell phone, took a deep breath, and said a prayer.

"*Allahu akbar, Allahu akbar, Allahu akbar.*"

He entered the number Ibrahim had given him. He stared at the phone for a moment and looked toward the row house. Then he pushed the call button.

He listened. The phone rang. When it went to voice mail, he began walking towards Fourteenth Street, knowing he had three minutes before the explosion.

***

2107

As he walked away from the row house, he did not look back. If he had, he would have seen Elizabeth quickly exiting the front door with a very focused Tova. Bassem crossed Fourteenth Street and continued west on Corcoran Street. He felt remorse but kept on walking. Exactly 180 seconds after calling the device, he heard a loud explosion and felt a rumble that moved the air around him. He turned to see the initial conflagration. He could feel the heat of the flames from two blocks away. The light from the flames cast new shadows. Car alarms sounded throughout the neighborhood, and he heard screams from frightened residents. He texted Ibrahim: "Success." Then Bassem wondered again why he had killed those women. Perhaps he was not cut out for this job.

He reached Seventeenth and R Streets and saw a street drain leading to the sewer system. He threw his phone into the opening. He kept walking. His apartment was less than a mile away, and he would take this time to reflect on what he did.

He had triggered an explosive device that killed three strangers tonight, just because someone he did not know—but trusted—told him to do so. From his training, of course he understood that he was meant to kill enemies. He welcomed the opportunity. But these two young women and one old man. How were they enemies?

At his apartment, he showered. And then showered again.

***

2108

Just after she turned the lights off in the bedroom, Sandra's cell phone rang. She thought it might be Elizabeth but noted an unfamiliar phone number on the caller ID. She answered the call.

"Sandra Friedman," she said. She was shocked when she recognized the caller's voice.

***

2109

Elizabeth and Tova had just turned south on Thirteenth Street when they heard the explosion. It was louder than any wind tunnel test she had ever conducted. Then she felt a violent shock wave.

Tova cringed and pulled on the leash as he tried to flee the explosion. Elizabeth restrained him and ran back to the intersection of Thirteenth and Corcoran Streets where she could get a clear view of what had caused the blast. Flames spewed from the bay windows from the house she had just left. Her *dedushka*! Sandra! They were in there! She raced down the sidewalk toward the house screaming.

"Help! Help!"

She pulled her phone out of her coat pocket and dialed 911. She was put on hold. Neighbors had already flooded the center with calls. The fire station was only three blocks away. She quickly heard the wail of the sirens heading her way.

She tied Tova to a neighbor's fence and ran towards the front door. She struggled to unlock the deadbolt with her key. The blast had distorted the metal security door frame. She screamed.

"*Dedushka*! Sandra!" The heat from the spreading flames was overwhelming but she continued working on the lock. Finally, the bolt gave way to her frantic attempts and she pushed the door open.

"*Dedushka*!"

As she pushed into the house, strong arms from behind stopped her. There were three firemen on the steps to the house, wearing full fire protection suits with portable air supplies. Others were snaking hoses from the fire trucks to a nearby hydrant.

"Get back! Get back!" a fireman yelled, his voice near her ear. He pulled her away from the door and yelled above the din. "How many people are in the house? Which floors?"

"There are two people in the house, second and third floors—save them!" she screamed. He signaled to the others, raising two fingers to indicate the others in the house and pointed to the upper floors. As they entered the house, more firetrucks arrived, parking in the alleyway behind the house and along Corcoran Street.

Elizabeth watched from the sidewalk across the street as the flames spread from the ceiling of the first floor to the upper floors. She saw two more firemen enter the house while even more trucks and firemen arrived. She retrieved Tova and waited as close to the house as the heat from the flames allowed. The police had arrived and were backing away the onlookers.

"Miss, please, we need you on the other side of the street," a policeman directed.

"My grandfather is in the house, my friend is—" she cried.

"Please, we need you to stay out of their way. Wait over here, it's safer," he said, directing her behind his patrol car.

Three firemen rushed down the steps carrying a dark shape by arms and legs from the rapidly expanding flames. It was her grandfather.

An ambulance appeared on the street. The firemen carried Alexi past Elizabeth and put him on a gurney near waiting EMTs. He looked so small, so frail. Elizabeth rushed to his side and grabbed the arm of one of the firemen who had brought him out. "Oh my God, thank you, that is my grandfather. There is another person in the house, top floor."

The fireman's suit was hot to her touch and his helmet visor blackened with soot. He looked up at the roof. "We still have two men in there, it looks bad," he yelled to other firemen manning the hoses.

She watched the flames searing through the roof. Streams of water were now aimed at the homes next door, which had caught fire, too. She saw two firemen exiting the front door just as parts of the upper stories began collapsing. The firefighters had given up on Sandra's home and would let it burn. The old timber and construction techniques from the late nineteenth century provided few barriers to the rapidly expanding fire. The entire block was at risk.

Elizabeth turned to the ambulance and saw the EMTs beginning to step away from him. One stayed and covered Alexi's badly burned body with a sheet, pulling it up gently to cover her *dedushka*'s face. She screamed.

The flames continued piercing the night sky, more sirens blared in the distance, and the heat was brutal. Tova whimpered when he heard her scream and pulled at his leash to join her.

Water from dozens of hoses showered homes on the entire south side of Corcoran Street. As she watched, she saw the firemen stopping the fire's advance, but Sandra's home was completely destroyed and her two neighbors' homes badly damaged.

***

2111

Ibrahim had settled into his comfortable first-class seat on the Saudia flight from Dulles to Riyadh when his phone vibrated. A text message. He was enjoying a freshly squeezed glass of orange juice as the A-380 was taxiing into takeoff position on runway 19L for the late evening non-stop flight when he read the note from Bassem: "Success!"

***

2323

Elizabeth sat immobile on the sidewalk. The ambulance with her grandfather had pulled away, and her home had collapsed into a pile of smoldering rubble. There was no sign of Sandra. The conflagration continued to smoke and radiated intense heat. All of the floors had collapsed into the basement, leaving very little trace of Sandra's three-story row house. Tova sat stoically at her side, knowing something was very wrong but not knowing what to do. She was filthy, did not have anything thing in the world except her dog and the clothes on her back, and everyone she loved was dead. How could this have happened?

A neighbor from down the block whom Elizabeth recognized, but didn't know by name, approached her.

"I'm Joyce. How can I help?" she asked.

"I have nothing, I've lost everything. My grandfather, my friend—gone," Elizabeth said.

Joyce hugged her and said, "Please, come stay with me tonight."

"That is very generous of you, but I also need to care for my dog," Elizabeth said.

"Your beautiful lab is very welcome at our house. Come with me. Let's get you a shower to get the smell of smoke off of you. I'll find fresh clothes."

As she prepared to follow her neighbor, two men in uniforms approached her.

"I'm Detective Farris with the DC police department," one said.

The other said, "I'm Inspector Nelson, with the DC fire department. Do you feel up to talking with us about the fire now?"

"Maybe for a few minutes," she said reluctantly.

"I'll wait right over here," Joyce said as she stepped back from them.

"Ma'am, you were in the house before the fire? Can you tell us your name and what you heard and saw?" the detective asked.

Elizabeth started tearing up. "I'm Elizabeth Petrov. We'd just gotten back from dinner only twenty minutes before." Now she was crying. "My dog ate a chicken bone this morning and was not well today. I took him out for a potty break and was just down the block. When I got to Thirteenth Street, I heard a loud bang, a loud thud. I turned back to the house and saw flames coming from the first-floor ceiling in the front."

"Did you smell any suspicious odors in the house before you left?"

"None at all. Do you think it was a gas leak?"

"We don't know yet."

"My girlfriend, Sandra, went into work late this morning. The gas company had repairmen here today. She said to test the lines and meter. Was it gas?" she asked again.

"We really don't know yet, ma'am. We'll have to wait for the house to cool before we can conduct a complete investigation. The gas company is here now to turn off the supply line to the property, so I'll check with them," Inspector Nelson said.

"I know this is a bad time, but can you tell us who was in the house?" Detective Farris asked.

Elizabeth eyes welled up with tears. She wiped them, but the tears continued to streak down her cheeks. The smoke stung her eyes as she cried much harder. Her voice choked. "My *dedushka*, my *dedushka*... my grandfather. Alexi. Alexi Petrov. He—he's dead, they took him in the ambulance. He was in his bedroom. And my girlfriend. My roommate. We lived there together. Sandra, Sandra Friedman. It was her house. It was my grandfather, Alexi Petrov and my friend... my girlfriend, Sandra Friedman, who were in the house."

"We recovered one body..."

"I saw them bring my grandfather out. And, Sandra, I just never saw her," Elizabeth cried.

"I think we have enough for now, ma'am. I think you should try to get some rest, and we'll follow up tomorrow or whenever you are able," Inspector Nelson said softly. "One last question: Is there anything else that would aid our investigation or anything we should be aware of now?"

Elizabeth looked him in the eye and exhaled. "Yes. Sandra and I work for the CIA."

"I see," the detective said. "Thank you for that. We'll contact the security duty office and let them know there has been an accident. I expect they will have someone here within the hour." He held out a card. "My name and number. When you're up to it tomorrow, give me a call."

She nodded.

"And Ms. Petrov, I am deeply sorry for your loss."

"Thank you."

Joyce came close and took Elizabeth's hand. "Come on, honey, let's get you inside."

Elizabeth followed her without thinking and was soon showered and in a warm bed. *Is this a dream, a nightmare?* she asked herself. *I can't have lost my* dedushka. She also thought about Sandra dying in the flames but had a remote sense that maybe it was deserved.

Tova jumped up on her bed, put his head on her torso, and did everything he could to ease her suffering. But he couldn't.

CHAPTER 29

Friday, December 2, 2016
Logan Circle, McLean and OHB

Morning came quickly. Elizabeth went downstairs and saw Joyce in the kitchen. The smell of smoke from fire was in the air. The yoga pants and sweatshirt Joyce had given her fit well enough, but Elizabeth was still in her smoky underwear and socks from yesterday. Waking up in these circumstances was confusing, and she felt uncertain of her next steps. She had put Tova's leash on and brought him with her. He was happy to be going out.

Joyce heard them coming down the carpeted stairs and said, "I'm so sorry, what can I do to help?"

"Please, Joyce, you have done so much already. You are so very kind. I can't thank you enough," Elizabeth replied.

"I've made some bacon and eggs. Perhaps you and Tova would like a bit of breakfast?"

"I'm not hungry, but I know Tova is," Elizabeth said. "Just some coffee would be great. Let me take Tova out for a break. Do you have a newspaper bag or something I can use?"

"Sure, the *Post* came this morning. Maybe this is the best part of the paper," Joyce said, smiling, while handing Elizabeth the plastic bag the *Post* came in for Tova. Elizabeth and Tova went behind Joyce's house in the alley, avoiding the rubble from the fire across the street.

They returned after a few minutes, and while Tova enjoyed his bacon and eggs, Elizabeth had a cup of hot, black coffee.

"I'll call an Uber to take me to a hotel in McLean I've stayed at before. Then I'll get a rental car," Elizabeth said. "My phone battery died—you wouldn't happen to have an iPhone charger, would you?"

"No worries," Joyce said. "I've got an extra portable charger plugged in right over there. You take that for now. Drop it off whenever you are through needing it."

Elizabeth plugged in her phone while Tova enjoyed his eggs. She tried to think of who she should call first, but her thoughts just whirled. List. *Maybe I should make a list*, she thought. Texts and voice mail messages began appearing on her screen. One text message grabbed her attention. It was from Gordon Haver: "Emergency! Call ASAP!"

She left Tova in the kitchen and returned to her bedroom with the portable charger and called Gordon's number.

"Hello, Liz...?"

"Gordon. I got your message."

"I need to see you. Where are you?"

"I stayed overnight at a neighbor's house." She began to cry. "Gordon, my grandfather and Sandra are dead."

"I know, and I'm so sorry. Elizabeth, I think you are in danger."

"What are you talking about?" Elizabeth asked. She couldn't imagine that Gordon had figured this out.

"When the call came in from the DC police about you and Sandra having been in an accident, our security team pulled your personnel files. Or tried to. Sandra's was there, but yours was not."

"So, my file was missing?" Elizabeth asked.

"We traced it. It was pulled by the DCI last week. Why would the DCI want your file?"

"I don't know why. I can't imagine why he would be interested in me," she lied. "I have to go."

"How can I help? I'm off duty until four today. Let me help."

"Oh, Gordon, thank you—listen. This is a big ask, but I need to go into work. Can you look after Tova, my lab?"

"I love dogs; I would be happy to."

"Just until I get a couple of things arranged. You know, get some clothes, replace my credit cards and driver's license."

"Hey, I have an extra car. It's a beater, but you're welcome to borrow it. I have a cash stash here at the house until you can get to the Credit Union."

"Are you sure?" Elizabeth replied.

"No problem. Just watch your back," Gordon answered.

She took a deep breath and said, "Thank you. I'll call an Uber. What's your address?"

She thanked Joyce for the help and left the house. She stared at the still-smoldering ruins of Sandra's house. Bright yellow crime scene tape was strung around the gate and across the front door. The fire damage had weakened the brick of the row houses adjoining either side, so they were cordoned off, also. She and Tova walked down the alley to the back of Sandra's house. The garage was badly damaged, and although their cars were intact, the intense heat had melted the tires and vaporized the paint. Sandra's body could never have survived the inferno. The house had become her pyre.

The Uber arrived, and they quickly made their way out of the city on their way to Gordon's house in McLean, only a mile from the CIA headquarters compound. She mulled over the warning she had received from Gordon. Why had the DCI pulled her personnel file? Why was Sandra's in place and hers was not? Sandra had greedily claimed credit for finding the tapes of Putin describing the Russian's interactions and plans for the *bashka*, so the DCI and Keisha should be unaware of Elizabeth's involvement in the Klondike intercept translations. *Or, perhaps they had become aware*, Elizabeth thought.

Then, it became clear to her. Within hours of her calling the *Post* reporter and scheduling a meeting, the house on Corcoran Street had become an inferno. She and Tova had survived only because of his insistence on going out for a bathroom break. She had risked and lost everything to take on Plummer. She had been targeted and would be targeted again. Maybe Gordon was a threat?

The Uber pulled into the driveway of a modest brick colonial in the old part of McLean. Gordon came out of the house as she and Tova got out of the car.

"I am so thankful you are okay!" he said. "But I feel so terrible about your losses. Come inside."

The house was decorated with a bachelor's touch. No furniture matched, floors showed signs of not having been vacuumed in a while, and there was a massive TV above the fireplace.

"Gordon, I can't thank you enough for texting me this morning and warning me. He wanted me dead. All of us. The DCI wanted me dead!"

"I can't imagine why he would want you dead!"

"Neither can I," Elizabeth lied. "But there are a number of coincidences that all point in that direction."

"Sure." He handed her an envelope. "One thousand dollars, my emergency fund. I think this is an emergency."

"I need to buy some clothes and get into the office today. Can I leave Tova here for a few hours? I'll get a hotel room this evening afternoon. Just until I get a place to stay for Tova and I?"

"You both can stay here for as long as you need to," said Gordon.

"I can't thank you enough."

"Here are keys to the Ford pickup in the driveway. Keys to the house, too."

***

Bassem skipped class that morning and was glued to the local stations' coverage of last night's fire. Ibrahim had been right; the gas-fed fire destroyed the house and damaged the properties next door. The news listed two fatalities, but names were not available until next of kin were notified. The photograph of the rubble on the online edition of the *Post* showed a pile of smoldering ruins where the house once stood and significant damage to the houses next door.

Bassem sent an encrypted message via WhatsApp, obliquely indicating the project had been successfully completed, and there had been three people in the house, but the news was only reporting two deaths. He had not yet heard back from Ibrahim.

***

Plummer arrived at the office at 0600, very angry. The morning bag included a short summary of a local row house fire that resulted in the death of two people, including an undercover Agency employee, Sandra Friedman, and the grandfather of another employee, Elizabeth Petrov. He read that Petrov had not been injured.

He wanted to reach out to Yousef and find out what the hell had happened. The Saudis had failed him.

He knew he was dealing with the worst scenario imaginable. He had tipped his hand to Petrov, and she had not been killed. He contemplated what her next steps would be and concluded she would be coming after him.

Keisha was not in yet, and he did not want to talk to her yet. He needed some time to think.

***

Elizabeth wrestled the balky steering wheel of the old Ford pickup as she drove to her Tabard Inn appointment with Samuelson, the *Post* metro reporter. Back into the city. She made good time and found a public parking space nearby for the truck. She walked down N Street and entered the Tabard Inn promptly at noon. She walked past the reception area into the dimly lit lounge with real oak logs glowing in the fireplace. She saw a young man in a black cashmere turtleneck sweater sitting in one of the sagging sofas.

He stood, extended his hand, and asked, "Ms. Petrov? Robert Samuelson."

She took his hand, "Elizabeth Petrov. Thank you for seeing me here today."

"Ms. Petrov, it's my pleasure to meet you," he said. Elizabeth towered over him. He wore his long brown hair in a ponytail and had bright blue eyes. She liked his warm smile.

"Please, call me Elizabeth. And I insist that before we talk, I have your commitment not to ever use my name. I have to remain completely anonymous. Do I have your word?"

"Of course, Elizabeth, you have my word. We refer to a source like you as being on deep background. You'll never be cited, nor will we use identifiers about you that would disclose your identity. If I am subpoenaed and threatened, I will still not disclose your name. I will have to be fully open with my editor, however."

Elizabeth nodded. "Also, I am going to give you tapes and transcripts of conversations and photos of computer screenshots. These can never be released. You can use the information you get from them, but they can never be released to the public."

"That will be complicated."

"If you don't agree to these terms, this meeting is over."

"Okay. But with those limits, your story may not be told," he said.

"Would you like to get some lunch and discuss further?" she asked.

"I would. I Googled you. You have an interesting background, but I didn't see anything about you joining the CIA," he said.

"I have only been there since July," she said.

"Okay. I have arranged for a table out of the way so we can have some privacy and talk," he said.

After the waiter took their order, Elizabeth said, "Let me use your computer to log in to my email account. I emailed myself all of the documents that prove my allegations. The USB drives were destroyed in a house fire last night."

"That house that burned on Corcoran Street?"

"My grandfather and girlfriend died."

"Oh my God," said a startled Samuelson. "I'm so sorry to hear."

As Elizabeth logged on to the Tabard Inn Wifi and into her Caltech.edu account, she described the circumstances of how she joined the Agency and vaguely outlined the Cloud Spinner project she had worked on. She wanted to make sure he understood that she was on the inside of the inner workings of the Agency.

The files documenting all of the *bashka*'s briberies and criminal behavior and Plummer's treachery and blackmail were in her CalTech technical library. As she downloaded and opened the files on Samuelson's computer, she explained what each one of them contained. She also explained that some of the tapes were in Russian. "You'll probably want to get a translator from the paper to confirm my work, but I have included transcripts that are very accurate."

"Do you think they tried to kill you?" he asked.

"Who?" she asked.

"The CIA," he answered.

"I can't know for sure. But I think so," Elizabeth said.

"Have you been back to work today?" he asked.

"I'm meeting with you first. It's essential that you and the *Post* run a story exposing the scum."

"I can't make such a commitment," he said. "Until we validate what you've told me, the best I can do is promise to check it out."

They talked for the next hour, covering each of the files in detail.

As she got up to leave, she said, "Please call me if you need any more information about the files or me."

"I will," Samuelson replied. "I certainly will."

She took a step away from the table and then stopped. She turned back and said, "My grandfather and my friend died so this story could be told."

***

At the main vehicle entrance to CIA headquarters, Elizabeth told the guard via the remote audio and video system that she was an employee and didn't have her badge. It had burned in the fire, along with all her other identification. He asked her to enter the outer checkpoint where she was subjected to a quick fingerprint check and facial recognition algorithm. She passed both and was issued a new Agency badge. As the badge was being processed, a very concerned woman in uniform asked, "Would you like us to issue you a CIA ID card? It will work in almost every circumstance where you will need to show an ID."

"That would be great," Elizabeth said. "I am not sure when I will be able to replace my driver's license."

"No problem. This will only take a few minutes."

At her cubicle, she was surrounded by caring co-workers who expressed their condolences for her losses and offered their help. Frank gave her a long, embracing hug and told her they were there for her. There was a fruit basket, flowers, emergency toiletries, and a pile of sympathy cards on her desk.

"Thank you all," she said. "You're so wonderful." Tears streaked her cheeks.

Frank brought her into his office and closed the door.

"I don't know what is going on," he said. "Security was here earlier this morning and removed all of your belongings, everything in your cubicle. Are you in trouble?"

"I may be," she said.

"Is it about the issue you raised to me in October?" Frank asked.

"Frank, I think it's best that this be my last day at the Agency. I'm afraid that some people here wanted yesterday to be my last day alive," she said.

"You think that the Agency had something to do with the fire?"

"It looks like they might have. I don't feel safe."

Frank could see the rage building in Elizabeth. He took her hand and pulled his chair next to her. She started to cry again. Tears fell off of her cheek and onto his hand.

He said, "I know you are in pain. With your grandfather dead, you should be angry. Please just take some time away from here. Let me look into this. You are a fantastic analyst. We are getting the coordinated comments back on the NIE, and all of the IC is agreeing with your assessment."

"I don't give a shit about that right now," she said.

"I know, I just don't want you to quit. Take an extended leave of absence. Give me a chance to do my job," Frank said.

Elizabeth stood up and moved toward the door. "Don't expect me back anytime soon. If at all."

"Understood," Frank said. "But please, check in with me now and then so I can keep you informed on what I can find out here."

"Goodbye, Frank," she said. She stopped at the credit union to get new credit and ATM cards and $5,000 in cash. She drove to the nearby Target and bought clothes and toiletries and dog food. She returned to Gordon's house.

"I didn't expect you here," she said. "Aren't you supposed to be at work?"

"Yeah, but I wanted to wait until you got home before I left," he said. "I told them I would be late coming in. It's all good."

"That was very thoughtful of you, and thank you again for being so generous," she said. She handed him back his cash. "And I have to ask you for an even bigger favor."

"Shoot," he said.

"Would you possibly be willing to keep Tova for a few days while I return to California? I need to deal with funeral home issues here tomorrow, and then go to Pasadena to sort out my grandfather's home and personal effects."

"Of course, I will," Gordon said. "Tova and I will be just fine. I'd love to have the company, and he'll be well cared for."

"I can't thank you enough," she said.

She contacted a Pasadena funeral home—to arrange for her grandfather's body to be moved from the DC hospital's morgue and sent to California so she could arrange a service there with their friends and neighbors—and learned they could arrange transportation within the next two days. Then, she pulled out the business card of the DC fire inspector.

"Inspector Nelson? Elizabeth Petrov," she said. "Do you have any further information on the fire? Did you recover Sandra's body? Was it a gas line explosion?"

"Ms. Petrov, the building is still warm, and the structures next to it were severely damaged by the intense heat, so we haven't been able to start any of our forensic work. I'll call when we have more."

"I understand. I'll be out of town for a few days, but please reach out when you know more."

Lastly, she called Samuelson.

"Robert, Elizabeth here. Have you been able to validate the materials I gave you?"

"It's only been a few hours. We need at least two or three days to confirm the materials you provided and write a story of this magnitude."

"Okay, but if I don't sense some movement quickly, I am going to the *Times* with the story and the documents."

"I hear you," he said.

Elizabeth said, "I'll call tomorrow from California. I'll be making arrangements for my grandfather; it'll be late. Is that okay?"

"Not a problem. Call whenever suits you," he said. "But I may not have much more by then."

Elizabeth lay down on the sofa with Tova and fell sound asleep. She awoke at 1 a.m., when Gordon returned home from work. He grabbed a blanket and carefully placed it over her as she nodded off again.

CHAPTER 30

Sunday, December 4, 2016

Pasadena

She hesitated at the door of the home that she and her grandfather had happily shared for almost ten years. There were flowers and candles on the front stoop from friends and neighbors. She carried the cards into the house and stacked them neatly on the credenza in the hallway. She carefully read each note and sorted them alphabetically to make certain she would efficiently respond to each one. She left the flowers on the stoop. She walked through each of the rooms without turning any lights on and then into the backyard, almost expecting to see her grandfather sitting there, looking over his roses. The quiet was deafening. As she stood in the garden, her straight shoulders slumped. She settled into his favorite chair.

The bountiful piney sweet fragrance of the eucalyptus relaxed her and took her back in time.

She was jolted back to reality when her phone rang.

"Hello," she answered, "Elizabeth Petrov."

"Good afternoon, Ms. Petrov, Detective Campbell from the DC police department here, investigating the fire from earlier this week."

"Oh, yes, detective. What have you learned?"

"First, how are you doing?"

"I am in California now, making arrangements for my grandfather's service this week and sorting out his personal effects."

"Again, I am so sorry for your loss."

"Thank you."

"A couple of things. First, are you sure it was repairmen from Washington Gas that were at the house the morning of the fire?"

"I wasn't there, but Sandra told me she had received a message from the gas company that a repair team would be there that morning."

"Washington Gas has no record of any work being done on the residence, that day or in the last six years since a major renovation was done."

"I don't know what to say," Elizabeth said. "Sandra said the gas company was sending people over. I had left for work before they arrived."

"Is there a record of you being at work at that time?" the detective asked.

"Many of them. Cameras, badge readers, security swipes. And I was in a meeting with my co-workers and boss at 0700," Elizabeth said. "Why do you ask?"

"Just following up on all of the angles," he said. "Lastly, most importantly, the fire department was able to get into the house today and conducted a search of the rubble. I can tell you that we have not found any definitive human remains. The coroner says the intensity and duration of the fire could have completely consumed her body—"

"Completely?" Elizabeth interrupted.

"Well, we're looking for only two or three of pounds of bone fragments and dust mixed in with tons of brick, mortar, building materials, rubble, and ashes. We have seen this happen before, but I just want to confirm with you that you are confident she was in the house."

"When I took the dog out, she was in our bathroom getting ready for bed."

"I understand. The coroner will be issuing death certificates for her and your grandfather."

"Thank you, detective," Elizabeth said. "Anything else? How did the fire start?"

"We are still investigating. We really don't know yet."

"Understood. Please call when you do."

"Thank you for your help. Again, I am very sorry for your loss," he said.

Elizabeth hung up the phone and saw a message waiting from an earlier call she had not heard. She pressed voice mail and heard Samuelson.

"Ms. Petrov, could you call me back at 555-797-7221? I have a couple of short follow-up questions about the material we discussed."

***

"I know we agreed not to reveal your name and not to publish the audio files or the transcripts, but our lawyers want to know what the origins of the tapes are," he said.

"No fucking way," Elizabeth responded. "We had a deal!"

"I know, but the goddamn lawyers are concerned that the tapes may have been taken in violation of US law."

"Are you kidding me?" she asked. "In violation of US law? These were collected by the CIA in violation of goddamn

Russian law! I can't tell you how they were collected; I need to protect that source as much as I can."

"Okay, I'll pass that on. Second, do you think they were trying to kill you?"

"Yes, I think so—but keep that out of the story. I cannot be in the story in any way. They should be held accountable for the things we know they've done and can prove."

"Look, we have the initial story final edit right now, and we plan to publish on Tuesday. Where will you be? Will you be safe?"

"I'll be here in California. I can take care of myself. Hell hath no fury like a physicist scorned," she said.

"If the story makes it through the lawyers, we'll be reaching out to the DCI and the president-elect late tomorrow afternoon to comment on the story. It'll be available online tomorrow around midnight," he said.

"Thank you, Robert. Really, thank you. Good evening."

She hung up the phone and went to her grandfather's study. She looked at his library of math and science books in both English and Russian. She would keep them all. As she opened the center drawer to his desk, she noticed a sealed envelope prominently positioned on top of all the papers neatly piled on the desktop. Her name was written on it in Cyrillic. Her grandfather's handwriting. She brushed a tear from her eye and opened the envelope.

It was in Russian, neatly printed in her *dedushka's* careful handwriting.

She read.

Elizabeth,

If you are reading this, then something has gone wrong. If this is not Elizabeth reading this, then something has gone very, very wrong. I write this on the occasion of leaving with you to go to Washington in a few hours to help you with the problem you have found. I asked you if the outcome you sought was worth risking everything and you

*answered yes. I can only pray that you are achieving the outcome you
are seeking.*

*I have not prepared you well for this day. A day when I am gone and
have left so many things untold. I have done everything I could to see
that you were educated and ready for your future life, but I have failed
to tell you of your past. About me, about your parents, and about your
brother."*

"A brother...!" she said aloud.

*... you have a brother who is three years younger than you and still
alive in Moscow. Your parents are still alive also but divorced and, I am
sad to say, have not been interested in either you or me for almost thirty
years. Your brother works for the FSB and has operated under many
names, the most recent being Fedor Litke. I think you two will have a
lot to talk about should you meet. The other area I have not been very
honest with you about is my background. Yes, I worked for the KBG and
yes, I was in the import/export business in New York, but what you are
not aware of is my success. I did not use banks or safety deposit boxes.
I kept much of my fortune in a fireproof safe under the carpet below
the chair you probably sitting in to read this. If you remove the carpet
and the mostly hidden wooden floorboards, you'll find a safe with an
electronic lock. The three-digit combination is from the math game we
played when you were younger. You loved to tease your friends with it.*

Elizabeth remembered the riddle fondly. An insurance
salesman walks up to house and knocks on the door. A woman
answers, and he asks her how many children she has and how
old they are. She says, I will give you a hint. If you multiply
the three children's ages, you get thirty-six. He says this is not
enough information. So, she gives him a second hint. If you
add up the children's ages, the sum is the number on the house
next door. He goes next door and looks at the house number
and says this is still not enough information. So, she says she'll
give him one last hint, which is that the oldest of the three
plays piano.

Elizabeth loved to challenge her friends with it. Hardly
anyone could solve the problem.

If you enter the incorrect combination, the lock turns off for twenty-four hours with the first incorrect guess, forty-eight hours for the second incorrect try, and so on. If this is Elizabeth reading this note, I know you will open it on the first try. Please put the contents of the safe to good use.

I love you, Yelizaveta.

Your Dedushka

Elizabeth was stunned to learn she had a brother in Moscow who was working for the FSB. And a safe under the floor?

She got up from the chair and pulled the small oriental rug back. She noticed irregular cuts in the oak floor, which indicated work had been done there. She found a letter opener and was able to lift a corner of the floor panel and pick it up. A safe embedded in concrete was exposed. It looked as though it had been there for a long time. She entered 2-2-9 into the digital lock and then pushed the enter key. She heard a whir as the lock retracted. She lifted the hinged door and placed a book at the hinge so it wouldn't fall back closed. Elizabeth saw two boxes in the safe. She took the first box out and opened it. It was full of neatly stacked and banded $100 bills. She had never seen that much money in her life. She set the box aside and extracted the other, a little smaller than the first. It contained eight silk bags. She opened one and found it to be full of what looked to be diamonds. The other bags were the same. There were hundreds of diamonds in the safe. Elizabeth knew this was one of the best ways to store wealth: compact, untraceable, and an easily exchanged commodity in many places in the world.

She had no idea her grandfather had been wealthy. Now she was. How he had come into the wealth she would never know, but she would honor his request for her to put his resources to good use. She carefully repackaged the money and the diamonds and put them all back into the safe.

She then went to her old room, pulled the shades, and lay fully clothed on her bed. She fell asleep immediately.

Elizabeth never dreamed, or if she did, she didn't remember. Around midnight she awoke in a sweat with a vivid memory of being chased by people. Many people. She was fast, and they could not catch her, but they kept chasing her. When she stopped to confront them, they stopped, not closing the distance. When she began running again, they followed, step for step, for as long as she could run. In her dream, she turned and ran toward them, and they fled from her. She was tormented by a chase that never ended, followed by pursuers who couldn't catch her.

She lay in bed awake for the rest of the night, unable to fall back asleep and unable to get up and confront her reality.

At sunrise, she got out of bed and made plans. First, a stop at a local jeweler to test a couple of the gems. She knew the test, measuring the thermal conductivity of the material, which only took a few seconds and was 100 percent accurate. Then, a visit to her bank in Pasadena to get a safety deposit box. While her grandfather did not trust banks, she did not trust personal safes and math quizzes. Then she would visit a nearby funeral home to finalize the arrangements for her grandfather.

By that afternoon, all of her tasks were completed. She stopped by a local Von's and picked up groceries for dinner and wine to help soften the pain.

She was wide awake at 11:30 p.m. PST when the *Post*'s online edition was released. She felt like a ball of adrenalin. Coiled and ready to spring.

She went to the *Post*'s website on her laptop and saw the headlines: "President-elect blackmailed by Russians—clear violations of the Foreign Corrupt Practices Act." And below that: "DCI Plummer directed cover-up."

The stories were mostly accurate and added new elements of the story she had not been aware of: travel details, Moscow building project details, and statements from the Department of Justice and the current attorney general about opening an immediate investigation into violations of the FCPA. The second story specified how the DCI had used his knowledge of the president-elect's misdeed for his own benefit.

The *Post* had contacted the president-elect's office and the DCI's office but received only "No Comment."

Elizabeth turned on the television news shows to watch the story unfold.

After thirty minutes, it was clear there was no more news to be had, only a continual rehashing of what was already reported and an endless series of expert guests voicing their opinions about what this meant. She put her phone on mute and fell back asleep.

***

She woke up and made a cup of strong tea, went to the garden, and reflected on what she had done since June and what she would do now. She felt returning to the Agency would be a mistake and going back to JPL would be unfulfilling. She wanted to go to Moscow and find her brother and perhaps her parents. She was now wealthy, so she did not really need a job. However, she knew she would be unfulfilled without one. She felt a deep sense of satisfaction having stopped the *bashka*, and a terrible sense of regret over having lost so much in the process.

She made another cup of tea. She felt lonely. No lover, no friend, and no confidant.

The television was on but muted. She read the scrolling headline at the base of the picture: "President-elect announces resignation, vice president-elect to take oath of office."

She turned the volume up and began listening to the confused commentary.

"Could he resign from a job he didn't have?"

"Was the vice president-elect in on the corruption?"

"Who would the electoral college electors vote for?"

***

Suddenly, one of the talking heads reported a breaking story.

"Director of the CIA, James Plummer, found dead on the George Washington Parkway."

There were no details, just the banner repeating over and over again.

She had dozens of calls on her phone. She ignored them all and called Gordon.

"Are you okay?" he asked.

"Yes, I just saw the news," she replied.

"Are you really okay?"

"Yes, I really am alright. How is Tova?"

"Oh, he is doing great. I think he is missing you, though."

"All I do is ask impossibly huge favors of you, Gordon, but I have yet another one. Can you keep Tova for a few weeks? I need to take some time away."

"I would be happy to look after him," Gordon said. "We're a good team. Take all the time you need. Do you think you'll be coming back to the Agency?"

"I don't know that yet. I need some time to consider my options."

"Just let me know," he said. "I'll do anything I can to help."

She hung up and called Frank. He quickly answered.

"Oh my god, you're okay, I was worried about you. There are a lot of people here trying to find you. You've seen the news..."

"Slow down, Frank," she said. "I am fine, more or less, and I have seen the news."

"I can't believe this is what you were working on in your spare time," he said. "Where are you now?"

Elizabeth hesitated before telling him, "I'm at my home in Pasadena. I'll be taking care of my grandfather's service and things around the house for the next week or so, then I'm going to take some time to myself. I'll let you know what I plan to do as soon as I figure it out."

"Elizabeth, we need you here at the Agency. Please come back." Frank said.

"Thank you, Frank, I'll think about it," she answered.

CHAPTER 31

Tuesday, December 13, 2016 to
Friday, December 30, 2016

The week after the service, she booked a flight to Sorong, Indonesia where she would spend eleven days scuba diving off of a liveaboard dive boat, the "Calico Jack." The boat was named after the infamous pirate, John Rackham, famously executed on November 18, 1720 in Jamaica after plundering and pirating the region for years.

The wooden, handmade vessel was launched in 2014 and built in the centuries-old tradition of boat construction practiced by the *bugies*, Indonesian sea pirates. Elizabeth learned from the crew that this was the origin of the term "Boogieman." The boat had five cabins and a crew of fourteen. They cruised through Raja Ampat to the ends of the Indonesian islands, searching for perfect diving conditions. And they found them. Unspoiled reefs, sharks everywhere, and millions of fish, rays and sea life of every size, shape, and color.

Elizabeth felt she had found her element: neutral buoyancy, calm waters, and spectacular scenery.

She swam with the fish, the dolphins, the mantas and the sharks. She had never felt such joy in her life. The time she spent in the glorious waters of Raja Ampat allowed her to reflect on what was important to her, re-establish the priorities in her life, and analyze the options she may have going forward. After eleven days and almost forty dives, the boat returned to Sorong, and she was finally able to re-establish contact via text and phone. Being isolated from her electronic connectivity had brought a newfound peace and quiet to her life.

She carried her phone up to the sundeck of the boat and dialed.

"Good evening, Frank."

"Great to hear your voice. What have you been up to?' he asked.

"I've been at sea for two weeks, scuba diving in Raja Ampat."

"I'm glad to hear you are well."

"Thanks, I really needed some time away, far away."

"It looks like Plummer's EXEC was deeply involved in the cover-up, too. I think she's cooperating with the DOJ. And it looks like we'll have a new, different president in two weeks," he said.

"The country's better off for it," she replied.

"Yeah, we all probably dodged a bullet," he said. "But you know your release of the records to the *Post* pissed a lot of people off. The current administration has issued a blanket order protecting you. I'm told the president wants to meet with you before the new president is inaugurated."

"I'm not sure when I'll be back. But that's why I called."

"We need you back here. You made a difference, on Cloud Spinner and uncovering a corrupt president-elect and DCI."

"I'd like to return to the Agency, Frank. But under my terms," she said.

"You know I can make almost any assignment work. Tell me what you want."

"Moscow," Elizabeth said. "I want an assignment in Moscow."

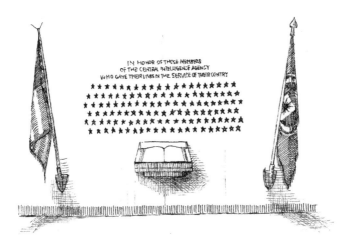

CHAPTER 32

January 2017
CIA Headquarter, Virginia

Elizabeth's first day back at the Agency in January left her conflicted. It had been less than a year since she had been approached at JPL by the men in suits, only seven months after she had begun her career there, and only two months since the calamitous events in Washington. Her requirement to return to the Agency had been met... an assignment to Moscow that she would be starting soon. Once she was settled in Moscow in her new assignment, she could begin her search in earnest for her brother and her parents.

This day, as on her first, she crossed the main lobby towards the badge-reading turnstiles and looked at the CIA Memorial Wall of Heroes. She saw that a new star had been added to the CIA officers who had died in the line of duty. There were now

127. She stopped and said a quiet prayer. Sandra Friedman's star was now on the wall.

After an internal review, the Agency had concluded it had been Plummer who ordered Sandra's death and that she had died in the line of duty. The Agency had ample direct and circumstantial evidence to conclude the Saudis were responsible for Sandra's death but did not follow up with them and let the issue wither so as to not cause more friction with an intemperate ally.

Upon her return to the Agency, Elizabeth had been directed to proceed to the Office of Medical Services for mental health screening and a full physical. She would need to pass these before a tour in Moscow. Then, case officer training at an undisclosed location for six weeks... she was confident she would be in Moscow soon. Hell really has no fury like a physicist scorned.

EPILOGUE

May 2017

Moscow

Elizabeth was enjoying a very nice glass of champagne at the Four Seasons Hotel Moscow with colleagues from the US embassy. The hotel was just steps from the Kremlin and the Red Square with a telling motto, "An Icon Reborn on the Doorstep of the Kremlin." It was a favorite among businessmen of all nationalities because of its location and elegance. She was standing in a large room with ornate inlaid marble on the floors and walls, brought to Russia from both Carrara, Italy and Turkey in the eighteenth century when Peter the Great was exploring Europe. There were many antique ornate tapestries on the wall, celebrating Russian nobility.

She was engaged in a spirited conversation about global climate change with her hosts, a group of US oil industry executives, and facing eastward, looking towards St. Basil's Cathedral, when she heard a familiar sound—spike heels striking marble in a particular, authoritative, confident pattern, indicating a woman was walking into the room behind her. Elizabeth turned, looked up from her half-empty champagne flute into a familiar face, and said, "You look really good as a blonde."

Up Next: *The Sewer: Deceit and Corruption in the Kremlin*
An Elizabeth Petrov Thriller (Book 2)

About the Author

Jeff Grant served for 21 years at the United States Central Intelligence Agency (CIA) in positions at the CIA and National Reconnaissance Office (NRO). While at the CIA, he worked in the Directorate of Science and Technology, and Directorate of Intelligence, Office of Scientific Intelligence. In his most recent assignment at the NRO, he served as Director, Office of Plans and Analysis. During his time at the NRO, Grant also served as a program director for a satellite, launch and ground segment development. In addition, he was the Chief Systems Engineer on two space intelligence collection projects involving spacecraft in both geosynchronous and low earth orbits. Grant also led an advanced technology division to develop and test advanced imagery, communication, and data processing technologies.

Grant left the CIA in 1997 and began working in the private sector and was most recently the Sector Vice President and General Manager of Space Systems at Northrop Grumman Aerospace Systems.

Grant is the recipient of numerous awards, including the CIA's Distinguished Intelligence Medal, Intelligence Medal of Merit, Engineer of the Year, and the NRO's Gold Medal for Distinguished Service. Grant received a Bachelor of Science in Ocean Engineering from the Florida Institute of Technology.

Grant lives with his wife, Margaret, and two daughters, Allison and Kristen, in Southern California.

About the Publisher

The Sager Group was founded in 1984. In 2012, it was chartered as a multimedia content brand, with the intent of empowering those who create art—an umbrella beneath which makers can pursue, and profit from, their craft directly, without gatekeepers. TSG publishes books; ministers to artists and provides modest grants; designs logos, products and packaging, and produces documentary, feature, and commercial films. By harnessing the means of production, The Sager Group helps artists help themselves. To read more from The Sager Group, visit www.TheSagerGroup.net

MORE
From The Sager Group

THE SAGER GROUP

Artifex Te Adiuva

Made in the USA
Las Vegas, NV
24 October 2021